SHE SHOULDN'T WANT A MAN LIKE HIM

Bless her heart, Rose Sinclair thought he was noble. She made no demands on him. She didn't judge him. She simply wanted a child. She wanted *his* child, and she would—Steven had no doubt—cherish that child as deeply and passionately as if she'd given birth to him.

Steven had a sudden urge to kiss her, to unpin her raven hair, sweep her into his arms and never let her go. Perhaps if he held her tightly enough, some of her goodness would seep into him.

Tentatively, for it was difficult to believe that she wanted him to kiss her, he lowered his head to her neck. To his surprise, she rose on her tiptoes and her hands caressed his back. As he fit himself against her, breathing in her scent, he experienced something he had never felt with another woman.

He felt safe.

"Dear lady," he whispered. " 'Twould be a mortal sin if I denied this haven to a child. How can leaving little Stevie with you be anything but right?"

He kissed her then, full on the lips. And before he could draw away and apologize, her lips parted and she kissed him back, as passionately as any woman ever had.

Dear Romance Reader,

Last year, we launched the Ballad line with four new series, and each month we'll present both new and continuing stories set everywhere from medieval England to the American West—the kind of passionate, romantic stories you love best, written by the most gifted authors. At the back of each book, we'll tell you when you can find subsequent books in the series that have captured your heart.

This month, the fabulous Suzanne McMinn returns with the second installment of her *Sword and the Ring* series. **My Lady Runaway** is determined to escape marriage to a cruel nobleman, but she never expects a face from her past to become her knight in shining armor. Next, Lori Handeland continues *The Rock Creek Six* with **Rico,** a man who has a way with women—until he meets the one woman who refuses to believe that love is possible.

In the third entry of rising star Cindy Harris's charming *Dublin Dreams* series, a widow meets her match in a brooding attorney and wonders if she can convince him that a true romance is certainly not **Child's Play.** Finally, reader favorite Alice Duncan concludes the smashing *Dream Maker* series with **Her Leading Man,** as an actress who dreams of medical school learns that even the smartest men can be stupid when it comes to love. Enjoy!

Kate Duffy
Editorial Director

Dublin Dreams

CHILD'S PLAY

Cindy Harris

ZEBRA BOOKS
Kensington Publishing Corp.
http://www.zebrabooks.com

ZEBRA BOOKS are published by

Kensington Publishing Corp.
850 Third Avenue
New York, NY 10022

All Kensington titles, imprints, and distributed lines are available at special quantity discounts for bulk purchases for sales promotion, premiums, fund-raising, educational or institutional use.

Special book excerpts or customized printings can also be created to fit specific needs. For details, write or phone the office of the Kensington Special Sales Manager: Kensington Publishing Corp., 850 Third Avenue, New York, NY 10022. Attn. Special Sales Department, Phone: 1-800-221-2647.

First Printing: November 2001
10 9 8 7 6 5 4 3 2 1

Printed in the United States of America

This is a story about a damsel in distress who falls in love with a lawyer, but ultimately learns that only she can save herself. Therefore, it is only fitting that I say thank you to some of the lawyers who have helped me learn that lesson.

So, to Nicholas Chiarkas, Arthur "Buddy" Lemann, Steven Scheckman, Phillip Wittmann and Lanny Zatzkis, thank you . . . and Hail to the Dragon Slayers.

Prologue

Fontjoy Square, Dublin, 1865

Devon Avondale lay beside his wife, nuzzling the side of her neck, tentatively caressing her bare shoulders. In the final stages of her illness, she was so frail and fragile that he was afraid to touch her, much less press his weight against her.

"It's all right, Devon. I won't break, you know."

"But I don't want to hurt you. I love you, Mary," he whispered.

"You used to say it in words far more provocative than that, dear."

He smiled. Mary's attempt at levity, indeed at normalcy, moved him. God, how he longed for the days when they would tease each other for hours, then practically rip each other's clothes off and make mad, passionate love for half the night.

But those days were gone forever. For weeks, Mary had lain in bed, wilting feverishly beneath the counterpane, moaning for nothing more than morphine, or whiskey or, on increasingly rare occasions, her diary. Her lung disease had progressed to the point where her breathing was labored and her chest ached constantly. Pain had replaced Devon as her faithful companion.

Raised up on his elbow, he gingerly kissed her lips.

"Make love to me, Devon." Her gaze snapped. "The way you used to!"

She wrapped her arms around his neck and pulled him to her. The familiar warmth of her kiss soothed Devon, piquing his ardor, inviting him to reach beneath the sheets and stroke his wife's alarmingly thin body. He would have done anything he could to make her happy. He would have given his life to make her well.

She took his hand and guided it to her breast. But Devon could only think that she was dying and that he would not be able to live without her. Making love to her seemed selfish and greedy. Suddenly, his movements were as timid as a schoolboy's. His heart ached to claim Mary, but his body was unresponsive.

"Come on, darling," she purred in his ear. Reaching between them, she slipped her hand beneath the waistband of his trousers. She knew what to do. She knew what he liked. No woman in the world knew Devon as thoroughly as Mary O'Roarke Avondale. Within seconds, he was hard and desperate to sheathe himself inside her.

Mary also knew what *she* wanted. Years of marriage had not dimmed her imagination or curiosity. Illness had not daunted her beauty or sexuality. What Mary lacked in physical strength, she made up for in sheer invention. Surprisingly willful, she told Devon precisely where she wanted him to touch her, and how.

She enjoyed her release—several times—before she allowed her husband his.

He hovered over her, uncertain and afraid to take his pleasure.

"Come on, then, darling, don't be afraid." Her voice was husky from desire, raspy from illness. Yet the sound of it sent tremors of erotic desire up Devon's spine.

"I am afraid." He remembered the first time he had ever made love to Mary. He had been afraid of hurting her then, too. God, how he longed for that moment, for that sweet, innocent moment when life stretched ahead of them like an endless road.

"You'll be all right, Devon."

"Not without you, I won't." Emotion cracked his voice, embarrassing him. Mary was stronger than he. He ought not to worry her by showing his weakness. But he could not help himself. He was terrified, and Mary was the only person in the world who could understand exactly what he was losing.

"You'll love someone else, Devon." She parted her legs and guided him inside her.

"Never." The moist heat of her body surrounded him. His physical need for her engulfed him. Lowering himself into Mary's body, Devon rocked his hips slowly against hers, intoxicated by the grip of her inner muscles, desperate to possess her and keep her with him always.

After a moment, their movements synchronized. Devon kissed Mary—*hard*—as the two reached their climax together. Then, carefully, he withdrew and rolled to his side. Mary's face was unnaturally flushed and her breathing dangerously shallow. For an instant, Devon was afraid he had actually hastened her death.

At length, she offered him a wistful smile. "I have already told you about my diary, Devon. Now I want you to promise me something."

"Perhaps the doctors in Paris—"

"Stop it!" She swallowed hard. "We have consulted every doctor in Ireland, England and the entire European Continent. It is time you faced reality."

"I promise to read the diary," he assured her for the tenth time. But he could not imagine how he would be able to. Indeed, he could not imagine how he would continue breathing once Mary was gone.

"There is more." Her sentences grew shorter by necessity, so that everything she said had meaning. "My friends. I want you to find them."

"Which friends, Mary? You have a hundred friends, or more."

"Real friends. Girls I grew up with. Four of them. They loved me. I loved them."

Beating back his tears, Devon nodded his grim assent. "How will I find them, Mary?"

She shrugged. "Use your head, dear."

"And when I do locate these four mysterious women, what shall I do then? Knock on their doors, and tell them I was married to Mary O'Roarke, their childhood friend who has just—" He choked on the words.

"Who has just died," she said flatly. "Get used to it, Devon."

He thought the fever had finally robbed her of her senses. *"I cannot!"*

A hollow silence ensued, and after a couple of hours, shadows lengthened and slid along the ceiling. Just when Devon thought Mary was sleeping peacefully, she spoke again. "Whatever they need, Devon, give it to them."

Her eyes were closed, but her lips were curved in a mischievous smile. "But do not tell them about me," she added. "Not at first, anyway. I would like for them to know one another. See if you can arrange that, will you, darling?"

He had almost forgotten whom Mary was talking about. Belatedly, he recalled the four women friends she had referred to. Bewildered, Devon asked, "Why do you want me to do this thing?"

Turning her head on the pillow, Mary looked him square in the eye and stared at him so fixedly that Devon feared for a split second that she had drawn her last breath. Her skin was as pallid and perfect as a wax mannequin's. The stillness in her expression frightened him.

Her voice was barely audible, but her meaning was unmistakable. "Because I want you to live, Devon. And to live, you must love."

He opened his mouth to protest, but her disapproving look quickly silenced him.

"I am asking you—"

"Anything, Mary."

"If you love me—"

"I do, you know that."

"Than you must love these women . . . who once loved me."

Even on her deathbed, Mary O'Roarke Avondale

did not mince words. Terrified of upsetting her, Devon agreed to find the four women who had befriended her during her girlhood and help them in any way he could. He would not tell them he was married to Mary O'Roarke, but he would bring them together as friends—in what manner and by what ruse, he had not a clue.

He put his arm around his wife, hugging her as tightly as he dared. "I promise, Mary."

She smiled. "One more thing, Devon."

"What is it?"

"Tend to the houses in Fontjoy Square, darling. Don't allow the houses or my garden to fall into disrepair." With a sigh, she added, "I have loved living here with you, Devon. I want you to be happy here. And Devon?"

"Yes, Mary?"

"Children would be nice."

One

Dublin, Fall 1870

Situated in Mabbot Street, in "Monto," Dublin's notorious prostitution district, and wedged directly between the bright red front of a pub called The Shebeen and the nondescript brick facade of a whorehouse, was the headquarters of the Dorcas Society for the Aid of Illegitimate Children.

Like many of its neighbors, the Dorcas Society did not advertise its presence, solicit visitors or hawk its services. No brass street numbers accented the tarnished doorknocker of the three-story former milliner's shop it occupied; no address was stenciled in black across its smudged transom. No painted board or marquee swung above its portal to verify or even identify its purpose.

Housed in a building so grimy and neglected, with windows so greasy and smeared, that passers-by paid it no more attention than they would a street beggar, the Society was a place to which no one bragged of going, or even admitted they'd been. Even in Monto, its existence was somewhat of an embarrassment.

It served a purpose, but one of small significance

and dubious importance to Dublin's strictly polite society. Run by an army of about fifty women, many of whom donated their efforts in defiance of their husbands, it helped unmarried women feed and clothe their children. It provided rudimentary medical services to children who would not otherwise receive them. And it arranged for the adoptions of children who were unwanted or who, in some cases, were loved dearly enough by their mothers to be given away to a family better able to care for them.

The Dorcas Society reached out to the most abused and beaten down of Dublin's female population—unwed mothers, frightened girls, ladies of the night—and their children. And it did so without moral judgment, religious proselytizing, political agenda—or outside contributions.

Though the Mayor of Dublin had probably never heard of the Society, and could never have found its offices even if he had, every prostitute in Dublin knew how to find the Dorcas Ladies, as they were affectionately called.

So it was that on a chill Monday morning, in the musty-smelling ground floor reception room of the Society's headquarters, Mrs. Rose Sinclair sat behind a scarred wooden desk. She shouted "Next!" as she adjusted her starched white cap, a distinctive peaked affair knocked askew by her previous visitor, a fragile boy who looked no more than three years old, but, as Rose had learned during her initial interview of his mother, was actually nearer five.

The child had not been pleased when his frantic-faced young mother had summarily tossed him into

Rose's lap. And he'd been far less pleased—absolutely panicked, in fact—when his mother had turned toward the door, making to flee before she could reflect upon her decision to abandon him to the collective custody of the Dorcas Ladies.

"Come back here at once," Rose had ordered.

But the young mother, practically a child herself, paused in the threshold and said over her shoulder—rather dramatically, Rose thought, like an actress on the stage—"He's better off without me, see. I can't give him proper clothes or even food to eat! Find another family for him, will you? One of them families with a regular father and a mother and a nanny like to chase after him!"

"What makes you think there is such a family?" Rose had asked, rising from her chair, clutching the tow-headed parcel that had now become a little machine of flailing arms and legs.

"You must know of some wealthy family who'll take him in. He isn't very big. He wouldn't be much trouble."

"I'm afraid it doesn't work like that. You can't just bundle up a child like a package and drop him on the doorstep of some unsuspecting family."

"It's that, or he'll be a climbing boy, like his pa."

The thought of the child's being turned out as a chimney sweep made Rose shudder. She looked him in the face. For an instant, his struggles stopped; frozen, he stared back at her. *And he was small and spindly.* Just the right size to be forced down the narrow passage of a clogged flue regardless of whether the bricks were red-hot or a flame still smoldered on the hearth below. He'd be lucky if he wasn't burned to death or severely maimed before he reached his tenth birthday.

"But you can't leave him here," Rose said, softening her tone. It wouldn't help to scold the young mother. She was desperate and confused. If she loved her child enough to keep him out of the sweepers' clutches, perhaps she could be persuaded to give up her role as a prostitute, acquire another skill and obtain a decent job. "Come now, sit down and we'll see what sort of assistance we can offer you."

Reluctantly, the young woman took her seat and reclaimed her child. A long consultation ensued. At length, Rose scribbled the name of an employment agency on a piece of paper and handed it across the desk. "Mrs. O'Conner is a member of the Society. She'll help you find a respectable job."

The young mother took her child home with her, but not before receiving an armful of secondhand clothing and a basket of food. It wasn't what she'd come for, but it was what she got.

Watching her leave, Rose sighed, sadly aware that her young client might never see Mrs. O'Conner and that the blond rascal who'd knocked off her cap might end up in the chimneys anyway. But there just weren't that many families in Dublin who were willing to adopt a five-year-old child in poor health and of dubious lineage. Abandoning one's baby wasn't as easy as some mothers tended to think it was.

Rose called out "Next!" this time a bit louder.

Another young woman, not much older than the one

who'd just left, but far more voluptuous, poked her head in the door. "Are you Nurse Sinclair?"

The ladies of the Dorcas Society were often mistaken for nurses. But Rose had no formal medical training, and very little informal experience with children. Her reasons for joining the Dorcas Society were borne of an inner need rather than a professional calling. She loved children and she couldn't have any. Caring for Dublin's neediest ones made her happy.

"I'm not a nurse, but I am Mrs. Sinclair, so perhaps I can help you. Come in."

The young woman, a pretty redhead with creamy skin and startling green eyes, slipped through the door with three children—twin girls who looked to be seven or eight years old and a boy of about five—clutching at her hands and skirts. Instead of sitting in the chair, she stood before Rose's desk, the children huddled about her, her shoulders square, her gaze direct.

Too direct. In the awkward silence, Rose stood and met the other woman's gaze. She was not entirely unaccustomed to brazen females storming the Dorcas Society's offices, demanding to be given food or money or to be relieved of the burden their children had become. There were many prostitutes who, toughened up by their unrelentingly harsh past, didn't know how to be gracious or polite; they'd never been given anything, or shown the slightest kindness, and so they didn't know how to go about asking for help without resorting to churlish threats and demonstrations.

At first, Rose thought the young lady standing in front of her was one of those, *a tough crumpet,* as she sometimes put it. But a long perusal of the woman's expression, not to mention her costume, told Rose this woman was not looking for a handout.

"Name's Clodagh Tweedy." She wore an expensive gray walking dress that was cinched tightly at the waist, accenting luscious hips and bosom. And as her gaze flickered over Rose, clad in a conservative dark blue frock and white apron, a superior little smirk played across her rouged lips. "So you're the widow Sinclair."

"Yes, and why would that be of any interest to you?"

Instead of answering Rose's question, the young woman slanted a glance at the children surrounding her. "These here are Katie and Mollie, and the little one's name is Stevie."

For the first time, Rose peered closely into the children's faces, or into the twin girls' faces, anyway. Stevie's head was ducked, and he was rubbing the toe of his boot on an imaginary spot on the floor. Katie and Mollie, however, gazed back at her with wide hazel eyes, their identical little mouths pursed in tight, fretful frowns.

Looking at the redhead, Rose couldn't suppress a pang of envy. "Your children are beautiful, Miss Tweedy. You're a lucky woman."

Miss Tweedy chuckled throatily. "Oh, they're not mine, Mrs. Sinclair."

"Tell me, how is it that you know me?"

"You're well known about this neighborhood, Mrs. Sinclair, didn't you realize?"

Spots of heat prickled at Rose's cheeks. She donated

her efforts to the Dorcas Society because it made her feel good. She had no interest in recognition of any sort. In fact, she preferred total anonymity. On the other hand, she was gratified to learn that the desperate young mothers who needed the Society's help knew where to find her.

"All right then, tell me what you need. No need to play this silly game of cat and mouse. If the children aren't yours, then whose are they? And why did you bring them here?"

"Because they need a home, lovie. They're orphans, see. And I been taking care of 'em because I was, er, friends with their mother."

"What happened to their mother?" Rose's patience was growing thin. The children—even little Stevie—were now staring at her with blank, emotionless expressions. They looked as if they didn't expect a speck of charity from anyone, including Rose, and she had the terrible premonition that she wasn't going to disappoint them in this respect.

"She died. Couple of months ago, actually. They've all but forgotten who she was by now!"

Rose sighed her disbelief. The children might have suppressed their bereavement, but she doubted seriously that they had forgotten their mother. "Yes, I supposed their mother had passed away when you told me they were orphans, Miss Tweedy. I mean, what did she die of? And why did she leave them in your cafe?"

"Like as I said, we was friends. Worked together. In the same establishment. If you know what I mean."

"I'm quite certain I do."

"At any rate, their mum, she went and got herself

with child again. Don't know why Katherine couldn't figure out how to—"

"Is that necessary?" asked Rose. "In front of the children, I mean."

"Well, you was the one who asked, lovie." It was Miss Tweedy's turn to sigh. "Katherine died in childbirth, like I said, just a few months back. And ever since, the young'uns, they been living with me, in my room, like."

"In your room? In a whore—" Gasping, Rose covered her mouth.

"Is that necessary?" Miss Tweedy mocked her. "In front of the kids, I mean?"

Recovering her wits, Rose clasped her hands at her waist and said quietly, "Dear woman, surely you know that you cannot raise children in an establishment of that nature."

"Well, ain't you the smart one! Now you're catching on! I know I can't raise 'em, Mrs. Sinclair. That's where you come in."

"I'm afraid I cannot take the children off your hands. The Dorcas Society does not have the facilities to house unwanted—" Even as the words spilled from her lips, Rose regretted them. It was bad enough that the children had been orphaned and left in the custody of a prostitute. Calling them *unwanted* seemed an entirely gratuitous act of cruelty.

"I'm sorry," she said more softly, daring a glance at Stevie which, as she had suspected it would, nearly broke her heart. "We just don't have the resources to care for these children, no matter how unfortunate their circumstances."

"This here's the Society for the Aid of Illegitimate Children, ain't it?"

"Yes, of course it is. But—"

"And you give food, clothing and other handouts to young'uns born out of wedlock, don't ye? Even them who's got mothers who are streetwalkers?"

"Unfortunately, children cannot choose their parents. But we can't take them all in—"

"I'm not asking you to take 'em all in." Miss Tweedy cocked her head.

"We can't take any one of them in, I'm afraid."

"Even if I tell you I can't afford to keep 'em no more? See, I'm going to be evicted from my house if I don't get rid of 'em. And then I won't even be able to feed meself. They'd starve right along with me. So I wouldn't be doin' 'em any favors by keepin' 'em, now, would I?"

"I presume their mother trusted you. Caring for children is a huge responsibility, Miss Tweedy. I'm not surprised you feel overwhelmed. But we can help you find honest employment. We can give you clothing, if you need it." Rose hesitated, suddenly mindful that Miss Tweedy's morning gown was made of finer stuff than her simple frock. The redheaded woman obviously wasn't destitute.

"I don't need clothing, dearie. Nor money. Nor food."

"Why did you come here, then?"

"I came to see *you,* Mrs. Sinclair. I came to prove to you that what you've long suspected is absolutely true. If you won't take the children in out of the goodness of your heart, perhaps you'll take 'em out of respect for your dead husband. A right virile man, he was, wasn't he?"

A needle of fear slid up Rose's spine. "I don't know what you're talking about."

Miss Tweedy grasped one of the twin girls' chins, turning up the child's face for Rose's perusal. "Look familiar?"

"I beg your pardon?"

"Don't Mollie here remind you of someone?"

Rose stared at the child's big hazel eyes, flecked with green, set a bit too close together so that she would always appear to be brooding. Her dark-brown hair was smooth and straight, of a fine texture, not coarse. Her lips were well shaped, but thin, as Rose's husband's had been, like his father's and like all the Sinclairs that Rose had ever known or seen in portraits.

A sick premonition roiled through Rose's body. For a moment, she was afraid she might faint. With one hand pressed to her stomach and the other gripping the edge of the table for support, she swallowed the bile that rose at the back of her throat. "What are you trying to tell me, Miss Tweedy?"

"These here children are yours, Mrs. Sinclair."

"That is impossible."

"Physically, that may be true. I ain't saying you give birth to them. Katherine did that."

"What *are* you saying, then?"

"They're your husband's children, then, Mrs. Sinclair. See, he was Katherine's best cust—"

Miss Tweedy smiled wickedly, and glanced at the children. "No use sayin' it in front of the kiddies, is there? He was Katherine's best *friend.* And now that he's dead, lovie, the way I see it, the children are yours."

The arrival of children in Fontjoy Square brought a wave of excitement and curiosity to the neighborhood. They couldn't be hidden, of course, not from Rose's neighbors. The moment she paraded down the street with them, rounding the corner and passing the grand Palladian mansion at the end of the square, the children became the object of Mr. Devon Avondale's unabashed interest. Abandoning the rose trellis he was mending in the garden in the center of the square, he crossed the street and met Mrs. Sinclair at her front door.

"Well, what have we here?" The little girls smiled shyly while the boy stubbed his toe on the slate steps.

Mrs. Sinclair sighed. "You may as well come in. For that matter, you may as well gather Lady Kilgarren, Lady Dolly, and Millicent, too. As soon as I get the children settled, I should like to talk with all of you. No use keeping anything a secret around here. And I don't want to have to tell the story more than once."

By the time Devon returned with his coterie, the children had been fed and bathed and put to bed. Mrs. Sinclair sat in her drawing room, sleeves rolled to her elbows, face flushed and hair disheveled. She looked as if she'd had an arduous day, to say the least. But there was a certain glow about her, despite her weariness, that awakened Devon's interest. Leaning against the mantel, a snifter of brandy in his hand, he wondered whether his wife's prediction about Rose Sinclair had somehow miraculously come true.

"You aren't going to keep us in suspense any longer, are you, Rosie?" asked Mrs. Millicent Hyde-Wolferton. Seated on the sofa beside Rose, the younger woman could not disguise her excitement. She never could, Devon thought affectionately; Millicent was a woman who wore her heart on her sleeve.

Swallowing a chuckle, he recalled how deliriously happy Millicent had been at her recent wedding to Captain Alec Wolferton, the infamous Sea Wolf of the Crimea. The captain, regrettably, was now in London on business. Otherwise, he would have been at his wife's side, just as curious and concerned about the sudden materialization of children in Fontjoy Square as everyone else in the room.

"No, Millie, I'm going to tell you everything." Mrs. Sinclair squeezed the pretty brunette's hand. Since the two women had moved in next door to each other nearly nine months earlier, they'd become confidantes. "As I told Mr. Avondale, there's no use trying to keep it a secret. You'd all have it out of me in no time."

Lady Claire Kilgarren, the aristocratic blonde who resided at Number Three Fontjoy Square, poured herself another cup of tea and sank elegantly into a red velvet covered armchair. Unmarried and vociferous in her determination to remain so, she cast a sidelong glance at Devon before speaking. "Did I hear Mr. Avondale correctly? Did you really bring a pair of twin girls and a little boy home with you this evening, Rose?"

"Who are they?" asked Lady Dolly Baltmore, a petite but well-muscled woman with cropped blond curls.

Beside Dolly's chair stood her husband of some six months, Dick Creevy. Though Dick was a legendary pugilist, he was, in the opinion of Devon Avondale and everyone else who knew him, one of the most gentle and intelligent men in all of Ireland. His marriage to Dolly, after she had masqueraded as a boy and taken boxing lessons from him, had shocked the neighborhood. His devotion to her gave Devon a deep sense of satisfaction.

Suppressing a grin as he stared at Dick and Dolly, Devon silently shared his self-congratulations with Mary, his deceased wife, upon whose wishes he'd acted by bringing these four delightful women to Fontjoy Square. Though only one of them realized he was the anonymous benefactor who had donated the neighboring houses to them, they all, Devon was quite certain, were grateful for their improved circumstances. After all, the four ladies—Dolly, Millicent, Rose and Claire—had been on the edge of poverty when he located them.

His thoughts were interrupted by a heavy sigh from Rose, a signal that she was prepared to begin her story.

"Before I tell you who the children are, allow me to give you a little background. I suppose you've been wondering where I've been disappearing to these last few months."

Though Devon had heard the other three women

speculate, conjecture, debate and gossip for hours on end as to where Rose Sinclair mysteriously went three days each week, he was amazed to see them exchange looks and shake their heads. Collectively, they denied they'd ever noticed Rose's absences.

" 'Tis none of our business," said Claire primly.

"It is now," replied Rose. "Because I'm telling you."

"You're among friends, Rose." Devon raised his glass in salute, and everyone else murmured their encouragement to the pretty violet-eyed widow with raven hair. Nearing age thirty, and the oldest of the ladies who lived in Fontjoy Square, Rose was also the most beautiful, Devon thought—if you didn't include Claire, that is. "Come on, now, tell us your story."

"Shortly after I moved here, I joined the Dorcas Society."

"Dorcas?" Dick Creevy scratched his dimpled chin. "Wasn't she a biblical heroine?"

"She helped others despite being dirt poor herself," answered Claire.

"The full name of the organization," Rose continued, "is the Dorcas Society for the Aid of Illegitimate Children. Our headquarters are in Mabbot Street."

"In Monto?" Millicent gasped.

"Most of the children we help are the offspring of streetwalkers. We give out clothing and food, and do what we can to get the children medical attention if they need it. We try to explain to the mothers the importance of cleanliness and a healthy diet. You'd be surprised how uninformed some of these young women are. Some of them, even those who make a living on their backs, lack even the most rudimentary knowledge required to prevent pregnancy!"

A moment of stunned silence followed Rose's remark. Devon noted with amusement that his neighbors weren't quite certain how to receive this frank intelligence. It wasn't unusual for ladies of leisure to donate their time to charitable organizations; that wasn't what had surprised everyone. What was unusual was for a well-bred woman to actually rub shoulders with prostitutes, rather than participating in some more elevating activity, such as passing out frames of needlework to the starving womenfolk of Dublin so that they could pass their wretched time with dignity. Rose's discussion in mixed company of a topic as controversial as the intentional prevention of pregnancy only doubled the shock of her admission.

To his credit, Dick Creevy took an enlightened, if not somewhat paternal, view of Rose's charitable endeavors. "Seems an admirable use of your energies, Rose. I must say I'm right proud of you. But is it safe, you going down to Monto three times a week without an escort or chaperone to see you safely to and fro?"

"Quite safe. Oh, and we also assist young mothers in finding honest employment, if that's what they want, if they're willing to take it."

"If they won't, why bother with them?" asked Claire.

"Because we can't force a woman who has known nothing but hardship and tragedy all her life to look at the world from our point of view. We can wish and pray that there exists some tiny little spark of hope and decency inside her that will catch fire when she sees an opportunity to better her situation. But it doesn't always happen that way."

Claire wrinkled her nose. "I don't think I could stand working with women who are willing to sell their bodies—"

"You mustn't judge them, Claire." Rose smiled. "Besides, when you help the mothers, you help the children. And there's no hope for a better tomorrow if we don't help the children, is there?"

"You sound like one of those suffragist reformers," observed Dick. "I suppose you're going to next tell us that women should have the vote."

"Why shouldn't they?" piped his wife.

"I haven't a political bone in my body," Rose said. "I simply have a soft spot for children, that's all."

"All right, then," Dolly said. "Mind telling us how you came to bring three of them home today?"

"They're not the children of *a prostitute,* are they?" Millicent's face was pink with astonishment.

"As a matter of fact, they are. A woman named Clodagh Tweedy brought them to the Society offices today. She said their mother was a friend of hers, but she's dead now. Before she died, she asked Miss Tweedy to take care of the children. Miss Tweedy kept them with her at an establishment that is overseen by a woman named Mrs. Bunratty."

"The children have been raised in a brothel?" Millicent and Dolly asked in unison.

Rose nodded. "But Miss Tweedy cannot keep them there anymore and she asked me if I would take them in."

"Why you?" Devon asked, unable to quell his suspicions.

Rose seemed to falter. "Well, not me personally. She thought she could just leave them at the Society headquarters. I told her she couldn't, of course, and she threatened to leave them there anyway. I couldn't let her do that, now, could I? For that matter, I couldn't let her take the children back to the whorehouse where they'd been raised up till now. She must have seen what a soft spot I have for children. At some point, she asked me to take them myself."

"What on earth did you say?" Dolly asked.

"I suppose I said no, at first." Rose lowered her gaze. "But she saw me for what I was, and she knew I would give in and agree to take them."

Millicent slid across the sofa and wrapped her arm protectively around Rose's shoulders. "They're not your responsibility, you know. You don't have to keep them. You can turn them over to the authorities, or take them back to Miss Tweedy."

"You're much too kind-hearted, Rose," Dolly inserted. "This disreputable woman—Tweedy, did you say? She played on your sympathies and emotions—"

"No doubt she has a great deal of experience doing that," suggested Claire.

"You can take the children back to her in the morning." Millicent looked about the room, searching for support of her idea. "I'll go with you, Rose. You can't be made to keep three children that you don't want."

"I'll go too," Dolly and Claire said.

Devon nodded at Dick. "We can't let them go alone, now, can we?"

"Hardly." Dick chuckled warmly. "I suppose we'll all go, Rose. It isn't going to be a pleasant task, taking these children back to Monto, but none of us appreciates what this Tweedy has done. Why, she's taken advantage of you in the most shocking way. Once she sees Avondale and me—the whole lot of us, for that matter—she'll think twice before she tries tossing this bit of gammon to anyone else."

"No, you don't understand!" Squeezing shut her eyes, Rose violently shook her head.

For a moment, everyone, including Devon, stared at her in wonderment and discomfiture. On the mantel, a gilt clock encased in a glass dome ticked conspicuously. Devon met Rose's gaze and knew what she was thinking.

I'm not getting any younger, I'm not married and I desperately want children.

Devon heard Rose's inner voice as clearly as if she'd spoken to him. He heard Mary's voice, too, and in his mind saw the delicate pen strokes that had committed his wife's memories of Rose to writing. His chest tightened empathetically. He and Mary had wanted children, too, but they waited too long. If only Mary hadn't gotten sick . . .

When at length Rose spoke, Devon was the only person in the room who wasn't surprised by what she said.

"You don't understand," she began slowly. "I do not want to take the children back. I want to keep them."

Claire sat up very straight, her bright blue eyes blinking in bewilderment. Millicent's mouth formed a perfect little oval. And Dick lifted his eyebrows questioningly.

"There, I've said it! I intend to keep them!" Rose gazed first at Millicent, then the others. Her gaze fastened on Devon, causing his stomach to knot with indecision.

He didn't know whether to be happy for her, or whether it was his obligation to dissuade her from such an outrageous notion. Setting aside his suspicions about this mysterious Miss Tweedy, he thought Rose had taken on a daunting challenge. Caring for three children was, even for a married woman, no small undertaking. As a widow, Rose would encounter a myriad of problems, not the least of which would be the additional costs of feeding her new family.

She answered his question as if she could read his mind. "Don't try to talk me out of it, any of you. I've made my decision. I only wanted to tell you all what I'd done so that you wouldn't think me crazed, or wonder where these children had come from."

"I think perhaps you are crazed," Claire said, not unkindly.

"You said the same of me once," Dolly pointed out.

Claire slanted her friend a knowing smile. "Yes, and I wasn't entirely wrong, was I? But you're happier now than I could ever have guessed. And so I hope you will be, too, Rose. I'm not certain whether you've made the right decision, darling—only you can know that for sure. But I think I speak for all your friends when I say that we'll do whatever we can to help you."

Devon felt a twinge of pride. Claire couldn't have disguised her highborn background if she tried, but at heart, she was one of the most generous and down-to-earth women he'd ever met.

"Are you certain you want to do this?" Millicent asked.

"I've never been more sure of anything," Rose said. "I'd like to adopt the children legally so that they'll be mine, just as if I had given birth to them." She dashed away a tear with the back of her hand. A wobbly smile replaced her worried look. "There's only one problem."

"Only one?" Devon quipped. "What's that, dear?"

"They haven't all three got the same father, I'm afraid."

"Which one doesn't?" asked Millicent. When everyone in the room stared disbelievingly at her, she blushed and said quickly, "Well, I suppose the twins share the same father, don't they?"

"That appears to be so." Despite her worries, Rose smiled. "I needn't worry about Mollie's and Kate's father. He's, er, dead. One of the ladies at the Society knows quite a bit about the legalities of adoptions. She's assured me there'll be no difficulties with the girls if no one comes forward to claim them."

Devon's doubts were taking hold. "Perhaps you'd better think about this, Rose. 'Tis a weighty decision you're making here."

"Oh, I've thought about it," she said passionately. "I've thought about it for years, Mr. Avondale. There's nothing you can say that will change my mind."

"If you're not worried about the girls, then, what's the problem?" he asked.

"It's the little one that I'm worried about. He says

he does not know who his father is. But he had this calling card in his pocket. The name on the card is Sir Steven Nollbrook of Landsdowne Road, Ballsbridge. Worse, there was a note attached to the card, and it is signed by Miss Tweedy. She has identified this Sir Steven as Stevie's father. I'm not certain she meant for me to find this bit of evidence, but, well, there it is."

"Does the child know who Sir Steven is?" Claire appeared skeptical.

From her apron, Rose produced a tiny ivory colored card, elegantly engraved with Sir Steven's name, title and address. "I asked him if he had ever heard of Sir Steven. He nodded, but he could not say anything else about the man."

Devon took the card and turned it over in his fingers. "Doesn't make sense. Why would the child have this man's card in his pocket?"

"Perhaps he has met his father," Rose suggested. "It's not unheard of for men to visit their illegitimate children."

"If Sir Steven Nollbrook has visited the child, then perhaps he is wondering where the child is. How long ago did the child's mother die, Rose?"

Rose shrugged. "Several months."

Claire's spine had gone ramrod straight. "If he had left his son in the custody of a streetwalker, I doubt seriously he'll want him now that she's gone. I shudder to think what sort of cad he is. I don't think he will object to an adoption, Rose, if that's what you really want."

"If he is the child's father, he does owe a duty of

support, however." Devon wondered whether Rose had given sufficient thought to the demands three children were going to make on her budget. He wondered, too, if the bank draft he sent in the post each month—anonymously, of course—would have to be increased.

"I don't want the man's money," Rose said. "But if he is Stevie's father, then I must go and see him."

"I think you need to consult with my solicitor first," advised Devon.

"If this Sir Steven doesn't know where the child is, he can't object to an adoption, can he?" Dolly asked.

"Oh, he must be notified," Rose said. "I'm afraid my friend at the Society has done a bit of research, you see, and it seems that all fathers, even alleged ones, must be properly notified of any adoption applications. If I fail to notify Sir Steven, and later he objects to the adoption, it will undoubtedly be overturned. And what a horrid mess that would be for poor little Stevie!"

"A horrid mess, indeed," agreed Devon, though he tended to agree with Claire that any man who would leave his child in the custody of a prostitute would most likely not object to an adoption. Glancing at the clock behind him, he started to tuck Sir Steven's calling card into the pocket of his trousers.

Rose, however, stretched out her arm. "Could I have that, Mr. Avondale? I'm afraid I may need it."

"I don't think you should call on Sir Steven alone."

"I can take care of myself, Mr Avondale."

Fully aware that the gentle Rose had a core of steel,

Devon returned the card to her, but not before memorizing the barrister's address.

"Never fear," said Rose. "If the need for my rescue arises, you'll be the first knight in shining armor that I call upon."

"Will you agree to see my lawyer first? Before you rush off to visit this Sir Steven?"

"You'd better have him here in the morning, then."

"All right." Bending down, Devon kissed Rose's forehead. His heart swelled as he thought how deeply affected he would be if Rose's plans went awry, or were thwarted by this promiscuous Sir Steven Whoever-He-Was—for he must be a scoundrel if he'd fathered a child by a prostitute and left him to be raised in a whorehouse.

The gathering broke up shortly afterward, and the neighbors drifted to their respective homes. Devon walked Lady Claire Kilgarren to the edge of her garden, staring wistfully as she entered her house. Then, guided by moonlight, he pensively crossed the length of the square, entering his own home with a troubled mind, uncertain what to make of Rose's startling news. It seemed, by some miracle, that she'd just acquired what she'd always wanted—children.

But there was something odd about the story Rose had told. Moreover, there was something fishy about the facts as Miss Tweedy had related them. And already, even without seeing him, Devon despised this character named Sir Steven Nollbrook. He could hardly wait for Rose to report back after her conversation with the barrister. If Sir Steven gave her any trouble, Devon would pay him a visit—over Rose's protests if necessary.

Because that's what Mary would have wanted him to do.

Two

Mr. Albert Finch gave his pocket watch a conspicuous glance as Rose entered her drawing room. Tucking the gold timepiece into the folds of his waistcoat, he smiled unctuously. "Mr. Avondale informs that you have an urgent legal matter that you wish to discuss with me, Mrs. Sinclair."

"Thank you for coming so quickly." Rose directed Mr. Finch to sit opposite her. Politely covering her mouth, she yawned as she sank onto the sofa. Thankfully, her servants had furnished a pot of hot tea, and she poured as she spoke. "I presume Mr. Avondale has briefed you concerning my situation?"

"His porter came round late last night," explained Mr. Finch, accepting a cup of tea. "I'm afraid I know nothing except that you wish to adopt three orphans."

In describing her encounter with Clodagh Tweedy, Rose scrupulously omitted the fact that the twin girls' father was Winston Sinclair. "As far as Miss Tweedy knows," Rose explained, "their father could have been one of dozens of men. Apparently, Katherine was a popular woman. At the time of her death, she had no idea who fathered her twins."

Though Rose felt a twinge of guilt at fibbing to

Mr. Finch, she simply couldn't bring herself to expose the fraud that had existed in her marriage. Publicly, she and Winston had appeared happy and there was no reason to rewrite history or befoul her husband's sterling reputation. He was dead, after all, having been felled by a heart attack in the lobby of Dan Lowrey's Stare Theatre on Dame Street, an establishment frequented by the most respectable of men, but not their wives.

Moreover, Rose thought that her husband's whoremongering reflected poorly on her. Clearly, she had failed him. Her inability to produce children had so disappointed him that he'd sought physical solace elsewhere. His fraternization with a prostitute humiliated Rose, not just because it was scandalous, but because it illuminated her failures as a woman.

No, Rose could not, and would not, reveal to Mr. Finch the tawdry details of her private life with Winston. She'd simply tell him the girls' father was unknown. Since both Katherine and Winston were deceased, no one would ever contradict her. No one need ever know the twins' true parentage.

"I see no difficulty in adopting the children if their mother is dead and their father is unknown," Mr. Finch said.

"There's a slight problem . . ." Rose's voice trailed as her mind spun. How much should she tell Mr. Finch? How much should she keep to herself? Above all else, she wanted those children to be hers, and she didn't want to jeopardize the legality of the adoption process by omitting necessary details. On the other hand, she didn't want some disreputable barrister named Sir Steven Nollbrook objecting to her raising the children together. "They need to stay together," she murmured.

"By all means, they do!" Mr. Finch leaned forward. "The courts strongly favor orphans staying together. Mrs. Sinclair, are you all right?"

She drained her teacup and fortified her nerves. The three hours of sleep Rose had managed the night before would ordinarily have left her too tired to engage in an intelligent conversation. But this morning her mind was sharp. The many nocturnal trips she'd made down the hallway to look in on the children, and the hours she'd spent tossing in her bed and fretting about their futures, as well as what she would tell Mr. Finch, had not completely sapped her energy. It was strange, she thought, how taking care of little ones could actually empower a woman.

"I'm afraid the situation is a bit complicated. You see, they're not all orphans," Rose said. "The girls' father is dead, but the little one may actually know the name and whereabouts of his father. He had the man's calling card in his pocket."

A small, rotund man with a balding pate and thick spectacles, Mr. Finch pursed his lips. "The law in Ireland is clear. In the case of illegitimate children, if the mother is dead and the father is either dead, missing or unknown, a third party acting from the goodness of her heart should have no difficulty whatsoever in obtaining adoption papers. However, if the little boy's father is known—"

"We can't be certain this Sir Steven Nollbrook is actually Stevie's father," Rose inserted. "Perhaps the child is mistaken. There's no telling what sort of nonsense he heard in that horrid whore—"

"Sir Steven Nollbrook? The famous barrister?"

"Do you know him?"

"Every lawyer and jurist in Dublin knows Sir Steven." Mr. Finch's eyes had gone as round as his belly. "Well, Mrs. Sinclair, that puts a new complexion on the matter, doesn't it?"

"Does it?"

"Sir Steven is not a man to be trifled with."

"Mr. Finch, he left his child to be raised by a prostitute! I can't imagine what sort of man would do such a thing! Surely, he won't object to the child's being adopted."

"I'm afraid we can't presume that." Mr. Finch cleared his throat and placed his cup and saucer on the table beside his chair. "I wouldn't want to be the man who told Sir Steven that his son had been adopted by a stranger. *Without his consent.*"

Rose's face burned. The idea that a man could abandon his child, then prevent that child from being adopted by a loving parent, offended her so deeply that for a moment, she could barely speak. At length, after blinking back the tears that stung her eyes, she said, "Mr. Finch. Let me understand this. You are telling me that for the adoption to be valid and binding, I must obtain Sir Steven's consent."

"If he is the father."

"Let us say, for the sake of argument, that he is the child's father."

"Yes, ma'am." Mr. Finch had grown nervous since Sir Steven's name had come into the conversation.

"Then he will either give his consent to the adoption, or he will oppose it. If he opposes, the adoption will not take place, ma'am."

"Suppose he denies he is the child's father."

"Then that is the end of it. We inform the court that the child's father is unknown, and the adoption goes through without question. And there is a very good chance Sir Steven will deny paternity! Let us hope that is what happens."

Sighing, Rose pressed her fingers to her throbbing temples. "All right, Mr. Finch. Suppose that we do not tell Sir Steven that I intend to adopt Stevie, and we inform the court that the child's father is unknown. Who can say that we are lying? Who would question such a thing? We do not know for a certainty that Sir Steven is the father."

"You said the child said—"

"But he is a child!"

Mr. Finch shrugged. "It poses many risks, Mrs. Sinclair, chief among them the possibility that Sir Steven is the child's father and does not want to see him adopted."

"I would wager that he doesn't even know where the child is." Rose gazed with deepening wonder as the fat solicitor squirmed and fidgeted on the chair across from her. "No one will tell him, I am certain."

"Miss Tweedy, perhaps?" Mr. Finch drummed his fingers on his well-padded knees.

"More than likely Sir Steven will never ask her where Katherine's children have gone to. Even if he does confront her, she was the one attempting to rid herself of the children. She'll tell him nothing." Rose hoped she was right, but even as she spoke, she recognized the glaring flaw in her logic. Sir Steven would only have to press a wad of notes into Miss Tweedy's palm to loosen her lips.

Mr. Finch's face darkened and his jowls shook. "That's a bit risky, Mrs. Sinclair."

"Yes, I suppose it is." Rose's stomach turned over, and a sickly feeling swept over her. "Well, then, there is only one thing for it, and that is to visit this Sir Steven myself."

"Oh, I don't advise that." Mr. Finch twisted his fingers. "No, I don't advise that at all. Sir Steven is not the sort of man a woman wants to anger."

"Are you suggesting that he might become physically violent?"

"Oh, no! Sir Steven would never strike a woman. And I don't suppose he would go out of his way to fight a man, either. I don't think there's many who would dare raise their fists to Sir Steven. If a man ever did, though, I think Sir Steven would be up to killing him without so much as wrinkling his trousers."

Rose absorbed this bit of information with bewilderment. "Would you accompany me to Sir Steven's offices, then, Mr. Finch?"

"To accuse him of fathering a prostitute's child?" The man's legs appeared wobbly as he pushed up from his chair. "I don't think so, Mrs. Sinclair. I'm terribly sorry that I'm unable to assist you. I'll send round a note to Mr. Avondale, explaining everything."

"Don't bother," Rose said, standing. Grasping Mr.

Finch's hand, she shook it firmly. "I can take care of this situation myself."

"Good luck," the solicitor said over his shoulder. He was out of the drawing room, down the stairs and out the front door before Rose reached her bedchamber.

Dusting her palms, Rose murmured, "Coward." Then she pulled the bell cord and summoned her maid. "Go and fetch a cab, will you?" she asked the stooped woman who worked partly for her and partly for Mr. Avondale. Dimly, she wondered how she would run such a large house without the assistance of Mr. Avondale and his large staff of servants.

But as she dressed warmly, donning cape, gloves and wide-brimmed hat, Rose's thoughts turned to this enigmatic Sir Steven. Finch might be frightened of him, and she might very well have been frightened of him, too, before she resolved to take Mollie, Katie and Stevie into her home. But something magical had happened to Rose overnight. She had made a decision not to turn her back on these children who needed her. Though it was a decision made quickly, it was not a decision made lightly.

And it was a decision even Sir Steven Nollbrook would not be able to reverse.

No matter how unpleasant or terrifying a man he was.

It was half past nine in the evening by the time Sir Steven Nollbrook emerged from his cab and trudged up the walkway leading to the red brick town house that he leased in an affluent section of suburban Dublin known as Ballsbridge. With a leather valise clutched in one hand and a bundle of newspapers tucked beneath his arm, he fumbled with his keys, muttering a benign oath as he finally managed to push open the black lacquered door.

A woman's voice startled him. "Are you Sir Steven?"

Turning quickly, and dropping his papers as he did so, Steven peered into the semidarkness. From the shadows stepped a woman, her face obscured by a large hat. In her dark cape, nondescript dress and gloves, there was little to distinguish her from the many women who had visited Steven's home before. And, as she mounted the few steps that led up to the small porch, he thought he knew why she had come. For the thousandth time, Steven cursed his former recklessness and the physical urges—urges that he still felt, but now fastidiously controlled—which had gotten him into this mess.

"Go away," he growled.

"I must talk to you," she countered, without a trace of fear.

"About what?"

"I'm afraid it's of a rather personal nature."

"If it's about Katherine's brats, I don't want to hear it. I've had enough of your kind," Steven added. It was his instinct to fight back, to lash out at anyone who threatened him.

"My kind?" she echoed.

"I know what you're about," he said curtly. But in the glow of the gas lamps that flanked the front door, this woman bore little resemblance to the last one—*Miss Tweedy, was that her name?*—who popped in on Steven to discuss the parentage of Katherine's children. His voice softened more than he intended it to when he repeated his demand that she leave at once.

"Sir Steven, you don't want me to say what I must on your doorstep, do you? You don't want a passing stranger to hear your private business, do you?"

With a derisive snort, Steven scooped up his papers, then laid them atop his valise on a small table inside the foyer. When he turned again, the woman had placed the toes of her leather boots in his doorway. "Didn't you hear me? You'll have to go."

Though he could see but little of this woman's face, as it was obscured by both flickering light and a wide hat brim, he saw that her shapely lips were not rouged, her complexion was not ruddy and her features were far from course. For a prostitute, she was unusually pretty and dignified.

Her prettiness, however, did nothing to diminish Steven's determination not to talk to her. He tried to shut the door, but her toes were in the way, and, as vicious as Steven could be in court, and often was, he couldn't bring himself to slam a door on a woman's toes. With a sigh, he yanked it open again, thinking that if rudeness would not dissuade her, a masculine display of anger might intimidate her into going away.

"I said you must go! Now leave, woman! And never darken my doorstep again. I've had enough of you all, and I shall not hesitate to call the police if you continue harassing me in this manner! I know quite a bit more about the law than you do, mind you!"

"I'm sure that I do not know what you are talking about," his unwanted visitor replied archly.

Her prim manner surprised Steven. She really was rather unusual for a prostitute, not at all like the foul-mouthed women he'd grown accustomed to. "You know precisely what I'm talking about," he shot back. "That's why you're here, isn't it? To blackmail me?"

"Blackmail?" She lifted her chin then, so that her hat tilted and her eyes came into view. "Someone's trying to blackmail you, Sir Steven?"

"Don't be coy, woman. Miss Tweedy and Mrs. Bunratty have been trying to get into my pockets for weeks now."

"My name is not *woman,* sir." She held out her hand. "Apparently, you have mistaken me for someone else. My name is Mrs. Rose Sinclair."

Grudgingly, and with a very carefully contrived look of disdain, one that he often turned on his legal adversaries, he shook her hand. Disturbed by the warmth it conveyed, he spoke callously, hoping to so offend her that she would turn her back on him and never return. "Mrs.? Old Lady Bunratty employs married women these days? How charming."

"I'm afraid I don't know a Mrs. Bunratty. If she is associated with Miss Tweedy, however, I imagine she is not a Sunday school teacher." The woman bristled. "I'm here to discuss a very serious matter with you."

"Let me guess." Angered, Steven spoke through clenched teeth. "You've come to talk about my alleged only son and heir to my fortune."

Mrs. Sinclair, if that was really her name, feigned

surprise. "Do you mean to tell me that Stevie *is* your son? You do not deny it?"

"On the contrary. Didn't you hear me? I called him my *alleged* son. Because the truth of it is, Mrs. Sinclair, that I have no son."

Her gaze widened now, and in the gloaming, Steven could see that her eyes were a rare shade of violet, fringed by thick, sooty lashes. She really was quite beautiful. For a moment, her jaw worked and her lips trembled, as if she was on the verge of a reply, but couldn't quite decide what she wished to say. "Well, that is very fine, then, Sir Steven. I won't be troubling you further."

"You'll have to go now, or I shall have no option but to send for a constable."

"Happily." Her chin lifted a notch, and tears glimmered in her eyes. "Thank you, sir."

"For what?"

"For being honest." She took a step back and half turned, then stopped. When she looked at him, her gaze was full of gratitude. Gratitude that Steven didn't deserve, gratitude that made him feel like a lout. "I don't know why the child says you are his father. The silly delusions of a child, I suppose. Or perhaps someone lied to him, poor mite. He even had one of your calling cards in his pockets."

"That is ridiculous."

"And I'm sorry for you if you were the victim of Miss Tweedy's greed. It wasn't she who sent me here, that I can promise you. 'Tis the law that requires you be given an opportunity to acknowledge paternity. But you've put my mind at rest, Sir Steven. Now that I know you are not Stevie's father, I am free to adopt him and raise him as my own. Thank you."

"Adopt him? Adopt Katherine's son? Who are you?" Suddenly, Steven's gut tied in a knot. So this woman really was not a prostitute like Clodagh Tweedy. The realization that she was not Miss Tweedy's accomplice, and that whatever her motives were, they were probably sincere, hit him like a thunderbolt. And strangely, he had the urge to admit to her that he *was* the boy's father. Even though he wasn't. Or at least, he didn't *think* he was.

Blast it to hell, how am I supposed to know whether that little urchin is mine!

Raking his hand through his hair, Steven wondered if he would ever know the truth about Katherine, about why she wouldn't allow him to help her, and whether this child of hers was, in fact, his.

"Sir Steven, before I leave, might I ask you a question?"

"I don't suppose anything I say will stop you, will it?"

"I do not always get what I want, sir, but no one ever accused me of being timid." She gave him a self-deprecating, wistful, thoroughly feminine smile. "You can't imagine how much peace of mind you've just given me, just by admitting that Stevie is not your child."

Steven felt an unbidden wave of attraction for this brazen little minx, dressed as conservatively as a Puritan, a good ten years older than any woman he had ever courted or even dallied with, and far too respectable a female ever to trifle with the likes of him. A heaviness tingled in his groin, but a tocsin rang in his head, and an inner voice warned him off. She was not for him.

"I'm pleased I was able to make you happy, Mrs.—"

"Call me Rose." She extracted a tiny vellum card from her handbag and handed it to him. "And if Miss Tweedy continues to trouble you, tell her that this is where she can find me."

He looked up from the card, puzzled. Why had this woman given him her address? He didn't want to know where she lived. He didn't want to know anything about her. Seeing her address made him curious about her. Curiosity made him hunger for her society. And the last thing Steven needed was to become infatuated with a woman who was adopting his *alleged* son. That was a scenario that had more pitfalls than Miss Tweedy's extortionate suggestions.

"Your question, ma'am?"

"I'll need a representative, won't I? To formalize the adoption, that is. I realize you're a barrister, but you must work closely with one solicitor or another, and I thought perhaps you could recommend me to someone knowledgeable about these things."

He felt as if he had cotton stuffed in his head. *What the devil is she talking about?*

Seeing his confusion, Mrs. Sinclair said, "You see, if you are not Stevie's father, then there's no reason I can't adopt all three children at once. Is there?"

"All three children?"

" 'Twould be a tragedy if the twins, Mollie and Katie, were to be separated from their younger brother."

"Twins?" In a dim corner of his mind, he grasped at the fuzziest of memories, an impression, really, of twin girls running about Mrs. Bunratty's. He had not paid them any mind. And Katherine had never told him she had other children. She had told Steven that the infant boy was her first child. For that matter, Miss Tweedy had only ever mentioned one child. Was he to believe now that there were more? Would he also be accused of siring those children, too? "I'm afraid I don't understand, Mrs. Sinclair."

She opened her mouth to explain.

But Steven couldn't bear to hear more. His senses were overloaded, his intellect was overwhelmed and his emotions were overtaxed. Regret and self-loathing knifed through him as he slowly shut the door. He watched Mrs. Sinclair's pleasant expression turn to disappointment as he shut her out. But he had to.

Sir Steven was not a man who showed indecision, vacillation or weakness. He was a man of action and conviction. Better to appear rude and boorish than vulnerable. Better to push Mrs. Sinclair away than give her the opportunity to learn the truth about him.

And in the few minutes she'd been on his doorstep, Steven had sensed that she *could* learn the truth about him, that she was just that sort of woman, the sort he might fall in love with, the sort who would break his heart.

The door clicked shut, locking him inside his house with nothing but loneliness and bitterness. Mrs. Sinclair's boots cracked sharply on the bricks outside, then faded from earshot. She was gone; Steven breathed a sigh of relief. He'd escaped whatever trap she'd intended to lay for him. He was free of Katherine, Miss Tweedy, that pathetic little bastard ironically named Stevie and a Puritan named Rose who had the sweetest smile and loveliest eyes he had ever seen.

He hoped he never saw any of them again.

And he was terrified by the thought that he wouldn't.

Three

He is Stevie's father.

For the hundredth time, Rose tried to put that thought out of her head. But the mental pictures wouldn't go away; Sir Steven and the boy shared the same coloring, the same broad forehead and—as fate would have it—the same cleft chin.

A chill wind blew through the open casement window of her bedroom. As she leaned out to pull the window closed, a movement on the street below caught her attention. Rose smiled at the sight of Mr. Avondale strolling past the garden, hat pulled low over his eyes, hands tucked inside the pockets of his greatcoat. It wasn't unusual to see him patrolling the neighborhood, even at this late hour. He said he had insomnia and enjoyed the fresh air. But he invariably paused in front of Number Three, where Lady Kilgarren lived, and stared up at the second-floor windows as if he were attempting to divine what was going on inside.

With a sigh, Rose drew shut her white lace curtains and got into bed. She wasn't the sort to worry about another woman's business—not unless it was Millicent Hyde, of course, who, since the two had moved into

Fontjoy Square some nine months earlier, had become Rose's best friend.

However, Millicent, after one of the most unconventional engagements Rose had ever witnessed, was now happily married to Captain Alec Wolferton. She didn't need Rose's maternal protection; she was quite grown up and, despite an obviously consuming passion for her husband, quite an independent young woman. The thought should have cheered her. But Rose missed Millicent's late night visits and tortured confidences. She missed feeling as if Millicent needed her.

She missed having someone to talk to.

Burrowing beneath the covers, Rose tried to will herself to sleep. Having assisted in bathing the children before bedtime, she was physically exhausted. Stevie, it appeared, held a deep conviction that soap was bad for his health and water was for swimming. Getting him in and out of the tub had required more strength than Rose thought she possessed. She'd had little rest in the past two days and she was physically and emotionally exhausted. She should have fallen asleep before her head hit the pillow. She would have—if her mind hadn't refused to release those pictures of Sir Steven juxtaposed with little Stevie.

Restless, she got out of bed, threw on her wrapper and went below stairs. A single taper lit Rose's way through the darkened house until she reached the kitchen. There she lit an oil lamp, as well as the fire in her new Gold Medal Eagle Range, delivered several weeks ago from Maguire & Gatchell department store with an unsigned note that simply encouraged her to enjoy using it.

Padding from the pantry to the big wooden work table in the center of the kitchen, arms laden with cannisters of flour, cartons of eggs, crocks of butter and blocks of yeast, she reflected on her move to Number Four Fontjoy Square. She still didn't know who had donated the house to her, installed the modern plumbing, sent the fancy modern oven, and furnished a stipend each month generous enough to allow her to pay her bills and maintain her red brick house. She couldn't even *think* of anyone who might owe her a kindness.

It wasn't as if she had a very wealthy father who could have given her the house, as Lady Kilgarren's had done hers, or even a doting one, like Millicent Hyde's, who, despite his estrangement from his daughter, had seen to her creature comforts by installing her in Fontjoy Square.

And it wasn't as if Rose's husband had died and left her a home in which to live, as Lady Dolly's had done for her.

No, Rose lacked connections, money *and* breeding. No one owed her anything, and no one had ever given her anything. She couldn't imagine who had snatched her from the edge of poverty and given her Number Four Fontjoy Square. But to whomever had, she was eternally grateful.

She cracked an egg and dropped it in the center of the flour well she had created. Baking bread was hardly expected of her. Rose had a maid now, and a cook, too. As soon as she could make arrangements, she'd hire a governess for the children. But the work relaxed her, and the creative process, the ability to take a pile of raw ingredients and shape them into a loaf of fragrant, chewy bread, gave her a sense of accomplishment and well-being.

That she could offer her loaves of bread to the women who visited the Dorcas Society offices made Rose feel useful and needed. Not for a minute did she consider what she did as altruistic or charitable. On the contrary, the pleasure she obtained from feeding others, and helping those less fortunate than she, left her feeling self-indulged and greedy.

With a fork, she expertly incorporated the egg into the flour. While she worked, she forced her thoughts away from Stevie's resemblance to Sir Steven. The mystery of her benefactor gave her something else to mull over. Not for the first time, she considered the odd coincidence of four unmarried women moving to Fontjoy Square at the same time. The others, of course, had explained how they'd acquired their homes. Rose had no such explanation.

So, while it was against her nature to lie, Rose had told her neighbors that her deceased husband had bequeathed her this house. But that was a bold-faced clanker if ever there was one. Mr. Winston Sinclair had left nothing for Rose but a battered heart and a legion of creditors.

Forming the sticky dough into a ball, she felt a quickening of her pulse. What would have become of her if the strange man dressed in black and wearing a black mask hadn't come to her house and given her the envelope that contained the invitation to live in Fontjoy

Square? Where would she have gone to escape the bill collectors? How could she have survived any longer?

Shivering at the thought, aware of how close she had come to being one of those women who stood in line for soup at charities similar to the Dorcas Society, Rose pressed the heels of her hands into the dough. Pushing forward, pulling back, working the dough, she transformed it into a flat, supple oval. She folded the dough in half and tirelessly kneaded it some more. The certain result of her efforts comforted her; it was reassuring to have some control over something in her life, even if it was baking bread.

She oiled the inside of an earthenware bowl, then placed the dough in it. Insofar as her mysterious benefactor was concerned, Rose knew only that he wanted her to live here, and, in exchange, all she had to do was care for the Georgian house—which was slightly run-down except for the incongruous modern fixtures—and refurbish the neglected garden in the center of the square.

Luckily for her, since gardening was not her *forte,* Rose's neighbors seemed equally intent on rejuvenating the garden. Though the fall weather had been keeping the ladies indoors of late, they had made tremendous progress in the spring and summer months. A rose trellis was half built, the bordering hedges were trimmed and tulips were planted in concentric patterns around the roots of Japanese dogwood trees. Barring a harsh winter, the garden would be in full, riotous bloom by next year.

As she draped a linen towel over the bowl, Rose wondered if the two new male additions to the neighborhood would expedite the gardening project. Lady Dolly Baltmore, the first of her neighbors to get married, could certainly enlist her husband, the famous pugilist Dick Creevy, to pull a few weeds.

And perhaps Miss Millicent Hyde's new husband, Captain Alec Wolferton, could lend a hand as well. Mr. Avondale really couldn't be expected to do *all* the heavy work. It was merely fortuitous that he had taken up the gardening project with as much, if not more, zeal than the four ladies.

With nothing more to do for the moment besides allow the bread to rise and double, Rose climbed the stairs and peeked in on Mollie and Katie. For a long time, she stood at the door, watching them sleep, her chest aching with affection. Then, she walked the short distance to Stevie's room and looked in on him.

In the faint light that filtered through the window, the child's pale cheeks glowed like a cherub's. Unable to resist, Rose smoothed the covers over his shoulders and kissed his forehead. *God, he looks so much like Sir Steven!* And, inexplicably, the similarity in their features endeared them both to Rose. As Stevie wriggled beneath her touch, Rose's heart squeezed. Then, careful not to awaken the child, she tiptoed from the room. A wave of yearning swept over her as she returned to her bedchamber.

She supposed some might wonder how a woman could form such a strong attachment to children in such a short time. But Rose knew that any loving mother would understand; though she barely knew anything about the children's background, personalities, likes and dislikes, talents and intellect, she knew she loved them. That was all she had to know. She'd walk over broken glass to keep those children with her. They might not know it, but they needed her. And she needed to be needed.

Clutching the counterpane to her chin, Rose closed her eyes. If she didn't get some rest, she'd be dead on her feet come the morrow. But sleep eluded her. Her conversation with Sir Steven Nollbrook haunted her. His hazel eyes and cleft chin tormented her. The way his voice had softened when she smiled, the wounded look in his gaze when he closed the door, totally confused her. She was relieved that he'd denied paternity, but he was lying, she was certain. And though she knew she should simply forget about him, she couldn't erase him from her thoughts.

What sort of man would reject his own son?

When dawn came, Rose was back in the kitchen, shaping her dough into long, thin loaves. Shortly after, the homey smell of baking bread wafted through the house. Stevie materialized like a little wraith, his hair tousled from sleep, his eyes blinking. Rose chuckled at the sight of his wrinkled nightshirt, far too big and dragging the floor, having been lent by one of her servants, a good-natured woman with a dozen children of her own. His tiny bare feet alarmed her; he would develop a cough if she didn't get some warm stockings on his legs.

But his gaze was fixed on the warm loaves she'd just taken from the oven. Without a word, Rose broke off a chunk of bread, buttered it and slathered it with strawberry preserves. The child, eyes lit with joy, ate greedily. Rose couldn't have been more pleased if she'd invented a cure for plague. Watching Stevie eat, she studied his features—the straight nose, the intelligent intensity in his eyes. He was his father's son, all right.

Licking the crumbs off his fingers, he stared frankly at her. "When is Father coming to get me?"

Rose felt a sharp pain in her chest. "I—I do not know. Would you mind terribly if you stayed here with me?"

The child's brows knit together. "Mummy said he would be coming to get me some day. He's an important man, though, very busy. But I expect he'll come and get me soon, don't you?"

Uncertain how much the children knew about Katherine's death, or her occupation for that matter, Rose hesitated. "When did your mummy tell you those things, dear?"

"Before she went away." He shrugged lightly. "She's never coming back, is she?"

"No, darling." Rose gathered him in her arms and squeezed him. He smelled of jam and soap and little boy. "Come on, then," she said, releasing him. He grasped her hand as she led him from the kitchen. "Let's wake your sisters and get ourselves dressed. We've got a busy day, I'm afraid."

"Are we going to see Father?"

"Not just yet."

"When?"

Rose tried to sound reassuring. "As soon as possible, dear. I shall look into it, I promise."

* * *

The judge's gavel banged the courtroom session to an end. Steven's client, ebullient with his legal victory, gushed his gratitude.

"You might not be so grateful when you receive my bill," Steven replied.

As the courtroom cleared, Sir Steven glanced across the aisle at his opponent, Mr. Aloysius Letterfrack. For years, the two barristers had battled each other over controversies ranging from the mundane to the profound. But whether it was a landlord-tenant dispute they fought over, or the constitutional issues surrounding the extension of voting rights, they always ended their legal match with a gentlemanly handshake and a grudging word or two of admiration.

Lately, however, Steven had noted a marked change in Mr. Letterfrack's demeanor. The man's determination to best Steven seemed more personal, less professional. His written correspondence had taken on a vitriol out of proportion to the enmity their clients felt. The case at bar, a simple dispute concerning money owed to a creditor, should have been settled out of court. In insisting that the matter be brought to trial, Mr. Letterfrack had, in Steven's mind, created unnecessary legal fees for his client. And the fact that the judge ruled in favor of Steven's client did not brighten Mr. Letterfrack's mood.

Letterfrack crammed his papers into a leather valise, then shot Steven a malevolent glare. The two men stood at the wooden gate that separated the court officials from the spectators. For a moment, Steven thought Letterfrack would refuse to shake his hand.

At length, the older man grumbled, "Congratulations," and squeezed Steven's hand.

As they pushed through the swinging gate, Steven said, "As always, Letterfrack, you were a worthy opponent. The decision could have gone either way, in my estimation."

"Next time, Steven, next time." With that, the man trundled off, his broad back bent beneath his black barrister's robe.

In his office, Steven removed the heavy woolen wig barristers were required to wear in court. Tossing off his robe, he slumped into his chair, tired after a bitterly contested and hard-fought trial, but, as always, slightly enervated by the thrill of battle. Most men would have called it a day, but for Steven, hours more of paperwork, letter-writing and research lay ahead.

Letterfrack's recent coldness toward him was a niggling worry. But that was a small concern compared to the most troublesome of Steven's thoughts. Try as he might, he couldn't push Katherine's son—possibly *his* son—from his mind.

Staring at the pile of correspondence on his desk, Steven sighed. There was no use trying to read those letters now; he'd managed to concentrate on his case all day. Now his brain was free to grapple with his own conundrum.

Was it possible that the little boy Rose Sinclair had called Stevie, indeed all three of Katherine's children, were truly his?

It was possible.

Mentally, he ticked off his options. He could do nothing, keep his mouth shut, deny the child was his and go on with his dreary life as if Katherine had never existed. There was much to be said for that course of action. Mrs. Sinclair would be happy; she would adopt the children, and judging by the looks of her, she would care for them as if they were her own.

Yes, the more he thought about it, the more certain he became that denying paternity of Katherine's children was the right thing to do. He was not fit to be a father. He worked too hard, and he had grown accustomed to living alone. He had no family to support him in his efforts to raise a family, his own parents having passed on many years ago. He was too old to bounce babies on his knee or chase little ones around the park. He would be doing those children a disfavor by getting involved with them.

And denying paternity carried with it the added incentive of avoiding Miss Tweedy's blackmail scheme.

Rubbing the lids of his closed eyes, he groaned. He knew he was rationalizing his selfish behavior. He tasted the fear at the back of his throat.

But whether he could swallow that fear and confront his responsibilities was a different matter altogether.

"Don't be ridiculous, Steven," Katherine had said to him after she had given birth. *"The baby cannot be yours. I suppose I was foolish to name the child after you, but you have been so kind to me that I thought . . ."*

What *had* she been thinking? What had *they* been thinking?

Had Katherine lied to him outright about the identity of her child's father? If so, why?

Well, he would never know the answer now, would he?

Not if I walk away, I won't.

Pulling himself to his feet, Steven surveyed his office, crammed with books and filing cabinets, its walls covered with diplomas and certificates of award from academic honor societies. His life was in this office. Every ounce of blood and sweat he had expended during the last three decades, building his practice, honing his craft and earning his reputation, could be documented in the scraps of paper filling this room. But in the end, the scraps of paper gave him no joy. And Katherine had been right when she told him life was passing him by. Katherine had been right when she told him he needed to find someone to love and care for.

Regret descended on him, so that he moved like an old man as he shrugged into his coat and extinguished the lamps.

He had loved Katherine, and yet he had failed her. Perhaps if he had taken her to a doctor when he first discovered she drank . . . Perhaps if he hadn't been so absorbed in his own career . . . Perhaps, perhaps, perhaps. Well, it was too late now.

Or is it?

A half-buried desire to see his own features in the face of a child, a long-abandoned plan to have a family and share his life with a good, kind-hearted woman, a long-suppressed need to be loved . . . suddenly, all these things tugged at Steven's heart. He could spend an eternity trying to convince himself he enjoyed being a bachelor. But his heart would not cease aching.

And his conscience would not allow him to shirk his moral or legal obligation to his offspring. If any of Katherine's children were his, Steven owed them a duty of support and succor. Rational thinking, however, demanded that he investigate further before he disclaimed any relationship with them.

He considered another alternative. He could pay a visit to Mrs. Sinclair and meet the children. *He could just visit.* He did not have to make a commitment, not at first sight. There was always the option of *just visiting.* He had every right to do that. Indeed, having been accused of fathering these children, he owed it to himself, and to them as well, to investigate the matter further before making a decision.

Mrs. Rose Sinclair would not be pleased.

Her guileless expression flashed in Steven's mind. She—virtuous and a trifle stern—was the opposite of sensuous, frivolous Katherine. Yet, there was something about her, something so upright and straitlaced that Steven couldn't help wondering what she was really like when she unpinned that thick raven hair of hers. What was beneath that severe dark-blue gown with the prim high neck and the starched white shirt cuffs? What would it take to make Rose Sinclair swoon and gasp with unbridled passion?

His fantasy created an uncomfortable tingling in his lower body. Plunging into the harsh chill of a starless night, Steven realized he had not so much as looked at a woman in over six months. It had been over a year since he'd actually lain with one. His body thrummed with sexual need, and, worse, his spirit yearned for the comfort of a woman's embrace.

His arm flew up, and a hackney cab ground to a halt in the middle of the street, invoking a stream of invective from the driver of the carriage behind it. Climbing inside, Steven considered going to Mrs. Bunratty's. There were women there, plenty of them, warm and willing.

But the image of Rose Sinclair, little Puritan that she was, would not allow him to enjoy his lascivious urge. Directing the driver toward home, Steven threw himself against the squabs with a sigh of disgust. He thought it distinctly possible that he was going crazy. How on earth could one woman, a woman he'd met for no more than ten minutes, one who, in that short period of time, had accused him not only of fathering an illegitimate child, but of abandoning it too, inspire him to such emotion?

Pretty little minx! And she had not believed him for a moment when he denied he was the father of Katherine's son. He'd seen the disbelief in her violet gaze; it had penetrated him to the core, impaling him with guilt and remorse. She thought he was an amoral scoundrel, or worse, a coward!

Well, he might be a scoundrel, but he wasn't a coward!

She could not prevent him from paying a visit, just to look at Katherine's children, just to be certain they weren't his. He was sorry if his decision made Mrs. Sinclair unhappy, but he had legal rights and he intended to protect them.

Turning the key in his lock, he hesitated. This was where she had sneaked up behind him, ambushing him, as it were, on his own doorstep. The back of his neck prickled as his door swung open, and the loneliness of an empty house reached out to embrace him. He half expected Mrs. Sinclair to materialize; he half hoped she would. But she did not, of course, and he entered his home with a heavy heart, thirsty for a glass of whiskey and thoroughly bewildered by the mixed emotions swirling in his head.

Devon Avondale stood at the mantel, his hands clasped behind his back. For the better part of the morning, he'd been watching in amusement as Rose interviewed potential governesses. She'd have done better to leave the children out of this process, rather than allowing them to participate in interrogating the hapless applicants themselves, but it wasn't his place to tell her how to run her house. Besides, watching the children cope with their new environment was an education in itself.

Flanked by the twins on one side and Stevie on the other, Rose sat on the camelback sofa, consulting a list of questions she'd composed for the interview. Her jet black hair wisped negligently around her nape and forehead, just as it had been doing the past few days. She looked tired, but she looked happier than Devon had ever seen her.

Opposite her sat Mrs. Annie Bleek, a thin woman clad in clothes so severe that they made Rose's dark blue gown look like a harlot's *negligée.* Mrs. Bleek's silver hair was pulled so tightly into a bun atop her head that Devon wondered how she closed her eyes. As she eyed the three children, her gaze narrowed and her lips pursed. When Rose looked up from the notes she'd made, however, the woman smiled sweetly and tilted her head in Stevie's direction.

"What a precious little boy," Mrs. Bleek cooed.

Rose smiled. "This is Stevie, and these are Mollie and Kate. I know it is rather unusual for children to be present when a governess is being interviewed, but since you'll be spending all your time with them, it seems only appropriate they have a say in who is hired."

"Um-um." The older woman's spindly fingers formed a web on her lap. "Been working with children for nigh on fifty years, Mrs. Sinclair."

"My, that's impressive. I'm afraid I am new at this."

Mrs. Bleek's eyebrows rose. "Married their father, did you? Stepchildren?" Her gaze shot to Devon.

Caught off guard, he shook his head and cleared his throat while Rose stumbled through an explanation.

"We are not married," she said.

"Not married? You don't mean to tell me you are living in—"

"Don't misunderstand! Mr. Avondale is not their father. I was never married to their father."

"Never married?"

"They are orphans, Mrs. Bleek. I am in the process of adopting them."

An audible sigh of relief escaped the older woman's bony chest. "I understand." But it was evident from her tone that she did not understand at all.

"Well, none of that signifies at present, does it, Mrs. Bleek?" When the governess failed to answer,

Rose tapped her list of questions and said, "I hope you won't think me rude, but do you feel that you are physically capable of dealing with three children?"

"I am as healthy as a horse."

"Can you play catch?" interjected Stevie.

"Can you play hide-and-seek?" queried Katie.

"Can you ride a pony?" added Mollie.

"Can you chase a bill collector with a broom?"

"Can you dance the waltz?"

"Dance the waltz?" Mrs. Bleek's eyes widened. "Whoever heard of a governess dancing the waltz?"

Mollie, her dark-brown hair parted down the middle and plaited in two pigtails, gave the older woman a toothy smile. "When we lived at Mrs. Bunratty's, we danced most every evening. Stevie's a terrible dancer. He likes to stand on Miss Tweedy's toes and hug her about the waist. That's not really dancing, is it?"

"I want Miss Tweedy back," announced Stevie.

"I don't," replied Katie. To distinguish the twins, Rose had brushed Katie's hair straight back into one glossy ponytail. Now that all eyes were turned on her, she slumped back into the sofa cushions and self-consciously twirled that thick shock of hair with her fingers. "I'm glad we're rid of Miss Tweedy. Or she's rid of us. Either way, 'tis for the best."

"She liked Stevie," said Mollie. "She was nice to him."

"Who is Miss Tweedy?" warbled Mrs. Bleek.

"Their, er, former governess," Rose said.

Mollie plucked at Rose's sleeve. "So Mrs. Bleek is going to take Miss Tweedy's place? Is that it?"

"Well, not exactly," started Rose.

"Can you sing?" asked Stevie.

With a frown, Mrs. Bleek said, "I know a few songs, hymns mostly."

"Do you know 'Gertie Let Her Garters Down?' " piped Mollie.

"Do you know any clever limericks?" asked Katie. "Like the one that starts, 'There was a young woman from Horn Head—?' "

"That's enough!" Patches of scarlet appeared on Rose's porcelain cheeks.

Stifling his amusement, Devon dipped his head and studied the hearth beneath his feet. That the children were raised in a brothel had become abundantly clear. If he made eye contact with Rose, he feared he would erupt into laughter.

"Good heavens, what sort of governess did the children have before me?" asked Mrs. Bleek.

Rose swallowed hard and scrutinized her list of questions. "I would like to discuss your moral and religious values, if you don't mind. Do you consider yourself a particularly devout woman?"

To Devon's surprise, Mrs. Bleek squared her shoulders and gave all three children a long look before she replied. "I am not a prude, Mrs. Sinclair, but—"

"Good. That's a start, isn't it?" Rose proceeded to her next question. "Do you object to living in this house, with the children? As you can see, they do so need someone full-time. You would be free to do as you please on at least one night each week. And I can't pay you grandly, Mrs. Bleek, but I am prepared to meet the going rate for governesses, I assure you."

Mrs. Bleek's jaw worked as she considered her

response. She gave Devon a short, reproachful glance, as if she questioned the necessity of his being in the room. Then she turned an earnest gaze on Rose. " 'Tis time to be frank, Missus. I am not a young woman and I suffer from occasional bouts of fatigue. The doctor tells me my heart is weak. I cannot chase a ball or play hopscotch or jump rope. I cannot saddle a pony or run races. 'Tis why I was dismissed from my previous position, understand. And I may not be around to see the children through their schoolroom years."

Mollie hopped off the sofa and stood next to Mrs. Bleek's chair. Gently, the child touched the older woman's arm. "I'm sorry you're sick, Mrs. Bleek. Have you tried tincture of iodine?"

"Perhaps you're pregnant," suggested Katie.

" 'Tis the hazard of your occupation," said Stevie solemnly.

Devon pinched the bridge of his nose to keep from chuckling.

Nonplussed, the older woman's hand covered Mollie's. "But I do love children, Mrs. Sinclair. And I do not give a fig where they have been, really I don't."

"In that case, you are hired," Rose said.

Mollie threw her arms around Mrs. Bleek's neck and squealed with joy. Katie leaped off the sofa and did the same. But Stevie remained as still as a statue. Rose gave him a little nudge and whispered in his ear.

The child, arms crossed over his chest, sullenly shook his head.

" 'Tis all right." Mrs. Bleek gave the child a knowing look. "He'll come around."

Rose nibbled her bottom lip. "I hope you are right."

With Mollie and Katie holding her hands, Mrs. Bleek stood. "Would you girls like to show me my new quarters?"

"I'll have the maid take you above stairs and show you around," offered Rose, rising. She pulled a bell cord, and when the maid appeared, she introduced the new governess and instructed that Mrs. Bleek be shown the bedroom next to Stevie's. "It will be more convenient for you than the servants' quarters. This way, you will have fewer stairs to climb."

"Thank you, ma'am." Mrs. Bleek had a tear of gratitude in her pale blue gaze.

When the entourage, Stevie included, had left the parlor, Rose turned to Devon.

"Have I done the right thing, sir?"

He gave her a light hug. "I should think so. Mrs. Bleek seems to have summed up the situation rather quickly."

"Is it that obvious?"

The laughter Devon had suppressed now escaped him. "How many seven-year-old girls would recommend tincture of iodine at the first sign of illness?"

Rose was reluctant to share in his laughter, but she couldn't resist a smile. "I'm afraid they have received quite an unusual education thus far."

"My dear, I believe we are all about to receive an education."

"We're never too old to learn, are we, Mr. Avondale?"

"When we are, then it is too late, because we are dead," he replied. "On another subject, I am made to understand that your conversation with Mr. Finch was less than satisfying."

She colored instantly. "Oh, I do appreciate your sending him round! I didn't mean to be ungrateful!"

"Dear, I do not mind at all if you prefer someone else," he assured her. "But I have taken the liberty of obtaining for you the name and address of another attorney. This one is extraordinarily aggressive. Believe me, he won't shy away from a legal problem just because Sir Steven Nollbrook is involved. On the contrary, I rather think he will relish the thought of representing you in this matter."

"It shouldn't be too difficult a task," Rose said. "Sir Steven has denied he is Stevie's father. That will greatly simplify the adoption process."

Devon had an uneasy feeling about Sir Steven. While he was relieved to hear the man denied paternity, he doubted seriously that the adoptions of the twins and Stevie were going to be as effortless as Rose anticipated.

And because it appeared that the adoption was going to be a contested matter that would wind up in court, Rose needed the assistance of a barrister rather than a solicitor. That was why, after numerous inquiries among his business associates and acquaintances, Devon had carefully chosen Mr. Aloysius Letterfrack to handle Rose's case.

Mr. Letterfrack was well known for his silver tongue and brutal litigation tactics. And it was common knowledge that Mr. Letterfrack and Sir Steven Nollbrook were fierce adversaries. Letterfrack would chomp at the bit to take a case that might potentially embarrass his archenemy.

"How will I pay—"

"Let me worry about that," Devon said. "You have an appointment with Mr. Letterfrack at three o'clock this afternoon. My carriage will take you and the children to his offices just off Anglesea Street. I was told the children must attend. I hope it won't be too traumatic for them."

"After what they've been through, I shouldn't think meeting a lawyer would even faze them. You've been very kind and supportive, Mr. Avondale. I do thank you," Rose said demurely, her thick lashes fluttering while she blushed.

Moved by her emotion, Devon gave Rose an abbreviated bow. "Good luck, then, and keep me abreast of developments." He crossed the room, but hesitated in the doorway and grinned over his shoulder. "By the way, I should like to hear a round of 'Gertie Let Her Garters Down' someday. It sounds like a charming little ditty."

Blushing even more violently, Rose dismissed him with a wave. "You're incorrigible," she scolded. But he heard her giggle as he jogged down the stairs and out the front door.

Four

With Mrs. Bleek in the house, the afternoon acquired an amazing degree of calmness. After supervising the children in a luncheon of sliced meats and cheeses, the new governess set up a schoolroom on the third floor and immediately went about evaluating their reading and writing skills. Standing outside the door, Rose listened as Katie and Mollie labored to recite the alphabet. It would take many months, perhaps years, for the children to catch up academically with their peers.

Satisfied that the children were in capable hands, Rose returned to the drawing room, where she sat at a small rosewood refectory table, shoulders hunched over her journal as she composed another of her ubiquitous lists. Deep in thought, she answered absently when the maid knocked gingerly at the door. "I've had enough tea, thank you."

The door squeaked open to reveal the maid's puckered expression. "Sorry, ma'am, but they's a gentleman here to see you. Says his name's Sir Steven and that it's very important business he has with you."

"Show him up." Rose's pulse skittered. In the moment it took for Sir Steven to ascend the stairs, she concluded that his visit was going to be unpleasant. She hadn't liked the man when she first encountered him, and by the time he entered her drawing room, she liked him even less.

She could not, however, deny his attractiveness. The man was tall and broad-shouldered, with thick, wavy russet hair and penetrating eyes. His high forehead, so disturbingly like little Stevie's, was lined with experience and intelligence, perhaps even worry. His handsome black suit bespoke refinement, understatement and prosperity. By anyone's standards, Sir Steven was an arresting individual, a man who commanded respect and attention. *A man whom others feared.*

Mr. Finch's nervousness at the sound of Sir Steven's name, and his reluctance to anger the man, were now instantly explained. The man's eyes were as hard as stone. The sobriety in his features was unrelenting. Rose wondered whether he had ever smiled or laughed once in his life. Stiffening with apprehension, she considered ordering him from her home. But the impulse was eclipsed both by curiosity to hear what he had to say, and by the faint notion that her efforts to adopt Stevie would not be furthered by rudeness.

"Hello, Mrs. Sinclair. Sorry to have dropped in unannounced. Please forgive me."

His voice, deep-throated and as smooth as honey, raised the hairs on Rose's nape.

It had been many years since she had looked at a man with anything other than distrust and suspicion; indeed, Rose viewed Sir Steven with healthy amounts of both. Still, another, more mysterious element suddenly entered Rose's evaluation of the handsome barrister. She couldn't quite articulate her feelings. She knew only that Sir Steven's appearance in her home was certainly bad news, and yet she took guilty pleasure in seeing him again.

Predisposed to dislike the man, she could not make sense of her emotions. She was not the sort of woman who developed infatuations for strange men. She was a mature woman, entirely in control of her feelings and her environment. Why, then, did her heart thud so violently as the man crossed the room? Without thinking, Rose politely extended her hand, and as Sir Steven's fingers closed around hers, a shock of warmth flowed through her veins.

"Why did you come here?" she managed, despite the tightening in her chest.

His lips curved. A knowing look and a slight shrug deflected her question. "You piqued my curiosity, Mrs. Sinclair. I was troubled by some of the things you said during our brief conversation. I have some questions for you."

"I should never have given you my card," Rose replied quietly. "I thought that if Miss Tweedy bothered you again, you might refer her to me. You see, I was so relieved to hear that you are not Stevie's father that I thought I might repay your kindness by taking Miss Tweedy off your hands."

"Mrs. Sinclair, I'm quite prepared to deal with Miss Tweedy myself."

"She is a nuisance to you, though. You have made that crystal clear. And since I am going to retain the services of an attorney and adopt the three children as quickly as possible, by all rights, Miss Tweedy is my problem now. Not yours."

"It may not be that simple."

Rose's tight smile was a hedge against the trepidation creeping over her. "Did you say you have some questions for me?"

Sir Steven's hesitation was rife with tension, his penetrating stare full of challenge. He watched Rose sharply, instilling her with self-awareness. And though she was, by nature, unflappable even in the most trying of circumstances, her face tingled with heat beneath his scrutiny.

"You said Katherine had three children, Mrs. Sinclair. I should like to see them."

Her heart sank like a stone. "Why, sir?"

"Upon reflection, it has occurred to me that one or all of the children may in fact be mine. I should like to be certain before I allow any one of them to be adopted."

"You cannot stop me," Rose said through gritted teeth. Anger coursed through her body, emboldening her, knotting the muscles in her neck and shoulders. "You said the boy wasn't yours. Well, the girls aren't, either, I can assure you of that. You have no right to—"

"Show me the children, Mrs. Sinclair, or I shall take whatever legal action is necessary to see them myself. And that will not be pleasant for any of us, will it? Least of all, the children."

She bit back the words, *I hate you,* but the sentiment echoed in her brain.

The scant feelings of warmth and good will Rose

had harbored toward this man—along with the inexplicable physical attraction she had felt for him—vanished.

Stark terror splashed across her features. For an instant, Sir Steven regretted coming to Fontjoy Square. His visit brought nothing but pain and fear to a decent lady who was obviously attempting to do a good deed. Who was he to question her right to adopt three homeless, helpless children? Recriminations blared in his brain.

Why did I come here? Was it to satisfy my curiosity? Assuage my wounded sense of male pride? Or was it merely to get another glimpse of the beautiful Rose Sinclair?

His first instinct was to offer an apology and retreat, but his training as a barrister had long ago taught him to control such unmanly impulses. Besides, Mrs. Sinclair intrigued him. Inexplicably, he wanted to know more about her and her motivations. So he schooled his features in an impenetrable mask of arrogance and determination.

It was a look he often wore in the courtroom. Designed to intimidate and frustrate his opponents, his scowl was famous. Sir Steven fully expected Mrs. Sinclair to dash from the drawing room, gather up the children and march them back for his inspection.

Her sooty lashes blinked rapidly for a moment, and her skin, as fine as Japanese porcelain, blushed bright pink. Stunned silence, the sort of uneasy quiet that follows the blast of a cannonball, enveloped the room.

Then, slowly, as Sir Steven watched with fascination, Mrs. Sinclair tamped back her own fear, steeled her nerves and squared her shoulders.

Her nostrils flared as she drew a sharp inhale. "Why do you want to see the children, sir? Why now? You said you were not Stevie's father, and you made it quite clear that you did not wish to be bothered with the child. You accused Miss Tweedy of blackmailing you. So, why do you want to see the child now?"

"The children," he corrected her. "I want to see all three of the children."

"Nonsense. The twins have nothing to do with you."

"You said they were Katherine's."

"But they are not yours."

His gut twisted with embarrassment. But he forced himself to meet Rose's gaze and somehow he managed to make his admission with the equanimity of a totally guiltless soul. "If they are Katherine's children, ma'am, there is a chance, albeit a slim one, that I am their father."

"But . . ." She stared him down. "Sir, I was under the impression that Katherine was a—"

"She was a prostitute in the last few years of her life, Mrs. Sinclair. That does not necessarily exclude me from being the father of her children."

He felt her appraisal, her curiosity. And, even though it didn't show in Mrs. Sinclair's expression, he imagined her condescension and disapproval. What decent woman wouldn't disapprove of his conduct, and of Katherine's? What decent person wouldn't condemn him for allowing Katherine and her children to live in Mrs. Bunratty's brothel these past few years?

"You were a regular customer of hers, then?"

"Our association was a bit more complicated than that." But he didn't owe Rose Sinclair an explanation and he didn't relish offering her a synopsis of his sordid past and his failings insofar as Katherine was concerned. "I knew Katherine long before she met Mrs. Bunratty. She was a young girl when I met her, and, er, well, Mrs. Sinclair, we were in love at one time."

"In love?"

"Why not?"

"I am sure I don't understand, Sir Steven."

" 'Tis not necessary that you do, Mrs. Sinclair. But you owe me the courtesy of introducing me to the child you claim is mine, and you might as well show me the others also. Because, as I have stated, if they are Katherine's offspring, they might be mine as well."

"I do not believe you. You said that Stevie was not your child. Now you are claiming all of them!"

"Not so fast." Steven calmly patted the air. "I am not claiming to be anyone's father. I am admitting that I had a, ah, sexual relationship with Katherine, that is all. Our union may or may not have resulted in children. I am here to find out."

"The twins are seven years old, sir. I'm certain you are not their father."

"Seven?" Steven did some nimble math in his head. He and Katherine had met about eight years before, but she certainly wasn't with child when he first laid eyes upon her. *Or was she?* As his mind flashed on her face, he was swamped by nostalgia. "I should like to see them."

"They were raised in the brothel where Katherine lived and worked. If you visited her frequently, you would have seen them, would you not?"

He quickly considered Mrs. Sinclair's remark. It did seem unlikely that Katherine could have hidden a pair of twin girls from him. On the other hand, the birth of little Stevie had taken place under the murkiest of circumstances. Steven had not been aware of Katherine's pregnancy until the baby was due.

Naturally, he had noticed the slight thickening of her waist and the fullness of her face, but Katherine's weight gain lent an aura of health to her appearance. He had actually been pleased to see her looking a bit more voluptuous; he had construed the change as an indication of sobriety.

But he had been wrong. Katherine's duplicity pained him even now, years later. She would not even have told him she was with child if he hadn't been at Mrs. Bunratty's the night she began having labor pains.

After the birth, Katherine told Steven she didn't know who the father was. She meant to wound him by suggesting the child's father could be any one of a hundred men, and she did. Of course, he didn't believe her. She knew who the boy's father was; she just didn't want to tell him, and she was wise not to, for Steven would have been tempted to shoot the man.

In the succeeding years, he saw the little boy less than half a dozen times. Mrs. Bunratty's establishment was a big place, a rambling old house with dozens of tiny rooms. It was not difficult for Katherine to keep the child out of sight when Steven visited.

"Mrs. Sinclair, I could count on one hand the number of times I have laid eyes on Katherine's children. I wouldn't recognize them if my carriage ran them down in the street. But she did name the little one after me, did she not? And that is a fact I cannot ignore."

"You were all too ready to ignore that fact a few nights ago, Sir Steven."

"You caught me off guard. I thought you were an accomplice of Miss Tweedy's, bent on extorting money from me in exchange for her silence."

Not surprisingly, Mrs. Sinclair scoffed. "If you wouldn't admit to Miss Tweedy that you are the child's father, why would you wish to suggest to me the possibility that you are?"

It was a reasonable question, one that Steven had been wrestling with the past two days. Why did he suddenly have the urge to see Katherine's children? Why was he disturbed by the idea of allowing Rose Sinclair, an apparent paragon of maternal virtues, to adopt the children?

His feelings were as multifaceted as a picture puzzle with a thousand pieces. And though Steven ordinarily loved the mental exercise of solving such complex problems, he hated analyzing his own emotions. It would have been so much easier to throw himself into his practice, to lose himself in his clients' problems, to ignore his own feelings and focus on something more tangible—a case, a brief, or perhaps an oral argument before the chancery court—something he could master and control.

But he could not rid himself of the suspicion that one or three of Katherine's children might also be his. No amount of whiskey or beer would wash away the guilt he felt at allowing Katherine's children to be taken in by a total stranger. And while it was easy to slam the door in the face of a little grubber like Clodagh Tweedy, it was impossible to forget the pretty Rose Sinclair, and the refreshingly sweet look of gratitude that swept over her face when he denied he was Stevie's father. He had not stopped thinking about her, and what she had said to him, and the chance that he was a father, since she'd appeared on his doorstep.

"I suppose you have succeeded in shaming me, Mrs. Sinclair," he said, at length.

"That was not the intent of my visit to you, sir. If you say you are not the father of Katherine's son, I believe you." She chafed her palms, as if dusting dirt off them. "There. You needn't worry about them ever again. And I promise I shall never darken your doorstep again."

He wasn't so certain he wanted that. "I must see the children before I deny I am their father. The law, as well as common sense and moral decency, demands it."

" 'Twas wrong of me to come to your home." Her panic was evident, but her tone was that of a mother apologizing to a child after she'd wrongfully accused him of stealing a cookie from the jar.

"The solicitor said if there was any chance you were the child's father, I owed you both a duty to inquire. But I had only the calling card in Stevie's pocket and a scribbled note from Miss Tweedy to make me think you knew anything about him. 'Twas wrong of me to be so presumptuous."

"Do not forget that Stevie also bears my Christian name. Surely that means something."

"Not your surname, though. The children claim Rowen as their last name."

"Katherine's name," Steven observed quietly. Whoever the father of her children was, she hadn't burdened them with his name. Katherine would always be a mystery to Steven, and the frustration of attempting to understand her thinking would forever frustrate and haunt him. "At any rate, I should like to see them. Now, if you please."

"You cannot see them just now." Mrs. Sinclair stalled, her lashes flickering, her fingers twisting. "They are in classroom, and their lessons cannot be interrupted."

"I have not got all day, Mrs. Sinclair."

"You have not been curious about Katherine's children all these years, and now you want to have them paraded in front of you! Just like that!" To punctuate her point, Mrs. Sinclair snapped her fingers in the air. "You are undoubtedly accustomed to having your way, Sir Steven. I would wager that you order your employees around as if they are slaves! Well, you will not order me around in that manner! I am not your servant! I am afraid you will just have to be patient, sir!"

But his patience had reached the limit, not so much with Mrs. Sinclair but with Katherine Rowen, the elfish little girl he'd met eight years earlier, the lass with the loveliest hazel eyes he'd ever seen, the woman he'd intended to marry. Ever since then, Katherine had controlled his emotions, usurping every true and honest feeling he had, using him, teasing him, loving him, needing him, leaning on him . . . ultimately abandoning him. She had told him only what she wanted him to know, putting him on the shelf when she didn't want him around, taking him down when she did. He had watched her spiral into alcohol and opium addiction, and he had not been able to help her. And now, even after her death, she was confounding him.

He did not know whether any one or all of Katherine's children were his. He did not even know what his reaction would be if he determined that they *were* his. The responsibility of raising children was not attractive to him. The thought of having three, or even one, sniveling brat underfoot made his stomach churn.

A very finely honed sense of self-preservation urged Steven to leave this investigation alone. He ought to ignore the possibility that he was a father, forget about the troublesome Katherine and go on with his life.

It was what Mrs. Rose Sinclair wanted him to do now.

But some deeply buried instinct, an indefinable need to do the right thing, clawed its way past Steven's selfish desire to run away. "I want to see the children," he said, more gruffly than he intended, giving credence to Mrs. Sinclair's suggestion that he was used to being obeyed. "Don't worry, I have no intention of letting on to Stevie exactly why I am here. He need only know that I was a friend of his mother's."

"You are a cruel man," she replied, walking toward the bell cord. "I do not believe you have any feelings, Sir Steven. You disappoint me."

"You are not the first woman to say that."

Her disapproval of him injured him more than he wanted her to know, however. The insane desire to please her stirred him. He hated disappointing Rose Sinclair; he hated making her unhappy.

He could make her happy if he walked away.

But she would never respect him if he turned his back on these children without looking at them.

Worse, he would never respect himself.

Minutes later, Mrs. Bleek ushered the children into the room. At first glance, Steven knew that the twins, pretty brown-haired girls with round hazel eyes, were not his. There wasn't the slightest resemblance between his sharp, chiseled features and their soft round ones. "Hello," they said in unison as they perched primly on the sofa.

But the boy . . . He was thin, and his chary gaze was too world-weary for a child his age. Wedged between his sisters, he dangled his scuffed boots and fidgeted. His knickers, clearly castoffs, would have slid down his hips were it not for the leather braces he wore. His stockings were threadbare but clean, his shirt patched but tidy. He had a straight nose that would one day dominate his face, Steven predicted, and he had a high forehead that gave vivid expression to what was surely a serious nature.

Steven fought the urge to hook his finger under his

collar and yank off his restricting necktie. The band of heat that scorched his neck would have undone a man of lesser self-control.

For one horrific second, Steven feared he was going to explode with anger, anger at Katherine for having lied to him and betrayed him, anger at himself for having been so willing to believe her lies, anger at Rose Sinclair for having forced him to confront his inadequacies and his failings.

"Well, sir?" She hovered on the periphery of his vision, waiting for a response.

Stalking to the mantelpiece, Steven gave her and the children his back.

"That will be all, Mrs. Bleek," she said quietly.

He heard her whisper to the governess. Then there was the rustle and patter of the children's exodus and, finally, the soft click of the drawing-room door.

"They are gone now. You can dare turn around."

Slowly, his heart pounding like a bodhrán, he faced Mrs. Sinclair. *The child was the spitting image of him.* In his heart, he knew little Stevie was his son. Katherine had named the child after him, not out of some perverted whimsy, as he had long ago convinced himself, but because he was the child's father. He could see in Mrs. Sinclair's face that she knew the truth, also.

Oddly, the realization stunned him. It should not have, he reminded himself. He had asked Katherine years ago if that little boy was his. When she had said no, Steven was only too eager to believe her.

He wondered now why he hadn't looked more closely at the lad on the few occasions when he'd had the opportunity. As the drawing room swayed, Steven saw blurred images of a toddler waddling down a corridor at Mrs. Bunratty's only to be snatched up by that wretched Clodagh Tweedy. He saw the same child a year later galloping around a corner, his serious gaze locking on Steven for an instant before Katherine pushed him into the arms of a passing maid. That child was Stevie. He'd been a fool not to have known that child was his.

Anger seethed beneath his skin. Katherine hadn't wanted him to know Stevie was his. Yet he had been carrying Sir Steven's calling card in his pocket. How was that so? Who had given the card to the child? Clodagh Tweedy, perhaps?

And what was Steven to do now that he had discovered the depth of Katherine's duplicity and the dreadful extent of his own thinly concealed and selfish apathy? Oh, he was as guilty as she was, perhaps even more so. Katherine, at least, had her addictions to blame for her moral failings. But didn't he, as a man, as a barrister, as a decent human being, have the obligation to provide for his own offspring? His irresponsibility had made him Katherine's co-conspirator.

His resentment toward Katherine was so consuming that he could barely conceal it. It clouded his reason. He did not want her child. He did not want anything to do with Katherine Rowen.

"Sir Steven?" Rose Sinclair's voice, as refined and cultured as a pearl, drew him back to reality. "What do you think? Do you recognize the child? Do you believe you are Stevie's father?"

Unspeakable fear engulfed Steven. Outwardly, his

features were carved in stone, but inside he was a heap of emotional rubble.

"I saw not the slightest resemblance to me or any of my family members, ma'am. I regret troubling you on such an embarrassing matter. My first instinct was correct; the child is not mine. I don't know what made me think little Stevie might be mine. It appears that Miss Tweedy's blackmail scheme has unnerved me more than I thought."

She looked like a lottery winner who didn't want anyone to know she'd struck it rich for fear her winnings would be stolen. Her eyes rounded while her hands fluttered briefly. Then she clasped them together, reining in her elation.

Her tone was conciliatory. "I am sorry that I said you were a bad man."

'Tis easy to be gracious when your prayers have suddenly been answered.

"You have done what is best for the child, Sir Steven. He will be happy here, I promise. And I swear that I will cherish him and care for him as if he were my own."

As if he were your own?

"I wish he were," Steven said coldly, deliberately divorcing himself from the sadness that threatened to crush him. "For the child's sake. But none of us can pick our own parents, can we?"

He started toward the door, anxious to put some distance between himself and Rose Sinclair.

But she crossed the room quickly, and when he reached the threshold, she was there, looking up at him with those beautiful violet eyes, lips parted, hand pressed to his arm. "Wait."

"We've nothing more to discuss." He wished he could turn off his feelings as easily as he could school his features. He was weary of projecting indifference while his insides churned. For once, he wished he could honestly express what he was feeling. But how could he? His feelings—fear of responsibility, of losing control, of loving or being loved—were anything but noble and manly. Indeed, his fears were downright childish.

"I think I know what you are feeling, Sir Steven."

"Dear lady, you cannot possibly know what I am feeling."

"I work at the Dorcas Society for the Aid of Illegitimate Children, you see. Over the years, I have seen countless women give up their children for adoption. Many of those women loved their children beyond reason. They knew they could not give their children a proper upbringing. They gave their children up because they loved them so dearly."

"How saintly. But I assure you, Mrs. Sinclair, that is not my motive in denying that I am Stevie's father. If he were mine, wild horses couldn't drag him from me."

The tiny sigh she exhaled raised the hairs on Steven's neck. "You needn't lie to me, Sir Steven. I will not betray your confidence. I am not Miss Tweedy."

"You would lie to the court, Mrs. Sinclair? That surprises me. You seem to place such a premium on integrity and honesty."

She blinked, uncertain how to answer.

It was wrong to attack her. She'd done nothing to provoke his anger. Standing this close to Mrs. Sinclair, Steven could see the fine lines that crinkled at the corners of her eyes, the subtle dimple in her chin, the perfect arch of her thick black brows. Her lips tightened, and she drew back. At arm's length, he could see that he had wounded her.

"I do apologize, Mrs. Sinclair." A wave of guilt washed over him.

" 'Tis understandable that you are overset, sir. If it is any consolation, I believe that you are doing a noble thing. Giving up one's child cannot be easy. But I can provide a better home for Stevie than you, as a single man, can."

A dozen rebuttals to her argument surfaced in Steven's mind. He wasn't doing a noble thing; he was running away from his responsibilities, and he was lying. And he could give little Stevie the finest home in Dublin if he wanted to. He had far more money than Mrs. Sinclair, judging from the slightly shabby condition of her house.

"Thank you," he said, as matter-of-factly as he could.

She took a step closer, laying her hand on his arm again. This time, a strange warmth flowed through Steven's body. Stranger still, a well of gratitude sprang up inside him. Mrs. Sinclair, it seemed, was making it easy for him, giving him absolution, condoning his despicable actions. Bless her heart, she thought he was noble. She made no demands on him. She didn't judge him. She simply wanted a child. She wanted *his* child, and she would—Steven had no doubt—cherish that child as deeply and passionately as if she'd given birth to him.

Wisps of hair strayed at her temples, tempting him to brush them off her face. Her perfume, a heady mixture of freshly baked bread, lavender and soap, both soothed and aroused him. He had a sudden urge to kiss her, to unpin her raven hair, sweep her into his arms and never let her go. Perhaps if he held her tightly enough, some of her goodness would seep into him.

Tentatively, for it was difficult for him to believe that Mrs. Sinclair wanted him to kiss her, and the last thing on earth he wanted to do was offend or insult this virtuous creature, Steven lowered his head to her neck.

Reaching around him, she rose on her tiptoes. Her hands caressed his back. Her embrace was warm and strong, perhaps a bit maternal if Steven analyzed the entire range of emotions surrounding this phenomenon. As he fit himself against her, breathing in her scent, pressing into the softness of her breasts and belly, he experienced something he had never felt with another woman.

He felt safe.

"Dear lady," he whispered against her neck. " 'Twould be a mortal sin if I denied this haven to a child. How can leaving little Stevie with you be anything but right?"

Her fingers tangled in the hair at his nape. She kissed his jaw and murmured, "Thank you."

Unthinkingly, Steven shifted his head, finding Mrs.

Sinclair's mouth and kissing her full on the lips. Her surprise, manifested in the instantaneous stiffening of her body, gave him pause. *What the devil was he doing? Had he lost his mind?*

But before he could draw away, her resistance vanished, her lips parted and she kissed him back. She made a low, throaty, thoroughly feminine sound. And she clung to Steven, kissing him as passionately as any woman ever had.

Five

Am I losing my mind?

"Rose," he whispered against her neck. "I don't mean to frighten you."

The depth of his voice was reassuring, yet beneath the yards of dark-blue poplin that covered Rose's body, her skin rippled with gooseflesh. Tilting her head, she said, "Sir Steven—"

"Good God, woman, let us dispense with formalities."

"Steven." It felt good to say his name, to be so close to him, to feel his body pressed against hers. She could not remember feeling that way about her husband. "You do not frighten me."

Framing her face in his hands, he peered into her eyes. "You trust me?" he asked quietly, as if he doubted her.

"You are willing to give up your son because you want what is best for him. You are willing to entrust me with the care of your son. How can I not trust you in return?"

"Ah." His forehead touched hers. "But you do not understand—"

She pressed her finger to his lips. For the first time

in years, perhaps in her entire life, she felt comfortable and safe in a man's embrace. She did not want to ruin the moment by ladling guilt atop Steven's head. He did not deserve to feel guilty. By agreeing not to press for his paternal rights, he had given her the one thing she wanted above all else—a child. *His child.*

How could she not want to draw him close to her? Her gratitude to him was overwhelming. Her compassion for him, her respect for the sacrifice he was making and her sorrow at the pain he was experiencing filled her with emotion.

His lips were a compressed line, his jaw a slab of stone. Rose's strongest instincts, to comfort and protect, were aroused. Her need to be needed was blindingly urgent.

"You owe me no explanations, Steven." She ran her fingers through his hair. "Just kiss me."

With a sigh, he did. He lowered his head and covered her mouth with his, groaning as his arms tightened around her back. A flood of warmth and wellness spread through Rose's limbs. She thought she'd never felt as alive, as womanly or as wanted. Her husband, God rest his soul, had certainly never inspired these emotions in her. He had viewed sex as a sort of stress reliever, a necessary bodily function, like deep knee bends, that he performed to improve his circulation. His kisses were perfunctory; his embraces cold. Nothing he'd done in twenty years of marriage had ever excited her as much as Steven's kiss.

This is just a kiss! Rose struggled to maintain some modicum of control, to regulate her increasingly irregular breathing, to suppress the little mewling sounds that bubbled up her throat. But as the kiss deepened, as Steven's tongue explored her mouth, and his hands caressed her shoulders, and the warmth of his body seeped into hers, she realized she wanted more.

Her breasts tingled; her knees wobbled. The thoughts that danced in her mind, graphic images of Steven's naked body entwined with hers, shocked her. She had never entertained such wicked thoughts. This was the sort of thing women like Mrs. Bunratty, Miss Tweedy, and Katherine Rowen did. This was not appropriate behavior for a woman who had just taken on the responsibility of raising three children.

Summoning all her moral strength, she pressed her palms against Steven's chest and pushed herself away. "Steven! This is not right."

Stepping back, he took a deep breath. His face and neck were mottled, betraying his physical arousal, but his gaze was hooded. He was, Rose recognized, a man who could turn his emotions on and off like a spigot.

"No, 'tis not right." His voice was no longer low and velvety; now he sounded like a barrister, analytical and unsympathetic. "I do apologize. It will not happen again."

That was hardly any consolation, but Rose nodded demurely, as if she were satisfied with Steven's promise that he would never hold her in his arms and kiss her again.

He started to leave.

She touched his arm, holding him back again. "I want to thank you. My attorney will inform the court that the children's father is unknown. You will not be troubled for financial support. You need never give this matter another thought if you wish."

"Your attorney?" His brow furrowed and his shoulders tensed. "You have already retained an attorney to represent you in this matter?"

"Yes."

"Very well," Steven replied. Then he turned to her, offering naught but a cold, tight smile. "Good day then, Mrs. Sinclair. Thank you for your understanding."

When he was gone, Rose returned to her desk and the list of errands and chores that she had been composing when Sir Steven arrived. A compulsive list maker, she bent over her paper and frantically scratched down items of clothing needed by the children, as well as foodstuffs necessary for the pantry and supplies for the classroom.

In the past, organizing her thoughts had always given her the illusion of controlling her life. But tonight, she could not fool herself into believing that she was at the helm of her future. She had fallen in love with three children and she had committed herself to caring for them. Yet it remained uncertain whether they would be legally entrusted to her care.

And as her pen flew over the paper, her emotions, like mischievous leprechauns, danced chaotically in her mind. Her body ached with pent-up desire for the man who had given her a child. And she prayed he never darkened her doorstep again.

* * *

A bell above the lintel tinkled as Rose entered the offices of Mr. Aloysius Letterfrack. Stevie clutched her hand while the twins tagged along behind, Katie frowning and Mollie stamping snow off her sturdy boots. A studious looking young man, obviously unaccustomed to the visitation of noisy children, looked up from his desk and swept a curious look over the shivering foursome. As he rose, his nose twitched convulsively and his lips quirked—much like a rabbit's, Rose thought, quelling a nervous chuckle.

"You are Mrs. Sinclair, I presume?"

"Yes, and these are Katie and Mollie and Stevie. I have an appointment with Mr. Letterfrack."

The clerk, whom Rose mentally dubbed Mr. Rabbit, took her cloak and hat, along with the children's outerwear, then bade them all follow him down a short passageway. Ushered into a large office, paneled in rich, dark wood, warmed by a gas stove and filled with stacks of musty smelling books, Rose found herself standing opposite Mr. Letterfrack's desk.

As the man lumbered to his feet, he gave her a stare that was as curious as Mr. Rabbit's, but far more challenging. With his thick white hair and massive shoulders, he was one of the most imposing figures Rose had ever encountered. But with a gulp, she silently concluded that it was better to have a gladiator on her side than a meek and timid mouse.

Instinctively, the children huddled against her legs. Forcing a polite smile to her lips, Rose extended her gloved hand to Mr. Letterfrack. "I trust Mr. Avondale explained my predicament?"

"Aye, and I understand you have quite a sticky mess

on your hands." His leather chair creaked as he lowered himself into it. "Sit, sit. Oh, Mr. Hare, why don't you take the children into the outer office with you? I prefer they not be privy to my conversation with Mrs. Sinclair."

To Rose's chagrin, the children readily accompanied Mr. Hare. Katie mumbled her dissatisfaction with the arrangement, and Stevie scraped his toes on the floor as he followed his sisters. But with the irrepressibly cheerful Mollie exhorting them to look lively, they quickly made their exit.

To the invisible list of things to do that she kept in her brain, Rose added another item: She must instruct the children to be more suspicious of strangers. They had undoubtedly grown accustomed to being bounced from one adult to another, to being left in the custody of relative strangers and to being introduced to new faces daily. Theirs had not been a cosseted, sequestered upbringing thus far. Living in a brothel had made them far too tolerant of situations which most children would view with terror.

"You wish to adopt the children." While he stated it as a fact, Mr. Letterfrack's tone held a degree of disbelief, as if he thought his new client was crazy to want to do such a thing.

"By all means. Indeed, by *any* means." Rose clasped her hands in her lap and met Mr. Letterfrack's steely gaze without flinching. "May I be frank, sir?"

"Please do, Mrs. Sinclair. In fact, I ask that you tell me everything you know about these children. Terminating a man's parental rights is not done without extensive inquiry and an investigation into the fitness of the party wishing to adopt."

"Will everything I say to you be reported to the court?"

He steepled his fingers beneath an alarmingly rosy and bulbous nose. "Your confidences will not leave this office, I assure you."

That was a relief. Marshaling her courage, Rose told her story, concluding with a sigh. "The twins look just like Mr. Sinclair, I'm afraid. And the little one looks just like Sir Steven."

"So your husband has given you children, after all."

"And Sir Steven has given me a son." Rose blinked back a tear. "I am certain he recognizes the child as his. He is not blind, and he is not an unintelligent man. He realizes that I can provide a more loving, nurturing environment for Stevie, and so he is willing to disclaim paternity and remove any obstacles to my adoption of the child."

"Are you sure that Sir Steven is not going to claim he is little Stevie's father?"

"I am sure."

Mr. Letterfrack's beefy lips glistened as a slow smile spread across his face. "And how do you intend to financially support these children, Mrs. Sinclair?"

"I will make do."

"Why not ask Sir Steven to assist you? He is a very wealthy man, you know."

"I do not want his money." Rose was offended by the suggestion. "Nor do I want his interference in this adoption process."

A silence enveloped the room as Mr. Letterfrack

studied the tips of his fingers. "I do not approve of a man avoiding his obligation to support his children."

"Stevie is not Sir Steven's child. Not in the truest sense of the word. He never wanted the child. He never cared for the child."

"He sired the child, Mrs. Sinclair. Trust me, it is difficult for a man of honor to turn his back on his only child, even if the child's mother is a prostitute."

"*Was* a prostitute," Rose corrected him. "Katherine Rowen is dead."

Abruptly, Mr. Letterfrack stood and reached across his desk to shake Mrs. Sinclair's hand again. "Mr. Avondale speaks highly of you, and I am pleased to take your case. However, you must allow me to proceed as I see fit. Which means it will be necessary to obtain a written statement from Sir Steven in which he denies any relationship to Katherine Rowen's child and consents to the adoption."

A bitter taste washed up the back of Rose's throat. She had assumed that if Sir Steven said nothing and did not come forward to protest her adoption, the court would not inquire any further into Stevie's parentage. Why did Mr. Letterfrack have to aggravate the situation by approaching Sir Steven for an affidavit?

"It is not so simple to adopt a child whose father is well known," Mr. Letterfrack said in response to her crestfallen expression, as he escorted her to the door.

"But it is not generally known that Sir Steven is the child's father—"

"There may be witnesses who are aware of Sir

Steven's relationship with Katherine Rowen and who know full well the nature of it."

"Like who?" She felt a twinge in the middle of her chest.

He shrugged. "Let us hope and pray that Katherine Rowen kept her sordid little secrets to herself," replied Mr. Letterfrack.

Rose's breath caught. She felt Stevie's hand tugging at her own and realized that she was once again in the reception area, surrounded, it seemed, by a cloud of confusion. Mr. Hare was fretfully handing out mittens and caps in an obvious attempt to expedite the children's departure. Mollie was chattering about the snow swirling outside the window, and Kate, her lips puffed out, tapped her foot impatiently while standing with one hand on the doorknob.

She drew comfort from Stevie's upturned face. Hiding her fright, Rose squared her shoulders. She had a hundred questions, but Mr. Letterfrack did not appear interested in entertaining them. Perhaps he was busy. Perhaps Rose's case was not the most important case Mr. Letterfrack was handling. Perhaps Rose's worries were out of proportion to the matter at hand.

"I suppose Mr. Avondale would not have recommended me to you if he was not entirely confident in your abilities," she said, accepting her cloak from Mr. Hare.

"Trust me," Mr. Letterfrack said.

As she guided the children outside and into the waiting cab, Rose experienced a crushing pessimism. The notion that Katherine Rowen would have confided in someone the identity of Stevie's father struck a chord of terror in her heart.

Nothing Mr. Letterfrack had said made sense to her. And yet he was the finest attorney Dublin had to offer, second only to the famous Sir Steven Nollbrook. Mr. Avondale had retained Letterfrack to represent her, and so he had to be the best. Inhaling deeply, Rose pulled Stevie to her side and squeezed him until he complained.

"You are going to spoil him," Mollie observed.

"He is already spoiled," Katie amended.

Rose's tension eased. "Is that such a bad thing? I hope to spoil all three of you, if the truth be known. A little bit at least. Not so you will be brats or grow up to be boorish and rude. But just so you know that I love you above all else."

"Why?" Katie demanded sullenly. "You don't even know us."

"Darlings," Rose assured her, "I loved you before I ever even knew you."

The tangle of streets between the south quays and Dame Street represented sanctuary for a man wishing to be anonymous. Settled at a corner table in a pub frequented by sailors and prostitutes, Sir Steven pondered his predicament. Half a pint of whiskey had numbed his senses, but failed to brighten his mood. A silent debate raged inside him.

Is it more noble to leave the child alone and spare him the pain and humiliation of having me—an absolute moral failure of a man—for a father?

Or should I embrace my paternal obligations and thereby snatch from Mrs. Sinclair the hope of being a mother?

As night fell, other customers sought refuge, filling the tiny room with laughter. Smoke from an open fire, over which a joint of mutton crackled on a turning spit, burned Steven's eyes, evoking the tears he promised himself he would not have otherwise shed.

He swiped his sleeve across his face, then drained his glass. Looking up for a bar mistress, he was surprised to find himself peering into Aloysius Letterfrack's hawkish eyes.

"Mind if I join you?" the white-haired lawyer said. Without waiting for an answer, he sat down.

Steven welcomed the distraction and the fresh round of whiskey Letterfrack brought with him. "I didn't expect to meet anyone I knew in this godforsaken hovel."

Letterfrack gave a gravelly chuckle. "It's no coincidence that I found you here, man. I have seen you here before. I came here because I hoped to see you again."

"If it is business you wish to discuss," Steven said wearily, "it will have to wait until Monday. As you can see, I've tossed off my robe for this week."

"Lucky for me." Letterfrack rubbed his bottom lip. "You're a worthy adversary, Steven. You have bested me in court time after time. But you have always played fair, and I judge you to be a man of integrity."

Struck by the irony of Letterfrack's remark, Steven poured another long drink down his throat.

Leaning across the table, Letterfrack lowered his

voice. "That is why I am giving you the opportunity to extricate yourself from a rather sticky matter. A potentially embarrassing matter, if you know what I mean."

"I haven't the slightest notion what you mean."

"I obtained a new client today."

"Good for you."

"Her name is Mrs. Rose Sinclair. It seems she has a benefactor, one Mr. Devon Avondale, who has guaranteed payment of her bill, up to a substantial amount. So there is no question that her case will be pursued zealously."

Fingers of ice clutched the back of Steven's neck. He would have liked to leap across the scarred tabletop and throttle Letterfrack, but he held his violent impulse in check, and drew back, repulsed, insulted and angered beyond measure. "What the hell are you getting at, Letterfrack?"

"According to Mrs. Sinclair, you are the father of a bastard child named Stevie Rowen, son of Katherine Rowen, one of Mrs. Bunratty's most successful prostitutes. Until she died, that is."

"You knew Katherine?"

"Dear sir, everyone in Dublin knew Katherine. Well, every man of a certain age and appetite knew her, I should say."

Beneath the table, Steven's fists coiled into lethal balls. Experience had taught him, however, that physical attacks were rarely as successful as carefully premeditated legal ones. Fury simmered just beneath his skin, but Steven's scowl was perfectly controlled. "Mrs. Sinclair told you that I am the father of Katherine Rowen's child? Just the little one? Or did she say I was the father of all three?"

"Just the little one."

"Why? Why did she tell you that?" Steven thought out loud. "If she wants to adopt the children, the most expedient way is to represent to the court that the children's father is unknown. Why would she tell you that I am Stevie's father?"

With a sigh, Letterfrack donned a sad expression. "Who knows?" he said with Shakespearean melancholy. "Perhaps she believed, as many clients do, that they should tell the truth, confess everything to their advocates—you understand."

Steven studied Letterfrack's shifting gaze. The man was a consummate liar, but a monstrously poor actor. "She might be wrong, you know. It has not been established that the child is mine."

" *'Admit nothing!'* Ho, that is what I would do, too! Isn't that what you tell your clients? You are wise to have taken your own counsel, Steven."

"I have nothing to admit."

"Um." Letterfrack drummed his fingers on the table. "If the inquiry ended there, 'twould be sufficient to ensure that Mrs. Sinclair's adoption application is approved. Believe me, sir, I would not voluntarily furnish your name to the court. I owe you that courtesy."

"Who else would say that I am the child's father?"

"There may be witnesses."

"Don't be ridiculous! Have you forgotten whom you are talking to? There are no witnesses—"

"What about Miss Clodagh Tweedy?"

"How do you know her?"

"Let us just say that she has made herself known to me. For some inexplicable reason, she intends to insert herself into this matter. What she will tell the court . . . Well, that is anyone's guess."

Pain pierced Steven's skull. "She has no credibility. She's a prostitute, for God's sake."

"Yes, that is true. I suppose her testimony would have to be corroborated by someone else if the judge were to give it any weight. Some of Mrs. Bunratty's other clients, for example."

"You wouldn't do that," Steven said, his voice menacingly quiet. "Why would you? Exposing the names of Mrs. Bunratty's clientele would ruin dozens of reputations, tear apart families, and embarrass countless people, some of them totally faultless."

Letterfrack put his hand over his heart. "Oh, I wouldn't do that, sir. But this Miss Tweedy . . . She seems to have it in for you. And once the cat is out of the bag, so to speak, there is no telling what sort of inquiry the judge might order."

"Clodagh Tweedy is a money-grubbing little blackmailer."

"P'raps."

Steven forced the tension from his back and neck muscles. The initial shock of Letterfrack's unpleasant news had faded, along with his whiskey haze. What remained was pure white anger and indignation. His mind sharpened. Speaking hastily, or allowing his emotion to shape his reaction, would only place him in jeopardy. He needed to appraise his situation. He needed more information before he committed himself to answering Letterfrack. He needed more time.

"What are you suggesting, Aloysius?"

The other lawyer smiled as he placed his palms on the table and pushed his bulky body to a standing position. "I prefer that you make the first suggestion, Steven. Think about it. What are you willing to do to silence Miss Tweedy's testimony and remove yourself from this entire tawdry affair?"

So that was it. First Miss Tweedy had attempted to blackmail Steven, and now Aloysius Letterfrack was doing it for her. Well, their scheme would fail.

"What am I willing to do to silence Miss Tweedy?" Steven raised his glass in mock salute to Letterfrack. "Why, nothing, my friend."

Letterfrack's jowls sagged and his eyes widened. "Nothing? Do you not understand what I am offering you, Steven?"

"You are offering me an opportunity to buy my way out of a scandal."

"And a lifetime of child-support payments."

"Ah, yes, I understand that children can be outrageously expensive. Particularly the intelligent ones who want everything from swift carriages to fine educations and tours of the Continent. If this boy is mine, I am certain he will be intelligent."

"If the boy is yours?" Letterfrack sputtered.

Steven arched one brow. "You thought I would leap at the chance to line your pockets in exchange for Miss Tweedy's silence?"

"You told Mrs. Sinclair—"

"Forget what I told Mrs. Sinclair," Steven growled. As he rose, the table wobbled and the whiskey bottle fell to the brick floor with a crash. A couple at the nearest table glanced over, but their interest waned quickly when Steven shot them a wolfish look of warning. Then, fixing his smile, he took a step closer to Letterfrack, so close that he could smell the man's perspiration beneath his sodden woolen jacket.

"You have denied you were the child's father," Letterfrack inserted hurriedly. "It is obvious to me that you do not wish to be saddled with the burden of a child, particularly a child you sired with a prostitute. And just think what this scandal will do to your standing at the bar. Victoria's reign has brought with it a peculiar striving for *rectitude.*"

"If you think you can intimidate me, Aloysius, you are less of a lawyer than I would have given you credit for. I care not a fig what Miss Tweedy has to say. Her word will mean nothing in a court of law. And you can take the testimony of every philandering banker, merchant and politician who ever set foot inside Mrs. Bunratty's establishment, for all I care. If they all say they saw me with Katherine—indeed, if they all swear under oath that they saw me at her bedside, holding her hand while she gave birth—I shall not be troubled by it in the least."

Letterfrack took a step back. "Think about it, Steven."

"There is nothing to think about."

"You do not have to give me your answer now."

"You have my answer. I will not be blackmailed."

"Then I suggest, sir, that you prepare yourself to be a father." The lawyer put on his black beaver hat and gave the brim a curt little tug. "Good evening to you."

"Good evening," replied Steven, returning to his table. He summoned the tap girl and ordered a plate of lamb-and-kidney pie. Eating heartily, his depression lifted. The dilemma he faced had suddenly resolved itself in a very unexpected manner. No longer was he choosing between ruining Stevie's life and dashing Mrs. Sinclair's hope for a smooth adoption process. Now he was confronted with the threat of a public scandal versus the constant demands for money that Miss Tweedy would make on him if he allowed her to blackmail him. Smiling around a boiled potato, he thought he owed Mr. Letterfrack a word of thanks. The man had thrown a great deal of light on a murky situation.

The garden in the center of Fontjoy Square was blanketed in snow. Standing in her parlor, Rose watched through the window as Mr. Avondale and the children built a snowman beside the half-finished rose trellis. Behind her, on the sofa, sat Mrs. Millicent Hyde-Wolferton, sipping hot chocolate and eating smoked-salmon sandwiches on black bread.

Without turning around, Rose said, "Darling, haven't you eaten enough of those things?"

"I'm ravenous," said Millicent. "Have been for weeks, ever since Alec left for London. Boredom, I suppose. And since we cannot work in the garden because of the cold, I have become as lazy as a cat."

"Come see. Mollie just poked a carrot in the snowman's face for a nose."

"Mr. Avondale has taken a shine to those children, hasn't he?" Millicent remained on the sofa, popping lemon cookies into her mouth. "Do you ever wonder what we would do without him, Rose?"

"I don't like to imagine it," Rose answered absently. She couldn't tear her gaze away from the activity in the garden.

"What did the lawyer say, dear?"

"Um? Oh, he said he would have to contact Sir Steven Nollbrook, the gentleman whose calling card was in little Stevie's pocket. He needs verification that the man is not going to assert parental rights over the child." Without turning her head to look, Rose knew that the younger woman had stopped chewing. "Don't worry, Millicent, the adoption will go through. I have talked with Sir Steven myself. He is a bachelor barrister. The last thing in the world he wants is children."

"Are you certain?"

"Darling, men never want children until it is their idea."

Millicent murmured something that Rose couldn't hear, adding, "What sort of man does not want children?"

"Either a very selfish one," Rose replied, "or a very honorable one."

"And which is this Sir Steven?"

A bubble of doubt welled up in Rose's throat. "I honestly do not know."

"Is he really Stevie's father?"

Rose shrugged.

"Does he deny he is the child's father?"

Rose hesitated. She hoped to God that Steven would deny he was the child's father. She did not understand why Mr. Letterfrack insisted on formally questioning the man, unless it was, as Mr. Avondale had suggested, to ensure that the adoption was irrevocable.

"You wouldn't want Sir Steven to show up a year from now and claim he had been unfairly denied the opportunity to assert his parental rights, or to object to this adoption, would you?" Those had been Mr. Avondale's exact words the night before, as Rose stood in her parlor, wringing her hands and recounting her conversation with Mr. Letterfrack. *"Let your lawyer do his job, Rose."*

But she could not cease worrying. There was always the chance that Sir Steven would change his mind when pressed by Mr. Letterfrack to make a stand on the issue of Stevie's paternity.

Turning from the window, she gave Millicent a wobbly smile. "Who can know whether Sir Steven is the child's father?" she said at length. "Who can ever truly know?"

"Is there a resemblance?" Millicent asked.

Rose's lips tightened. She met her friend's gaze, but said nothing.

"Oh, my," Millicent whispered, understanding all. She got up from the sofa and stood next to Rose. "Well, it doesn't signify, does it? If he doesn't want the child—"

"Yes, yes, that is what he said."

"He will tell Mr. Letterfrack he is not Stevie's father, and that will be the end of it." Millicent's words came out in a rush. "And you will have complied with the letter of the law, and the adoption will be finalized and no one can ever undo it, ever. Ever! And Mollie and Katie and Steven will be yours. The end!"

Shutting her eyes, Rose willed herself not to cry. "Oh, Millie, I will be so happy when the adoption is final and I know for certain that no one can take them away from me!"

Millicent wrapped her arms around Rose's shoulders, and the two women stood for a moment, quietly consoling each other while the snow softly battered the window. When carriage wheels sounded on the street below, they straightened and looked through the window. Mr. Avondale, who was in the process of holding Katie aloft so that she could place a top hat on the snowman's head, could be seen peering at a gleaming black equipage as it drew to a halt in front of Rose's house.

The carriage door opened and a tall, black-clad man alighted. Pausing, he returned Mr. Avondale's gaze, but did not throw up his hand in greeting, or nod, or even smile his hello. Grimly, he turned and headed toward Mrs. Sinclair's front door. She pressed her forehead to the cold glass, clouding the pane with her breath. The man's face, even beneath the brim of his hat, was easily recognizable. Her heart squeezed, and she grabbed Millicent's hand for support.

"Who is it?"

" 'Tis Sir Steven Nollbrook," Rose whispered.

"Why is he here?" Millicent asked innocently.

"I do not know."

But in her heart, Rose knew exactly why Sir Steven had returned. She had sensed his decency when she kissed him. He was not the sort of man who could turn his back on a child, a child that was undoubtedly his only son.

Six

Rose sent Millicent home with a promise that she would tell her everything once Sir Steven had gone. Then she went to the sideboard, pulled the stopper out of a decanter and threw back the first shot of whiskey she had drunk since Winston died. By the time her visitor was shown into the parlor, Rose had calmed her fluttering nerves and could greet him with at least a semblance of normalcy.

His face was pinkened by the cold, his lips set in firm lines. "Once again, I arrive uninvited."

"And unexpected," Rose said. "Please sit down, Sir Steven. Would you care for some tea, or hot chocolate?"

"No." A lengthy silence spun out. "I've been thinking about the children," Sir Steven said at length.

For once, Rose noticed, his gaze flickered away from her. He was unaccustomed to being out of control. He had no ready script for this occasion. Fearing her knees would buckle if she didn't sit down, Rose sank onto a sofa and waved Sir Steven into the chair opposite her. "What about them?" she asked, her heart thudding.

"The twins look nothing like me. But there is no

denying the resemblance between Stevie and me. The child is mine, I am certain. I should have said so before."

Rose's vision blurred. Her own voice sounded small and far away. "Did Mr. Letterfrack speak with you?"

"Yes."

"And you told him you think Stevie is your son?"

"Not exactly." Steven's brow furrowed. He looked as if he were going to say something more on the subject of Letterfrack, but then he changed his mind. "I understand my options, Mrs. Sinclair. *Rose.* I can deny paternity, but that would be a lie. I can agree to the termination of my parental rights. Or I can take the child and raise him myself."

Her throat constricted. "You wouldn't—"

"Not right away. The children are happy and safe here with you."

Blinking, Rose wondered if her hearing were impaired. Or had that shot of whiskey rendered her senseless? She did not understand what Steven was telling her. She tried to eke out a question, but all she could do was shake her head and turn up her palms inquiringly.

" 'Tis difficult for me to explain," Steven said, somewhat apologetically, though Rose thought he was not sorry at all for what he was doing to her. "After much reflection, I have come to the conclusion that I cannot walk away from Stevie. I have not yet decided what role 'tis proper for me to play in his future."

"I don't understand," she whispered.

"I did not expect you to, not really." When he looked at her, his gaze fixed on her so intently that she felt transparent. Even while he was robbing her of her most precious gift—*motherhood*—he somehow managed to soothe her with his dark, smoldering stare and his honeyed words. "I am sorry for the pain this causes you. I would not blame you at all for hating me."

Rose did hate him—for an instant. She held him responsible for the hurt she felt. He was the stronger one of them; he was the more experienced. He should know better than to trifle with the emotions of a woman and a child. He was the most feared and respected litigator in Dublin, a man sought out by other men for counsel and protection. Yet he was behaving as if he were as confused by this situation as she was.

But she could not hate him for long. Staring at him, Rose saw little Stevie's troubled expression and frightened eyes. Like his son, Sir Steven attempted to conceal his fear and his confusion. Rose, however, could see right through him. There was a vulnerability behind Steven's eyes that made her want to assure him everything would turn out all right. Exhaling a breath she hadn't known she was holding, Rose muttered a sanguine oath. She did not know whether she should embrace Steven and hold him close to her, or run him through with a hot poker.

"What did you say?" he asked, clearly startled.

"I would prefer not to repeat it, sir."

He almost smiled. "I did not think you were the sort of woman to use profanity."

"You are driving me to it."

She was relieved to hear him chuckle. The tension in the room eased. Sir Steven crossed his long, lean legs in a casual, elegant manner. Leisurely, as if he were studying a painting on a museum wall, he gazed at Rose. "I have never thought of myself as having the qualities required to be a good father."

She started to tell him she thought he would be a fine father, but she bit back the words. She did not know him well enough to say that, and she did not particularly want him to believe it, anyway. "Being a father requires a great deal of time and dedication," she replied.

"Yes, and I have fallen into the habit of working all the time."

"You are a dedicated lawyer. That is understandable."

"Recently, I have wondered whether life has passed me by. Other men my age have children in finishing school or university."

Rose wished desperately for another drink of whiskey. The intimacy she was feeling toward Sir Steven was disturbingly pleasant. He voiced the fears that she had lived with for years. Life had passed her by, too, cheating her out of the chance to give birth to children of her own. But now she had three children whose futures depended on how competently she maneuvered her way through the legal intricacies of this adoption process. And getting friendly with Sir Steven could not be helpful in that regard.

"Children tie a man down," Rose remarked.

"I suppose that is true. But a son could also be a great comfort to me in my old age. Or so I am led to believe."

Panic fluttered just beneath the surface of Rose's

composure. Serenely, she said, "Steven, what are you getting at? You can't possibly be toying with the idea that I should live with you."

"As I have said, I believe you are quite the proper custodian for Stevie. For now."

"*For now?*"

" 'Twould be traumatic to separate him from his sisters. *Now.*"

"Or at any time in the future, sir. Stevie should stay with me, and that is all there is to it."

"Well, now, I don't know about that." Steven uncrossed his legs and leaned forward. "You see, I am contemplating the merits of being a father."

"Versus the drawbacks?" Rose shot back. "Why don't you make a list, then?" Anger suddenly whipped her into a froth. She leapt up and ran to her writing desk. She snatched a pen and a piece of paper from one of the cubbyholes in the desk, then whirled and crossed the room, standing in front of Steven with her arms outstretched. "Here! If you are so bloody intent on analyzing this situation as if it were a boundary dispute or an inheritance problem, go ahead!"

"Rose, your language—"

"To hell with my language!" She thrust the pen and paper into his hands. "There, draw a line down the center of the paper!"

Slowly, probably because it was simpler to acquiesce in her demands than it was to defy her, Steven drew a line down the center of his paper. "All right, and now what would you have me do?"

"On the left hand side of the paper, we will list all the reasons you would *not* enjoy being a father."

"I do not think this is a useful endeavor."

"Do it!" She stamped her foot and jabbed the air with her finger. "Do it, or I will—"

"You will what, dear?"

Rose drew in a deep breath, but she could not, for the life of her, beat back her anger. Steven's endearment only made her angrier. Through gritted teeth, she said, "Do it, or I will have you tossed out of my house."

"You wouldn't dare."

Rose folded her arms across her chest. "Start writing."

"What would you have me write?"

"The first thing that pops into your mind—*why you would not wish to be a father.*"

Resignedly, Steven scratched his pen on the paper. "All right, I'll play your little game if it will amuse you. *'Why I would not wish to be a father,'* " he mused aloud. "Well, for one, it will involve a great deal of time. As you have pointed out, I have grown accustomed to working from daybreak until dark."

"On the weekends, too?"

"Of course. That is the only time when I can work in my office undisturbed."

Rose pointed at the paper. "Write that down. What else?"

"I am told that children are very expensive."

"Oh, yes!" Even to her own ears, Rose's voice sounded unusually shrill. "You wouldn't believe how much these particular three children eat. And little Stevie will soon sprout up like a weed and need an entire new set of clothes. I have noticed that he drags his toes on the ground and ruins his boots. No doubt he will need a new pair every few months!"

"The girls will wish to have seasons when they are of age." Steven's pen flew across the paper as he grumbled.

"Yes, and in London, too, *dear,* if you can possibly afford it." Rose nibbled her bottom lip. "Well, even if you can't, for that matter."

"Quite so."

"What else?"

"A man has got to be more circumspect when children are in the house."

Rose shot Steven a knowing look. "You cannot entertain floozies in your bathtub, and you cannot throw wild, drunken card parties that last all night."

"That would certainly crimp my style."

Uncertain whether he was joking, Rose said, "It would be unthinkable for you to remain unmarried. Necessity would demand that you take a wife—if for no other reason than to supervise the additional servants you would be forced to hire."

"I shouldn't think I would like that." Steven smirked devilishly. "I am not the marrying kind."

"No, I don't suppose you are," Rose murmured. "And then there is the small but remote possibility that you would become inordinately attached to the children. The girls will grow up and marry, most likely to someone you deem wholly unsuitable, and then they will fly away, leaving you perched in an empty nest, alone, without even so much as a visit from your grandchildren."

"Why don't my grandchildren visit?"

"Because Mollie moved to Paris with a penniless artist, and Katie married a shipping magnate from Liverpool."

"And Stevie?"

"Given the fact he spent his impressionable years in a brothel, you'll be lucky if he doesn't dedicate his life to whiskey and fast women."

"Yes, I see your point. A father is bound for disappointments. There is just no way around it."

"You are not cut out to be a father, Steven. Admit it now, and save yourself and the children a lifetime of heartache."

"We have not yet filled up the other side of our page," he chided her. "Now we must list the advantages to my being a father."

"There are none."

"Well, working less might not be such a bad thing."

"You would never get used to living a life of leisure."

"Chasing little Stevie around the house, teaching him to ride a horse and taking the girls to town to buy frilly gowns and bonnets hardly sounds like a life of leisure, Rose."

"What have the girls to do with anything? You are not *their* father, for heaven's sake!"

"I do not believe the children should be split up. Besides, I think it might be rather festive to throw grand birthday parties for the two of them. Twins are very special, you know."

"You are far too old to enjoy such things, Steven. Fatherhood requires youth and stamina."

"I am not much older than you, dear."

His audacity gave her a start. Gasping, Rose replied, "How dare you—"

But Steven was frowning hard at his list and writing furiously. "I think I should enjoy taking my boy to school, sending him to Eton—"

"He will never be admitted."

"My boy will be admitted," Steven said. "He is very bright, I can see that already."

Struggling to frame a response, Rose wrung her hands. Little Stevie *was* bright, and the girls *were* charming, and there was very little she could say to convince herself or anyone else otherwise. She had been foolish to insist that Steven sit down and analyze the advantages and disadvantages of being a father. Any simpleton with a heart would conclude that the joys of having children far outweighed the heartbreak of raising them.

"Mrs. Sinclair," Steven said, his voice as lush as velvet, "I do believe you have convinced me that turning my back on Stevie would be quite the wrong thing to do."

"You are going to take him away from me?" Rose asked in an almost inaudible voice.

"I am going to spend some time with my son. If, as you say, I ultimately decide that I am not fit to be a father, I will then sign over my parental rights to you. But if after spending a few weeks with Stevie, I conclude that my son and I should be together, I will oppose the adoption."

"You mean man!" Rose's hand flew back before she realized what she was doing. Purple spots danced before her eyes. Only once before had so much fury consumed her, and that was when she first learned of Winston Sinclair's infidelities.

But as the years passed and her husband continued to philander, confronting him became an exercise in humiliation and frustration. Eventually, Rose pretended not to see what was going on beneath her eyes, disguising her anger with unconcern and hiding behind a cloak of feminine martyrdom.

Yet the memory of that first time still filled her with rage. Rose had pounded her fists on Winston's chest until her arms were sore, and she had wailed at the top of her lungs until he had threatened to summon a constable to silence her.

Winston's love and devotion had seemed so important, then. Rose had thought her broken heart would kill her. But she had survived her husband's betrayals.

And she would survive this.

She would not, however, give up on Stevie, Mollie and Katie.

"I hate you," she breathed. But when she went to strike Sir Steven, he caught her wrist as easily as if he were cuffing a child. Their list slid to the floor.

Captured, Rose bent over Steven, her fingers inches from his face. He pulled her closer to him, so that their lips were nearly touching. "Let me go."

"Not until you promise to behave."

Rose jerked away, rocking back on her heels.

Steven reached around her waist and pulled her onto his lap. She placed her palms on his chest and pushed away, but he drew her back. They struggled, Rose thrashing about until the little bun on the top of her head came completely undone and her hair framed her face. It seemed like hours that Rose tried to free herself, but in reality, mere minutes ticked past.

"Do not fight me, Rose," Steven said gently. His arms slowly eased from around her middle.

Her breath came in shallow pants, and her heart raced. She could have escaped then; in fact, she supposed she could have escaped before. Instead, Rose went completely still, staring at Steven as the tension crackled between them.

She flinched when he brushed the hair from her eyes. After a moment, he slowly traced the line of her cheek and chin. His gaze swept over her face, and his fingertips followed, caressing her lips, lightly touching her eyebrows. Wariness pulsed in Rose's veins, but something else flowed into her bloodstream, too, something warm and pleasant. Her impulse to flee faded. Reluctantly, she relaxed.

"Would it be so terrible to have me around for a few weeks?" Steven whispered.

She started to tell him it would be unbearable. She did not think her nerves could withstand the constant confusion that just being near Sir Steven produced. But before she could say a word, he kissed her.

The heat of his lips on hers gave her a shock. Inhaling sharply, Rose closed her eyes and experienced a strange sensation of weightlessness and ecstasy. When she opened her eyes, Steven was staring at her.

"Shall we make a list, Mrs. Sinclair?"

"Um?" She felt the hardness of his arousal beneath her bottom. As an experiment, Rose shifted her weight and watched Steven's expression alter from one of fascination to one of pure agony. "What sort of list, sir?"

"Let us list all the reasons I should not spend a few weeks with you and the children."

A throaty, feminine giggle bubbled up Rose's throat, surprising even her in the erotic effect it produced. Steven's half-lidded gaze, his intimate whisper, and his irreverent attitude amused and seduced her. "All right, I will play your game," she said, nipping at his lower lip.

"Number one. You do not want me here."

"Number two. You have no right to be here. The twins are not yours, and you are not even certain whether you wish to take responsibility for Stevie."

He tipped her chin and kissed her hard. When their lips parted, his gaze looked drunken. After a sigh, he said, "Three. You think I am a callous, despicable, immoral cad."

"Four. You will disrupt their classroom."

"Five. My work at the office will suffer."

"Six. You will not have time to play with your floozies."

"Seven. I will be forced to spend an inordinate amount of time with *you*."

Rearing back indignantly, she saw the mischievous grin on Steven's face. Narrowing her eyes, she said, "Would that be so unpleasant, Steven?"

With a noncommittal shrug, he said, "Now let us list the reasons why I *should* spend a few weeks with my son."

"I know of none."

"One. I have a legal responsibility to financially support my offspring."

"How noble of you."

"Two. I have a moral obligation to him, also."

"I am willing to relieve you of that obligation. You needn't feel a sliver of remorse at terminating your parental rights. No one will love Stevie more than I."

"No doubt." Steven drew Rose's hand to his lips as he spoke. "Three. I have never tried on the mantel of fatherhood. Perhaps I am not as ill equipped to be a father as I thought. I should like to see for myself, I think."

"Take my word for it, sir, you are not cut out to be a father."

"Four." As his teeth scraped Rose's knuckles, she shivered. "I want to do this. I want to try."

"You are playing with a child's emotions. You should be thinking of Stevie's best interests, not your own selfish desires. If you wish to test your character, find some nice woman to fall in love with and have a family of your own. But leave mine be, please."

"Number five, Rose." Steven turned her hand over and pressed a kiss into her palm. For a moment, he was silent, but when he finally spoke, his voice was hoarse and filled with earnestness. *"I want to be with you."*

Either he was a consummate actor, Rose thought, or he was sincerely overtaken by emotion. At this point, she was not entirely certain. Nevertheless, an unbidden wave of liquid heat spilled through her as Steven held her palm against his lips. Wrapping her arms around him, she pressed the side of his head to her breast. "All right, then," she whispered.

A tiny voice inside her head shouted back. *What*

are you doing? He will only take Stevie away from you! This man will break your heart in the end!

But he was the child's father. If he wanted, he could take his son home with him that very day. Rose had no bargaining chips whatsoever. And Steven did have a right—and an obligation—toward his child. Rose could not deny that.

"I do believe, sir, that the disadvantages to your plan far outweigh the advantages." Still, she could not resist running her fingers through his hair and breathing in the masculine scent of his skin and his clothes.

"I disagree." Steven ran one hand up her back, across her rib cage and over the bodice of her light woolen gown. Slowly, he massaged her breast.

His touch released an explosion of erotic pleasure in Rose's body. Suddenly, Rose's breasts felt heavy and full; her nipples tingled and ached to be squeezed and suckled. Involuntarily, she arched her back and moaned.

But sexual pleasure wasn't all that Steven's touch incited. Something else inside Rose came undone. Some locked-away desire inside her was unleashed. Her thoughts were foggy, but she vaguely wondered why Winston Sinclair's touch had never made her feel so feminine, so attractive, so *wanted.* Sex with her husband had been awkward, embarrassing and shameful. He had shown no concern for her pleasure—which was why Steven's next question both surprised her and aroused her.

"Do you like this, Rose?" His hand cupped her breast while his lips moistened the front of her gown.

"Does this give you pleasure? Do you wish for me to stop?"

"God, no." Cradling his head in her hands, she instinctively directed his mouth to her nipple. The wetness of his suckling, even through her gown, excited her. The urge to strip off her conservative dress was nearly overwhelming, and she might have done so were it not for the long row of cloth covered buttons that ran up her spine.

Gasping, Rose shifted her weight. Steven's body hardened impossibly beneath her thighs, and his breathing—warm against the dampness of her gown—grew more labored. "Rose, I want to make love to you," he said, peering up at her.

She wanted it, too. Reaching down, Rose ran her hand over Steven's erection, aching to feel it inside her. And his groan only intensified her yearning. "Do you like that?"

His head fell against the back of the chair, and a smile flickered at his lips as he stared at her. "Yes, and I do very much, Mrs. Sinclair."

"Do you like . . . this?" Through the fabric of his trousers, she gripped him more forcefully, wrapping her fingers around his shaft and stroking him slowly, up and down.

Steven's eyes fell shut and a look of sheer ecstasy came over him. "I am transported, my dear." A moment later, his brow furrowed, his hips bucked and he sucked air in through his teeth.

His fingers closed around her wrist. "If you do not stop that, however," he whispered, "I shall be tempted to ruck up your skirts and pull down your knickers."

"I dare you." The novelty of talking like this to a man, of describing out loud what she liked and what she wanted, struck Rose as wickedly thrilling. And outrageously naughty. She wondered when she had turned into such a wanton. Had the children's talk of brothels and bawdy limericks transformed her into a jezebel? Was she experiencing some kind of physical imbalance associated with her age? Was she mentally ill? Or depraved?

The proper thing to do was to release Steven's erection, climb off his lap, smooth down her skirts and ask him to forget about their indiscretion.

She did not want to do that.

Uncertainty assailed her. When Steven opened his eyes, she said softly, "This isn't proper."

"You are free to stop this whenever you wish, Rose."

"I am afraid I do not wish for it to stop."

Having never been hungry for a man, it seemed ridiculous that she was starving for this one. Her upper thighs were drenched with the evidence of her need for him. The mental image of Steven's naked body pressed against hers actually created a throbbing point of pleasure-pain between her legs. She would have liked to pull down her knickers and have him touch her everywhere. But that tiny voice in her head began to shout again, and she realized she could not completely abandon the caution and logic that ordinarily controlled her.

Just as Steven's fingertips caught the hem of her gown, she released his pulsing erection. "I do not wish for this to stop, Steven, but it must."

"Why?" he asked groggily.

"I fear that I will regret it."

His hand stilled instantly, his gaze sharpened and he withdrew his hand from beneath her skirts. "I do not want you to regret anything."

"Nor do I." Shakily, she stood. She wondered if she would regret not making love to Steven.

He pushed up from the chair and stood toe to toe with her. "I hope I did not—"

"No, of course not!" Her hands fluttered nervously at her waist. It was difficult to look Steven in the eye, and even more difficult to look anywhere else. Glancing down, she noted with horror the telltale spot of moisture above her right nipple.

"You spilled some tea."

"Yes." Heat suffused her face. Now that the spell of intimacy between them was broken, Rose did not know what to say.

"Well." Steven appeared equally at a loss for words. At last, he gave Rose's hands a quick squeeze. "When would you like for me to return?"

"Excuse me?"

"Would tomorrow night be too soon?" Seeing her reaction, Steven quickly added, "Don't worry, I shall return to my own home every night. I only intend to spend the days and evenings with you and the children. After supper, I shall take my leave."

"That is rather presumptuous of you, Steven."

He gave her an appraising stare. "Would you rather pack Stevie's belongings and send him home with me now? As much as it pains me to tell you, Rose, that is your choice."

"I feel as if I am bargaining with the devil."

His lips twisted. "Perhaps you are, dear." Taking a step toward the door, he said, "Tomorrow night, then, don't forget."

"How could I?" Rose whispered, relieved by his departure but saddened by it, too.

Below stairs, the front door opened and closed. Children's laughter sounded on the steps. As Mollie, Katie and Stevie dashed into the parlor, Rose opened her arms. The children, their noses and fingers cold from playing in the snow, stepped into her embrace. At once, they began telling her about the snow man Mr. Avondale had helped them build.

"He rather resembled old Mr. Smythe, didn't he?" Mollie chirped.

"Who is Mr. Smythe?" Mrs. Bleek asked as she entered the room.

"One of my uncles," piped Stevie.

"He wasn't your uncle," Katie corrected him crossly. "He was a big, unpleasant man with a red nose from too much whiskey. He was a friend of Miss Tweedy's, and he smelled bad and he tore up the place one time because he had a quarrel with Miss Tweedy and planted a fiver right in the center of her nose."

"She bled like a pig, she did," Mollie said.

Rose exchanged a look with Mrs. Bleek. *How long would the children continue to talk about their past life in a brothel?*

"All right, children, 'tis time to wash up for supper." She shepherded them out the door and into Mrs. Bleek's custody. Then she pulled the bell cord and while she waited for a servant to appear, quickly scratched a note to Mrs. Millicent Hyde-Wolferton. When the message was dispatched, she rested her elbows on her desk and dropped her head into her hands.

She had only one night to plot a strategy that would dissuade Sir Steven Nollbrook from wanting to be a father.

Seven

The snow relented during the night. In the morning, an unusually bright sun appeared, and by noon the streets were lined with a gritty slush composed of ice and soot. The carriage ride to Mrs. Sinclair's took twice the time it ordinarily did, so that Steven had ample opportunity to mull over his decision.

Twice, he raised his arm to knock on the ceiling and instruct his driver to turn around and go home. But lacking the guts to alter his course, he drew his arm back and continued onward. Slouched against the squabs, his temples pounding from the pressure building in his head, Steven wondered why he had ever said hello to Katherine Rowen.

She had been so beautiful, that was why. And in the beginning, when their romance was fresh and everything he knew about Katherine's background could have been written on the head of a pin, he adored her. How was he to know what lay ahead for the poor wretched girl?

If he had known, would he have behaved any differently? Would he have refrained from falling in love with her? Would he have been able to leave her alone?

He doubted it. Bitterly, he flashed on the memory

of his own mum's weathered face. He saw her standing in the doorway of their modest cottage in Portlaw, her eyes bright with unshed tears, her hands nervously wringing a linen square. Outside, the sky was streaked with black smoke. Even inside, the ubiquitous black dust, spewed from the stacks of the nearby Malcolmson Cotton Mills, settled on the furniture, on the crockery, even on a person's skin if he didn't bathe daily.

Steven's younger sister, aged ten at the time, clung to Mrs. Nollbrook's thickening waist. "Is Papa ever coming home?"

Steven's mother dabbed at her eyes, then turned a hopeful smile on her daughter. "Aye, and he'll be home before ye know it, child. He's workin' an extra shift, he is! So as we'll be able to buy that new pair of boots you've been hankering after."

Even then, Steven should have known better. It took five more years for Steven's father to drink himself to death, and by then Steven had saved enough money from working in the cotton mills to travel to Dublin where he obtained an education, was called to the Bar and quickly became a rich man. Too bad his mother and his little sister hadn't lived to see him prosper; in Steven's first year of practice, they died of a lung disease. He had not returned to Waterford since their funerals.

Shortly thereafter, Steven met Katherine Rowen in a public library. It was her choice of reading material, as much as her bright red hair and porcelain complexion, that first fascinated him. Closing a volume of Thomas Moore's poetry, he had stood and simply stared at her. She looked over the top of a radical newspaper called *The Nation,* met his gaze and smiled shyly.

By the time he realized she was addicted to opium, and that she could not get through a day without copious amounts of drugs and whiskey, he loved her. Most men would have abandoned her, but Steven, every bit as optimistic as his mother, wanted to help Katherine. It was his duty to care for her, to hold her head when she was sick over a basin, to spoon soup between her lips when she lay in her bed, shivering from the effects of too much or too little opium in her body. It was his duty, his obligation and his privilege. It was his lot in life.

Katherine's weakness made him powerful. At first.

His carriage slid to a halt in front of Rose Sinclair's house. Resignedly, Steven tapped the crown of his hat and stepped carefully to the ground. Trudging up the walkway, he reminded himself how foolish he had been to kiss the widow Sinclair. He would not touch her again. She was not a suitable woman for him; no decent woman was.

With a heavy sigh, he banged the brass knocker on her front door. His breath frosted the air. He thought of turning around and leaving. It was not too late. He thought how perfect he and Katherine truly had been for each other. They were equally flawed, and no one else would have them. He thought he was losing his mind. He had been insane to think he could father a child, *really father a child,* not just sire one.

He was as negligent a parent as Katherine had been.

And his father had been. And his father's father before him.

His boots made a crunching sound on the bricks as he turned.

But the door swung open before he took a step.

"Aren't you Sir Steven?" called out a little girl's voice.

Slowly, his chest aching, Steven executed an about-face. In the threshold, framed in the light that spilled from the gas lamps bracketing the door, stood Mollie. Or was it Katie?

Embarrassed, Steven nodded.

An identical face appeared beside Katie's. Or Mollie's. "Well, come in, then," the little girl with the slicked back hair and ponytail demanded churlishly.

"Don't be rude, Katie," said her sister. "Remember what Mrs. B. taught you, for heaven's sake."

As he stepped into the entry hall, a servant took his cloak and hat. Steven followed the girls up the stairs and into the parlor, where little Stevie hopped along the hearth beside a crackling fire, and Rose sat serenely on the sofa, a hoop of embroidery on her lap.

"Stevie, you are too close to the fire," Rose said. But when she saw Steven and the girls enter the room, she put aside her sewing and turned her attention to them. "We had almost given up on you, sir."

"I am sorry to have kept you waiting." Steven, keenly aware of Stevie's proximity to the fire, and slightly alarmed by it, made a little bow in front of Rose. " 'Tis slow going out there. The streets are dangerously icy."

"Would you care for a glass of whiskey, or wine?" Rose asked him.

"A wee bit of whiskey always lubricates the wheels of society," Steven replied, taking a chair opposite the sofa, where he could keep an eye on Stevie. "Is Mrs. Bleek joining us, by the way?"

"Under the circumstances, I thought it best to give her the evening off." Rose remained seated, and to Steven's immense surprise, Mollie and Katie went to the sideboard.

Steven stared as the two little girls, standing on tiptoe, unstopped a crystal decanter and poured two fingers of scotch whiskey into a glass. Evidently, the girls had acquired quite an education at Mrs. Bunratty's. He thought it entirely improper, however, that they should be pouring drinks for visitors in Mrs. Sinclair's home.

"Do you like your whiskey neat?" Mollie asked over her shoulder. "Or shall I add some water?"

"Or sugar." Katie dipped her finger in the glass, then in her mouth. "We could mix you a toddy, if you like."

"No. Neat is fine." Steven took the proffered drink from Mollie and watched in amazement as the twins perched on the sofa, positioning themselves on either side of Rose. He wanted to ask Rose why in the devil she allowed Mollie and Katie to pour whiskey, much less dip their fingers in it for a taste, but he would save that conversation for later, when the children were not in earshot.

Mindful of his purpose in attending dinner at Mrs. Sinclair's, Steven directed his conversation toward

Stevie. "Well, young man, how do you like living with Mrs. Sinclair? Are you getting accustomed to things in Fontjoy Square?"

Stevie leapt from the hearth and went to stand beside the sofa.

"You're tracking soot across the carpet," Katie pointed out.

Indeed, the child was filthy, his boots caked with mud, his clothing dusted with ashes, his fingers stained with grime. Rose clucked her tongue, but said nothing even when Stevie leaned against the crimson velvet sofa, stenciling the cushions with tiny black handprints.

"Touch my apron, and I will wring your neck," Katie purred in a way that sent chills up Steven's spine.

But her little brother was not so easily frightened. Mischief twinkled instantly in little Stevie's eyes. When Katie tossed her ponytail, huffed and turned her head, he very carefully laid his hand on her starched white apron, leaving on it an indelible imprimatur of filth.

Katie's head turned slowly. Her gaze lit on her soiled apron. A split second later, she was off the sofa and, having knocked her brother to the ground, sat on his chest and wrapped her hands around his throat. Her face was screwed into an expression of rage, while her skirts and petticoats were strewn around her legs in a most unfeminine manner. Gaping, Steven feared the child might actually strangle little Stevie.

As this horrific tableaux unfolded, however, Rose merely sighed, lifted her embroidery hoop and shook her head. She shot Steven a weary look and shrugged her shoulders as if to say, *What can one do?*

"Aren't you going to—"

"To what?" she asked sweetly, while the children rolled about on the floor, Stevie choking and gurgling, Katie emitting imprecations only sailors had a right to utter.

"Aren't you going to do something?" The hair on Steven's nape prickled. He could not believe what he was witnessing.

"What would you have me do? They have been up to this since they arrived, fighting, biting . . ."

"Well, I for one do not intend to stand by and allow the children to kill each other." Quickly, Steven rose, grasped Katie around the waist and lifted her off her brother. Unfortunately, he had not expected his captive to struggle so violently. When she kicked her feet, catching him on the shins, he inadvertently dropped her on the carpet.

Rolling to her feet, the child stood up to him, her fists propped on her hips. With her bottom lip poked out and her green eyes flashing, her resemblance to Katherine Rowen was so striking that Steven took a step backward and blinked his astonishment.

"I demand an apology, sir!"

"An apology? Why, you little—" Steven wisely bit back the words that sprang to his tongue. "You would do well to remember, Katie, that you are no longer living in Mrs. Bunratty's establishment. Different rules prevail under this roof."

Or so I thought.

"As much as it pains me to say it, what you need is a little discipline!"

Her eyes turned to squints and her leg bent at the knee. Katie drew back her foot, aiming to kick Steven. But he was bigger, faster and stronger than she. And he was not about to be intimidated by a child. As her boot flung out, he took a swift side step. Then he scooped Katie up in his arms and stalked toward the parlor doors. Her arms and legs flailed in his embrace; unaccustomed to discipline, she screamed her protests at the top of her lungs.

"Where are you going with that child?" Rose's voice was tinged with fright.

Turning in the doorway, Steven saw that she stood beside the sofa now, her expression changed from one of mild bemusement to panic. Her sewing was tossed aside again, and this time she clutched Stevie's and Mollie's hands. Her eyes were as round as saucers. And beneath her dark-blue gown, her breasts rose and fell with every labored breath she took.

He tore his gaze from Rose's breasts, annoyed that, even under the most chaotic of circumstances, he could not dismiss the thought of their near lovemaking. "I am going to take Katie to her bedchamber, where she will remain throughout dinner as punishment for her unacceptable behavior. A plate will be sent up to her so that she won't starve. All in all, I believe she should consider herself lucky that a worse fate did not befall her."

"She didn't really hurt me," Stevie whimpered.

"Come back with my sister, you mean man!" Mollie demanded.

Just then, a servant appeared and announced that dinner was ready. "I will join the rest of you in the dining room," Steven said, bounding up the steps. Though he was unfamiliar with Mrs. Sinclair's house, it was not difficult to find his way to the twins' quarters and deposit Katie's limp body on a bed, where she turned her face into a pillow and began to sob.

As he closed her bedroom door, Steven said, "Katie, dear, you must learn to respect your elders."

"I hate you," came her muffled retort.

Steven's chest squeezed. For a moment, he was tempted to relent and allow her at the dinner table. But instinct told him that Katie's best interests would best be served if he enforced a little discipline.

"I hope that will change," he replied softly, and closed the door behind him.

When he entered the dining room, Rose and the other children were already seated. A servant circled the table, ladling cabbage soup from a tureen into everyone's bowls. He took his place at the end of the table, looking opposite at Rose. "Sorry for the distraction. I hope this incident will not spoil anyone's meal."

Tears streaked Mollie's face. " 'Tis my fault. I should have been watching Stevie more closely."

"It is not your fault, Mollie. Each one of us is responsible for his own behavior. Now eat your soup. Katie will be fine."

Stevie and Mollie dipped their spoons into the soup. The slurping noises they made gave Sir Steven a start. Once more, he looked to Rose for a reaction.

She had none. Calmly, she sipped her soup, occasionally slanting an approving glance at the children as they ate.

Steven cleared his throat to gain her attention. "Excuse me for saying so, Rose, but don't you think the children could stand some instruction in proper table manners?"

"Most assuredly," she said. "Go right ahead."

A sudden wave of weariness overtook Steven. If this was what lay in store for him, he was not at all certain he had the stamina to do it. Handling clients, writing briefs, and trying cases was hard enough. But rearing a child might prove to be the most difficult task he'd ever attempted.

For the next half hour, he attempted to teach Mollie and Stevie the finer points of dining. By the time dessert arrived, however, he was too exhausted to complain of Stevie's eating the meringue off his pie with his fingers. When Mrs. Bleek appeared in the doorway and said she had returned home early and would be happy to take the children to bed, he felt like hugging her.

In the parlor, he stood at the mantel while Rose sipped a cup of hot tea. For a long time, Steven remained silent, his hands clasped behind his back. He was not at all certain how to broach such a ticklish subject with Rose.

"Something on your mind?" she said, at last.

"As a matter of fact, yes. I am concerned that the children are completely undisciplined and unruly. They have no manners whatsoever! They fight like ruffians and they answer their elders with a sassiness that would have earned me a switching across my backside when I was a lad! Stevie needs a bath and Katie needs to have her mouth washed out with soap. As for Mollie . . . well, poor little thing, she thinks she is responsible for everything!"

Rose sighed and placed her cup and saucer on the little table next to her. " 'Tis the manner in which they were raised, Steven. In time, they may learn to conform their conduct to higher standards, but they will never erase their past. They have been raised in a brothel, and it shows."

"They can learn to behave, and they will!"

"They won't change overnight."

"No, I wouldn't think so. It will take time." Exhausted by the thought, Steven rubbed his face.

"You look a bit pale, Steven. Are you tired?"

"I am at that."

"Imagine how tired you will be in a couple of weeks. You have been with the children for less than two hours and already you look as if you are worn out."

"Don't worry about me. I have tried cases for days with hardly an hour of sleep each night. Surely I have the energy to keep up with three children for a couple of weeks."

Her smile was angelic, and yet devilishly knowing. "I am certain you are correct."

Glancing at the clock on the mantel, Steven suppressed a yawn. "Now that the children are in bed, however, I shall retire to my own home."

"You're leaving? I hope you do not think my night's work is over, sir."

"They are not babes, Rose. I presume they will sleep through the night."

"Stevie has a tendency to forget where his chamber pot is. Katie has bad dreams which cause her to cry out in the night, and Mollie visits the water closet at regular three hour intervals. Last night, Mrs. Bleek and I hardly got a wink of sleep."

"I could stay here if you need me, Rose," Steven suggested, fully aware that his tone and sly smile would elicit a quick refusal.

Blushing, Rose crossed her arms over her chest. "I do not need you, Steven."

"Yes, I am certain you are correct." He made a short bow. "Well, then, I shall return tomorrow."

"Be here before ten o'clock," she told him as he stood in the doorway of the parlor. "Mr. Avondale is taking the children and me to town to do some shopping. I believe it would be a good idea if you came along."

"I shall be here at ten on the dot, Mrs. Sinclair. And I shall bring a pocket full of banknotes."

Her reaction was quick and surprisingly full of heat. "I do not need your money, Sir Steven. Nor do the children. If you think that is why I invited you, then please, do not come."

Irritated that she would spurn his offer of generosity, Steven shot back, "You need me more than you think, Rose. I only hope for your sake that when you figure that out, it is not too late."

A half hour later, Rose was propped against a bank of fluffy pillows, a cup of hot chocolate balanced on her lap. At the foot of the bed, clad in a flannel wrapper, thick woolen stockings and a nightcap, sat Millicent Hyde-Wolferton.

"I ran over as quickly as I saw his carriage leave," Millicent said.

"You'll catch your death of cold traipsing about in this weather, Millie." But Rose could not suppress a smile. Since the two women had moved next door to each other, they had become fast friends. And since Millicent had married Alec Wolferton just a few months earlier, Rose missed the younger woman's company. "If Alec knew what you were about, he'd tan your hide."

"As long as he is in London, what he doesn't know won't hurt him. Besides, I miss him so much, I can't sleep." Millicent sipped her chocolate and sighed. "All right, now, spill the beans. Did the children behave like horrid brats?"

"All according to plan." Rose chuckled as she recounted the tussle that broke out between Stevie and Katie. "Poor little thing, she missed dinner on account of her bad behavior."

"Do the children understand why they are being encouraged to act like wild animals?"

Rose shook her head. "I can hardly tell them the truth. They're too young to understand. They think Sir Steven is a former friend of their mother's and that we are playing a game. Of course, the game will end as soon as Sir Steven bows out of the picture."

"And when do you think that will be?"

"Who knows?" Rose shrugged. "He is an uncommonly stubborn man. The trick to controlling him, I believe, is to make him think it is his idea to terminate his parental rights. If he thinks I want him to go away, he never will."

"Typical man," snorted Millicent.

"Oh, but there's the rub, Millie. He is anything but typical."

Millicent tilted her head and peered at Rose through narrowed eyes. "Do I detect a bit of admiration in your voice?"

"He dealt with Katie rather efficiently, I must admit. The poor dear didn't know what was happening. One moment she was rolling about on the floor with her brother, and the next she was being carted off to her bedroom."

"He sounds rather cruel to me, darling."

"It wasn't cruel." Rose put her cup and saucer aside. "Under the circumstances, I'd say it was entirely appropriate."

"Rose . . ." Millicent's voice became a honeyed purr. "You are not getting sweet on Sir Steven, are you?"

"Don't be ridiculous," Rose scoffed. "Good heavens! That's the silliest thing I have ever heard! Me, falling for a man like that?"

"You're turning red as a beet."

"Am not!"

"Come on, Rose, out with it! You fancy the man, don't you?"

"Millicent, he is a committed bachelor. He has admitted as much. He fathered a child with a—"

"It happens every day, Rose. That does not necessarily make him a bad man."

"No, but he neglected the child. For years, he pretended the child wasn't even his! How could I be attracted to a man like that?"

"Perhaps he did not know the child was his."

"He would have had to be blind not to know."

Millicent put aside her chocolate, too, then drew her legs to her chest and propped her chin on her knees. "Haven't you ever pretended not to see something, Rose, even when it was right beneath your very eyes? Even when everyone else surrounding you saw it?"

Of course she had. It had required some real effort on her part to ignore Winston Sinclair's infidelities.

Suddenly ill at ease, Rose yanked up the covers and tucked them beneath her arms. Millicent's probing questions left her feeling naked and vulnerable. She had not intended for her attraction to Sir Steven to become so obvious or so intense that she could not control it. After their last encounter, Rose had resolved never to touch the man again.

When confronted by her best friend, however, Rose could not deny she liked Sir Steven. Merely being in his presence made her feel more alive than she ever had. The fact that she was conniving to get rid of him, *so that she could adopt his son,* made her feel like the very worst sort of villain.

"Oh, Millicent, am I so transparent?"

"You're as easy to see through as a stem of Waterford crystal, Rose."

"I do not even *want* to like the man," Rose wailed. "His very existence creates an obstacle to my adopting Stevie. One whisper of opposition from him, and I could lose Stevie forever. And that cannot happen,

Millicent! The children must stay together—with me!"

"Have you considered telling Sir Steven how you feel? About him, I mean?"

"Nonsense." Rose shook her head, frightened by the very idea that Sir Steven would know what sort of power he had over her. The only thing that had saved her from going insane during her marriage to Winston Sinclair was the eventual realization that he could not hurt her. Once she fell out of love with him, she was immune to the insults of their daily lives together. Inside her own carefully built fortress, she lived a relatively painless life. A man could not hurt a woman unless that woman loved him.

After a long while, Millicent said softly, "Rose, I know you are older and more experienced than I, but Alec has taught me something. And that is that sometimes we must take a big risk in order to be happy. You'll never know whether Sir Steven loves you until you give him the chance."

"Who said anything about *love,* dear?"

Millicent's forehead wrinkled. "You didn't blush because you *like* him, Rose."

"You don't have to love a man to be attracted to him," Rose replied, sniffing. "In the physical sense, that is."

"Are you telling me that you . . . and he . . . have been . . . *intimate?"*

"Not completely."

"Partially?" It was Millicent's turn to blush. Her head popped up in interest, and her eyes widened with curiosity.

Guilty pleasure, and perhaps a small measure of pride as well, puffed out Rose's chest. For years, she had suppressed her femininity. What was the purpose in dressing alluringly when the only man who paid her any attention was Winston Sinclair, and then only to pounce upon her, have his way, and deride her for being unresponsive once their lovemaking was through? It had been far easier to dress in nunlike garb and try to be invisible. As long as Winston ignored her, Rose could at least avoid being hurt.

But now she had the strange urge to brag to Millicent about how exciting her lovemaking with Steven had been. "It wasn't long ago, Millicent, when you told me how wonderful Alec's lovemaking was."

Millicent crossed her legs beneath her and leaned forward. "Turnabout is fair play, so you must tell me everything, Rose. And don't leave anything out!"

What she had done was bad enough, but confessing her deeds out loud gave Rose a wicked thrill. Describing the way Steven kissed her and held her made Rose edgy. Talking about him kindled her desire, and yet she could not hold her tongue.

If she did not tell Millicent everything, she left very little to the other woman's imagination.

She even allowed herself to wonder whether the ladies who worked for Mrs. Bunratty actually *enjoyed* what they did. If they got to make love to men like Sir Steven, perhaps their lot in life was not so horrid.

"Maybe little Stevie's mum taught Stevie's dad a thing or two," Millicent suggested.

Jealousy poured through Millicent like poison. With a shiver, she said, "I can't bear to picture that."

"You're in love," Millicent declared, sliding off the edge of the bed. She found her heavy coat and shrugged into it. " 'Tis as plain as the nose on your face."

"Don't even say such a thing," Rose scolded her. "I have already resolved never to kiss the man again. 'Twas a passing fancy, a fling! But it was wrong, and it will never happen again."

In rebuttal, Millicent merely giggled and pulled Rose's toe beneath the covers. "Keep telling yourself that, old girl. And perhaps one day you will believe it."

"I am perfectly capable of controlling my physical urges, Millie."

"Good night, then." Millicent started toward the door, then suddenly halted.

"Is something the matter?" Rose asked her.

As she turned, a slow smile spread across Millicent's face. "I felt an odd sensation in my belly. A sort of tickle. Like a tiny finger pushing at me from the inside."

At first, the implications of Millicent's remark flew right over Rose's head. Then, with a sudden burst of understanding, she *knew.* "Oh, dear, you are going to have a baby!"

"I'm not certain yet," Millicent said, applying her palms to her stomach. She smiled shyly. "But I think so."

Already the young woman had a sort of ethereal glow. "A *baby,*" Rose whispered in awe, as if a miracle had just occurred. Well, the birth of a child *was* a miracle, she reminded herself, one that, unhappily, had never visited itself on Rose, and never would.

But she felt not a twinge of envy. The thought of Millicent having a baby stirred in Rose a deep, instinctual need. Throwing off her covers, she went to her friend and wrapped her arms around her. Tears spilled down her cheeks, and emotion threatened to rob her of her voice.

"Does Alec know yet?" Rose managed to eke out.

"I thought of writing him in London, but his business will keep him there another month at least. I have decided to wait until he returns home. Then I will know for sure, and the news will be a happy homecoming gift for him."

"He'll be so happy." Rose gave Millicent a kiss on the cheek and walked with her down the steps and to the foyer. "Now go home and get in bed. No more running around at night! You've got to take care of yourself, lass! First thing tomorrow morning, I am going to have Cook send over a big bowl of oatmeal, a slab of bacon and—"

"Rose, I am feeding a baby, not an army!"

"I cannot help but fuss over you, Millie."

" 'Tis a man you need to be fussing over."

"Oh, Millicent, that child of yours is hardly more than a glimmer in Alec's eyes, and already I love it as if it were my own."

Millicent chuckled. "I wouldn't have understood that until a few days ago. But now I do. A woman falls in love with a man gradually because he is good and kind and they need each other. But a woman falls in love with a child instantly, for no logical reason whatsoever."

"And once you fall in love with a child, dear, you never fall out."

"Yes, I understand," Millicent said, somewhat wistfully. "They'll break our hearts, won't they, Rosie?"

"The men or the children?"

"Both."

That was a possibility with which Rose was only too familiar. "So what if they do, Millie? We can't quit loving them just because there is a risk we won't be loved in return, now can we?"

Millicent, her eyes shining, silently shook her head. Then she wrapped her coat more snugly around her middle and started home.

Rose stood in her open doorway, watching her friend carefully pick her way home along the icy walkway. The happiness she felt at hearing Millicent's good news was not tempered in the least by her own fears. After years of suppressing her feelings, and trying not to love anyone, Rose now felt the freedom to bask in the richness of her emotion.

And, like a bear emerging from hibernation, Rose Sinclair was ready to taste what the world had to offer.

Eight

Devon Avondale stood before the mantel in Rose Sinclair's parlor, his hands clasped at his back. Staring at the fire, he struggled to suppress his irritation. He was not at all pleased to hear that Sir Steven Nollbrook was joining the shopping expedition.

"I was under the impression that you held the man in low esteem and never wanted to see him again." Turning, he stared hard at Rose. He tried his level best not to snap at her, but he could not help questioning her judgment in allowing Sir Steven to accompany them to town.

"You disapprove," she replied flatly. Arms folded across her chest, she stood near the sofa. Below stairs, Mrs. Bleek could be heard coaxing the children into their coats and mittens. Sir Steven was expected to arrive any moment.

"I disapprove strongly. In fact, I must admit, Rose, I am bewildered by your decision. Why on earth have you invited Stevie's putative father to spend the morning with you?"

"Putative?"

" 'Tis a legal term. It means Stevie's alleged father. Whether Sir Steven is in fact Stevie's real father has yet to be proven or disproved. That is why I retained Mr. Letterfrack."

"Oh, dear." Her hand flew to her lips. "I hope you don't think me ungrateful."

Devon's irritation waned. No matter how frustrated he was with Rose, he could not deny that her intentions were wholly honest. He wondered if she was simply naïve. "No, of course, I don't. But Rose, I don't understand why—"

"Because he *is* the child's father," Rose blurted. For a moment, she stood as still as a statue, her lips tightly compressed, her pretty violet eyes unusually round.

Stunned, Devon drew in a deep breath, then slowly released it. "Well, how did you obtain that bit of intelligence?"

"He told me." Rose's hands fluttered in the air. "Oh, and it is so obvious, Devon. I suppose I knew it from the moment I laid eyes on Steven. Wait until you see the two together. They are father and son, there is no doubting it."

"And the girls?"

"The girls . . ." Rose's voice trailed.

"Is Steven Nollbrook their father, also?"

For some odd reason, Devon had rattled Rose with that question. Instead of answering, she shook her head and bit her lip.

"Are you certain?"

"Quite."

"Does Nollbrook intend to oppose your adoption application?"

"He hasn't decided yet."

"Hasn't decided!" Devon's anger surfaced quickly.

He slammed one fist into his open palm. "And does he know it's a child's life he's playing with here? If he doesn't, Rose, I shall tell him—"

"No need." Steven's deep courtroom voice boomed through the room. "I think I understand your point of view. What I do not understand is why the issue of Stevie's adoption concerns you in the least."

Rose gave a start and whirled around. But Devon, his body thrumming with indignation, met the other man's gaze straight on.

"Rose Sinclair happens to be a friend and neighbor of mine," Devon replied. "My name is Devon Avondale."

"I appreciate your concern," continued Steven, walking into the center of the room to stand beside Rose. There was an animal-like grace to his movements, and a proprietary tone in his voice. "But you are out of bounds, sir. Whether I choose to oppose Stevie's being adopted by Mrs. Sinclair is none of your business."

Devon rankled. For nearly eight months, he had been the unofficial overseer of the women of Fontjoy Square. Two of his charges, Dolly and Millicent, had married during that time, and Devon was as happy and proud for them as if he'd been their papa. He had nothing but respect and affection for both their husbands. He hoped that Rose and Lady Claire Kilgarren would one day find suitable men to marry, also. But he did not think Sir Steven Nollbrook, a man who had fathered a prostitute's child, then abandoned his son, was the right man for Rose.

"I beg to differ, Nollbrook." Devon took a step forward.

To his chagrin, the impeccably dressed lawyer shot his cuffs, rolled his shoulders and met him in the center of the room. The men stood an arm's length apart, staring challengingly at each other. Tension crackled in the air surrounding them. An eerie quiet fell over the room.

Through his teeth, Sir Steven said, "Mrs. Sinclair and I have reached our own agreement concerning Stevie. I am going to spend a few weeks with him, and after that, I will inform Letterfrack whether I oppose the adoption. Until then, there is nothing you can do about my presence here."

"Oh, there isn't?" Devon practically snarled. "I could beat the hell out of you, that's what I could do."

"Do you think so, old man?" A deep chuckle rumbled up from Steven's throat. "Go ahead, then, and try."

Devon's anger flooded his ability to reason and think. His arm shot out in a flash. The sound of his fist connecting with Steven's jaw sounded like a pistol shot. Steven reeled back on his heels, but quickly regained his balance and lowered his head. The punch he landed in Devon's midsection fell like a battering ram.

Staggering back, Devon struggled to fill his lungs. Searing pain shot through him, but the pain was nothing compared to the fury boiling in his veins. Warily, he straightened, his gaze fixed on his adversary. Sir Steven, red-faced and heaving like a bull, stared back at him.

"Had enough, Avondale?" Nollbrook sneered.

"To the devil with you," Steven returned through a grimace.

Nollbrook charged, and the two men wound up in a hostile embrace, grappling and wrestling with each other while Rose screamed.

Devon wondered if hitting Steven might not have been a bad idea. The barrister's fists were obviously as powerful and dangerous as his words. For a wiry man, he was dreadfully strong. And he would not easily admit defeat, but would rather fight to the death to defend his honor. Devon knew this because he felt the same way. As he fell to the floor beneath Steven, he felt a kinship and a strange respect for Nollbrook. He also felt a knife of pain slide between his ribs. Reaching up to wrap his fingers around Nollbrook's throat, he realized he might have to kill the man.

Steven—eyes bulging, temples pulsating—sat astride Devon. "Go to hell," he whispered as he drew back his arm.

Cursing silently, Devon braced himself while digging his thumbs ever deeper into Steven's Adam's apple. Amazingly, the man seemed impervious to physical pain.

To Devon's astonishment, Rose's face suddenly appeared at Steven's shoulder.

"Stop it, you two! I won't have this in my home!" Having leaped onto Steven's back, she now pulled at his arm, preventing him from delivering to Devon's face what would surely have been a decisive blow.

Seemingly stunned, Steven froze, his gaze locked with Devon's.

"You're acting like children!" Rose wrapped her

arms around Steven's middle and tugged at him with every bit of strength in her body.

Of course, he could have swatted her away. He was far too strong to be overpowered by the likes of Rose Sinclair. *She knew that.* But perhaps her intercession was enough to cause him to reflect on what he was doing. Or maybe Steven needed an honorable excuse to end the fight. Whatever the reason, Steven allowed himself to be subdued, and with Rose's arms wrapped snuggly around his middle, he rolled off Devon's body and lay on the carpet, his chest heaving, his skin hot and clammy from his exertions.

For a brief moment, Rose laid on her side, snuggled against his back, spoon fashion. She liked the weight of his body in her arms and the way his bottom fit against the curve of her lap. It might have been her imagination, but she thought she felt him sigh heavily and wriggle more closely into her embrace. His fingers closed around her wrists as if he meant to capture her. But as Devon lumbered to his feet cursing colorfully, Steven roused, too. On their feet, the men scooped Rose up in unison, apologizing in tandem for their lack of civility. Rose brushed her dress with her hands and patted her hair. Guiltily, she was somewhat flattered that she'd managed to shame them both so thoroughly.

She might have laughed, but she did not want Steven and Devon to know how deeply amused she was by their boyish behavior. Instead, she fixed a stern look on her face. "Have you both gone insane? Why, I might expect such unruly conduct out of the children, but you two are grown men! I ought to toss you both out on your ears!"

It seemed they couldn't quit bowing and apologizing. While cutting sidelong glances full of hostility at each other, they practically fell all over themselves to obtain Rose's forgiveness.

"It will never happen again," Steven assured her.

" 'Twas all my fault," Devon said. "Perhaps I was a bit overzealous in my urge to protect you, Rose. It is your best interests that I am concerned with, you understand."

"Are you suggesting that I am *unconcerned* with Rose's best interests?" Steven asked.

Anger flashed in Devon's eyes, and he opened his mouth to retort, but Rose cut him off. "Now, now! I'll brook no more of this foolishness! I dare say, we will have to cancel our shopping trip for today." She stared at two sullen, childlike expressions. "We will go tomorrow, weather permitting. Good day, gentlemen. Both of you."

Reluctantly, the men said their good-byes and departed. Devon Avondale heading for his home at the end of the square, Steven entering his carriage and rattling northward toward town.

"And what has happened now, pray tell?" In the parlor doorway, Mrs. Bleek blinked her confusion. "Are we going to town or aren't we?"

"We will go tomorrow, Mrs. Bleek. In the meantime, I believe I shall pay a visit to Mr. Letterfrack."

An hour later, Rose sat across from Mr. Letterfrack's desk, staring first at the silver-haired lawyer, then at his rabbit-like assistant. Their sour expressions were not reassuring.

"I know I didn't have an appointment," she said for the third time. "I've already said I'm sorry. But this is a matter of the greatest importance."

Letterfrack leaned back in his chair, laced his fingers over his belly and pursed his lips. "Go on, then."

"I am worried about Sir Steven Nollbrook." When the men staring at her said nothing, she took a deep breath and plunged into her story. "He has admitted he is little Stevie's father. But he has not yet decided whether he wants to be a father. He is spending the next few weeks with us in order that he might make up his mind."

Letterfrack rocked forward. "He has admitted he is the father?"

"Yes." Rose studied her fingertips because looking at Letterfrack was growing more unpleasant by the moment. "But he has not decided—"

"Yes, yes, I heard all of that. Well, that is most unfortunate."

"I don't know why it was necessary to approach him at all."

"Madam, if a putative father is not given the opportunity to oppose an adoption, then he might legally do so at any time in the future. You wouldn't want the man to snatch the boy away from you when the child turned twelve, would you? Better to do things the right way, dearie. Less trouble in the end, believe me."

"I suppose you are right." Rose nodded. Mr. Avondale had said pretty much the same thing. But while she appreciated the logic in the advice she was given, she couldn't suppress her resentment. It would have been so easy to simply inform the court that Stevie's father was unknown. "What shall I do now?"

"Perhaps you should consider giving up your plan to adopt the boy."

"That is out of the question!" Infuriated, Rose gripped the arms of her chair. "If you feel that is the proper course of conduct, then I shall be forced to retain other counsel, Mr. Letterfrack."

He patted the air with his beefy hands. "No, Mrs. Sinclair. Your benefactor has asked that I do everything in my power to help you, and I have no intention of abandoning my mission if you wish to proceed."

"I love those children," Rose replied through her teeth, certain that Letterfrack had no idea how passionate her feelings for them were. He could not.

"Are you willing to do whatever it takes to ensure that the court awards custody of the children to you?"

"As long as it is not against the law."

The lawyer's bushy brows arched. "I would not advise you to do anything that is technically against the law, Mrs. Sinclair. Now, listen carefully to what Mr. Hare has to tell you before you say anything else. And remember, there is more than one way to skin a cat."

Rose stared in stunned silence as Mr. Letterfrack pushed himself out of his creaking chair and left the room.

Mr. Hare, still standing, gave her a twitchy smile. "The law is such, Mrs. Sinclair, that even if Sir Steven convinces the court that he is Stevie's father—"

"Which won't be difficult to do. They look so much alike."

"He still has the burden of showing it is in the child's best interest that he be awarded custody."

"As the child's father, would there be any question as to his custodial rights?"

The rabbit's nose wriggled. "Now there's an interesting question. 'Twould be a rare case indeed if the court were to find that Sir Steven Nollbrook is unfit to raise his own son."

"I cannot imagine the circumstances under which the court would make such a finding," Rose said. "Sir Steven has a temper, 'tis true . . . and I suspect he has enjoyed quite a bit of success with the ladies over the years, but . . ." Bewildered by Mr. Hare's remarks, Rose's voice faded.

"None of that would be sufficient to deprive a man of his custodial rights, of course." Mr. Hare always looked as if he were about to sneeze. But he never did. "If it could be proven that he were a moral degenerate—"

"He is not!" Why Rose felt the need to defend the man who stood in the way of Stevie's adoption, she didn't know.

"But if he *were*. If he were an opium addict, for example."

"But he is not."

"Apparently, there is much about Sir Steven Nollbrook you do not know, Mrs. Sinclair. Mr. Letterfrack, however, has known the man for many years."

"What are you getting at, Mr. Hare?"

"I am afraid that Sir Steven has been known to consort with opium addicts. He has been seen in opium dens on many occasions in the past."

"I do not believe it."

"Mrs. Sinclair, your innocence is commendable, but your naiveté is rather tedious." The rabbit's ears moved back and forth at the sides of his head. Leaning forward, he pressed his slender fingers on the edge of the desk and stared at Rose as curiously as if she were a talking head of cabbage. "Witnesses can be produced who would testify to Sir Steven's association with certain members of Dublin's drug underworld."

"What sort of witnesses?"

"Clodagh Tweedy, for example. She has had occasion to witness Sir Steven's debauchery. And she is willing to testify." The whiskers above his thin upper lip twitched. "For a price."

Rose inhaled sharply. Her brain could hardly process the raw information Mr. Hare provided. But dimly, in the corners of her mind, she comprehended the reason for Mr. Letterfrack's absence. "You are suggesting that I pay a witness in order to testify against Sir Steven?"

"I am suggesting that Miss Tweedy is hardly the type of individual to volunteer her testimony. In her line of employment, she has a natural dislike for the court system. But she might be persuaded to reveal what she knows pertaining to Sir Steven's moral conduct . . . for the right sum of money."

"A paid witness is bound to say whatever her benefactor wishes to hear."

"At least you are not unintelligent, Mrs. Sinclair." Mr. Hare gave a self-satisfied smile and leaned back in his chair.

"Nor am I willing to be a party to this sort of chicanery." Insulted that Letterfrack and his minion would even remotely think she might be interested in bribing Miss Tweedy, Rose stood.

Mr. Hare, his cheeks bright pink, stood also. "I was under the impression that you wanted to adopt Mollie and Katie and Stevie more than anything else in the world."

"That is correct."

"Yet you are willing to allow your own foolish sense of integrity to stand in the way of a successful adoption application."

"I will not lie to the courts, Mr. Hare, and I will not pay someone else to lie for me."

Mr. Hare patted his palms together in mock applause. "How very self-righteous of you. I hope you are prepared to see two little girls have their heart broken, then, Mrs. Sinclair. Because when Sir Steven takes little Stevie away from you, Mollie and Katie will be crushed. The children have never been separated, have they? No, I thought not. 'Twill be gut-wrenching. I am glad I do not have to sleep with *your* conscience, Mrs. Sinclair." He gave her a limp-wristed wave of dismissal. "Good day."

Shocked, Rose turned on her heel and left. She could not wait to get home and tell Mr. Avondale what had occurred. Surely he would recommend another lawyer, someone who was intellectually equal to Sir Steven, but who had an ounce of integrity as well. On the other hand, perhaps all lawyers were as conniving and cunning as Letterfrack and Hare. She had not met one yet whom she would trust any farther than she could throw him.

A hour later, too nervous to sit, she paced the length of her parlor while Millicent Hyde-Wolferton and Devon Avondale looked on.

"Rose, dear, you look as if you are on the brink of violence." Millicent, a platter of sandwiches in her lap, was seated on the sofa.

Devon stood at the mantel, his gaze switching between the two women. "Did Letterfrack hear everything that Hare said to you?"

"Letterfrack conveniently left the room prior to Hare's abominable suggestion!" Halting, Rose propped her fists on her hips and stared at Devon. "Oh, I don't mean to appear ungrateful, Devon, but, really, I must have another lawyer."

Devon was puzzled. Aloysius Letterfrack was reputedly the finest barrister in Ireland. And Hare was widely known as one of the most clever solicitors in Dublin. It would be difficult to find any two lawyers who wielded greater influence at court. And with Sir Steven Nollbrook lining up as a potential adversary, Rose needed the best legal representation available.

"Perhaps you misunderstood what Mr. Hare said," Millicent inserted.

"On the contrary, I understood it all too well," Rose replied as she resumed her pacing.

"There is only one thing for it," Devon said. "I shall pay a visit to Mr. Letterfrack tomorrow. If he is in agreement with Hare's corrupt notions, we shall set about finding you a new lawyer."

Rose released a breath she hadn't realized she was holding. "Thank you, Devon. I don't know what I would do without you." Crossing the room, she held out her hands to him.

Devon squeezed her fingers, then drew her into a quick, brotherly hug. *I don't know what I would do without you, either,* he almost said.

Indeed, Rose and her neighbors, Dolly, Claire and Millicent, had saved his life just as Mary O'Roarke Avondale had promised they would. Before the four women moved into Fontjoy Square, Devon was so steeped in depression that he could hardly force himself out of bed each morning.

But somehow Mary knew that the four women and Devon needed each other. Even in death, she had managed to give her husband a greater measure of happiness than he deserved. And with each passing day, Devon's love for the women of Fontjoy Square increased. He loved them because at times they needed him. He loved them simply because they had once loved Mary.

Nine

In his darkened study, Devon sat before a dwindling fire, one hand clutching an empty brandy snifter, the other holding Mary's leather-bound diary. His eyes watered as he stared at the dying embers, seeing nothing. A log fell, and sparks flew, startling him from his reverie. Shaking his head, Devon looked at the journal in his hands, then held it to his nose, breathing in the scent of Mary's perfume, the ink and paper, the memories.

Before the ladies moved to Fontjoy Square, Devon had only once read the chapters that concerned Rose Sinclair. Those passages were the most intimate and private of Mary's writings. Devon had been saddened and disturbed the first time he read them. It pained him to read of Mary's tragic loss. He would not have revisited those chapters if it were not for Rose's present predicament.

Now he felt the need to understand more. He wanted to hear Mary's voice, so clear and strong in her writings. He wanted to soak up the compassion that had flowed from her heart to her pen to her paper. He wanted to be near Mary because he did not know what to do for Rose. And he did not understand why he felt a closer bond with Rose Sinclair than he did with any of the other women in Fontjoy Square.

Opening the journal, Devon dashed a tear from his cheek and began to read.

Dublin, Spring, 1865

Dear Diary, or Dear Devon, I should say, inasmuch as this collection of memories is compiled primarily for you,

It was during the summer of 1853, just after I graduated from finishing school in Switzerland, that I met him, and in this journal, he shall be known by the fictional name of Padraig, because when you, my dear beloved Devon, read these pages, as I hope and pray that you will, I fear that you will hunt the man down and kill him if you are able to determine his identity.

Indeed, my father would have killed Padraig himself had he known what transpired that summer. But no one ever knew, no one except Rose Humphrey, that is, whose family rented a seaside villa in Killiney just down the street from ours. Though Rose was far too quiet and conservative for my tastes that year—after all, I was a budding eighteen-year-old with aspirations of being the first female member of parliament, and she wanted nothing more than to marry a suitable man and raise children—we became best friends that summer, in part because we were thrown together by our families, who, it seems likely in retrospect, thought that our most extreme qualities (my radicalism and Rose's virtuous ortho-

doxy) would rub off on each other, improving the sum total of us both.

In the end, nothing of the sort happened, and when it was all said and done, Rose remained in Dublin as virtuous as she'd ever been, while I took off for my next European adventure with as much, if not more, joie de vivre than I had ever possessed.

I believe my determination to continue on in my characteristically intrepid manner may have been a reflection of my resolve to put the Padraig episode behind me. But Rose's character remained static. I am certain that none of her goodness rubbed off on me, and none of my wildness rubbed off on her. But we learned something, both of us did that summer, and in that respect, we were never quite the same.

Padraig was the oldest son of the wealthy hotelier who owned the big resort that attracted so many vacationing Dubliners to Killiney.

(I trust, dear Devon that as you read this, you won't rush off to Killiney in order to seize upon the clue I have just tossed you. It doesn't matter anymore really, it doesn't.)

At any rate, he was a big, strapping boy, though I suppose at age twenty, he was a man, despite there being little in his behavior to suggest he was any the more prepared for life outside the parental cocoon than I was. We were both well-to-do, cosseted and yet indulged, a dangerous combination that created in us a joint attitude of cocksuredness, when in truth we hadn't the foggiest notion what the world was all about.

I wonder if I ever did know anything about life before I met and fell in love with you, dearest Devon. 'Tis an irony that life most clearly shows its meaning when we are fading to the edges of our existence. That is why, Devon, you must read what I have written and act upon your instincts. Do not waste your time moping about what could have been. Do not wait for divine wisdom to visit you, or for some profound enlightenment to pop into your head, dear, because it isn't going to happen.

The secret of life—if I may be so presumptuous as to suggest that dying has suffused me with some little wisdom—is very simple; that is, there is no secret, and so you must create your own happiness and the only way to do that is to find someone to love. Someone else. Someone other than me because I will soon be just a memory (a precious one, I hope). And when you do, Devon, love your new love very dearly, because life is also very short . . . and when we are getting close to its end, as I am doing now, I can assure you that the only thing that matters a whit is whom you have loved.

Oh, Devon, I have loved you so well.

But I was talking about Padraig, wasn't I? When I first laid eyes on him, he was sailing a small boat along the coast, and he was all alone, his red hair flashing, his bare shoulders pinkish-bronze and freckled from too much exposure to the sun. I thought he was the handsomest thing I had ever seen, and devilishly smart to be piloting his own boat without benefit of crew or servants.

Of course, I didn't know a fig about boating or boys or anything, then. I was just so itchy to experience something, everything, anything. And Padraig seem just the sort of roguish lad to encourage me in my endeavors. When he moored his little boat at the pier down the beach, I told Rose I was going to meet him. She looked up from the book she'd been reading—who but Rose Humphrey would have been reading a book instead of watching the bathers in the ocean—and she said, "You'd best be careful, Mary, I have heard he is as wild as a buck rabbit."

That was all it took, of course, to fascinate me completely. I gathered up my blanket and the picnic basket packed for me that morning by my servants and, trailed by a reluctant and admonitory Rose, set off down the beach. I wish I could say that Rose's company was enjoyable, but in truth, it was neither requested nor preferred. I would have liked her to stay put on the beach, beneath the great canvas umbrella our parents had paid a local vendor to erect and under which we were ordered to stay.

But accompany me Rose did, and she insisted, too, because of the anger my being spotted unchaperoned in the company of a slightly older, slightly bad boy would surely invoke. (I am speaking of the anger of my father, dear Devon, but having met him, I am certain you deduced that without further elucidation).

Padraig, as it turned out, was quite delighted to see that he had attracted my attention. While Rose made a pretense of searching for seashells along the shore, Padraig and I flirted wickedly, he even going so far as to suggest a clandestine late night rendezvous on the beach. I might have done so, too, had I not instinctively understood that a quick agreement on my part would have been interpreted by Padraig as capitulation or victory or—Erin forbid!—a sign of promiscuity on my part. Even at my most reckless, you see, I was still constrained by the moral principles impressed upon me by my parents.

So, Padraig and I parted that day, after much eyelash fluttering and blushing and long, soulful gazes, only to be reunited a fortnight later at a dance sponsored by a local ladies' organization. The dance was held at Padraig's father's hotel, where a small symphony orchestra played Mozart in a ballroom grand enough for London or Bath. Against a backdrop of sparkling chandeliers, mirrors and potted palms, Padraig asked me to dance.

For a boy his age, perhaps because he'd been reared in the festive atmosphere of a summer resort, he was a graceful dancer. He was the first boy I had ever danced with who did not tread on my toes or whirl me around the floor as if I were a ten-pound sack of sugar. Instead, and in contrast to the arrogance he'd displayed on the beach when I first met him, Padraig was polite and gracious. He seemed a bit shy, in fact, and when I placed my fingers in his palm and he rested his hand on the curve of my hip, gently guiding me in the proper direction as all good boy dancers know to do, I thought I heard him inhale and exhale very quickly, as if the friction of our touching actually took his breath away.

It wasn't long before I began sneaking out of the house at night to meet Padraig on the beach. . . .

A groan broke the silence, startling Devon. His head jerked up and his heart thundered. The fire was getting low, and the single lamp on the table beside his chair made reading difficult.

Belatedly, Devon realized it was he who had groaned, perhaps in sympathy for his dear Mary, who had been so young that summer in 1853 when she met the "slightly older, slightly bad" Padraig, the hotelier's son. He groaned because he knew what came next; he'd read Mary's diary in its entirety and he meant to read it again. But reviewing it tonight was too painful in light of Rose's predicament.

And he knew that Mary would have preferred he focus on the problems of the living.

So, he closed the journal. Leaning forward, elbows on knees, Devon held the little book of memories to his nose, inhaling the faint perfume of Mary's touch. He missed her. *God, did he miss her.* His loss was inconsolable, his pain too deep to share. What made his life worth living was the knowledge that he had in some small way repaid the kindnesses shown to Mary by her four friends, Dolly, Claire, Rose and Millicent. He was doing everything that Mary wanted him to do. *Almost everything, that is.* He knew he would never find someone to love as well as he had loved Mary O'Roarke Avondale.

Standing on the steps of Rose Sinclair's house, Steven marveled at his complete loss of objectivity. Already, fatherhood had inspired him to act like a fool. The jealousy and anger that had caused him to attack Devon Avondale was evidence of his sudden insensibility. Perhaps that was reason enough to turn tail and run, he thought, as he knocked on Rose's door. Perhaps he would be wise to concede to Rose's request, deny he was Stevie's father, and go on as before. If his emotional investment in the child deepened, he was at risk for making a total jackass out of himself.

And I do not even know this child! He could be clever or stupid, mean or sweet-tempered, honest or deceitful. He could be a little monster, for all I know! Yet, I have become obsessed with the notion that he is mine! And I cannot rid myself of the thought that he needs me!

Footsteps sounded from within, drowning Steven's silent debate. Underscoring his determination to be admitted, he knocked again. This time, someone yelled, "No need to knock the house down, we're coming!"

Suppressing a chuckle, Steven waited. It was far too late to be paying a social call; once again, he would owe Rose an apology for violating the rules of etiquette. No doubt she was in bed, and her servants were scurrying about wondering what calamity had occurred that would justify such an unseemly visit.

If he had any sense, or any consideration for Rose's feelings, he would turn around, climb in his carriage and go home. But he could not force himself to leave. An overwhelming compulsion had brought him here. He would not be satisfied until he saw Rose and Stevie. He could not wait to see them. Tomorrow was too long to wait.

At length, the door swung open, and a wizened old lady with a single flickering taper in her hand squinted into the darkness.

"Sorry to disturb you," Steven said, removing his hat. The cold at his back swept away the remaining vestiges of his manners, prompting him to quickly cross the threshold and close the door behind him. "I would appreciate it if you would inform Mrs. Sinclair that Sir Steven is here to see her."

"At this hour?" the woman squeaked, retreating.

"Tell Mrs. Sinclair I will wait in the parlor." Steven followed the maid up the steps, but at the landing, he made his way to the parlor, while she continued to the next floor.

He stood at the sideboard, pouring himself a glass of port, when Rose, clad in a woolen wrapper, entered the room.

"Sir, do you have no decency? It is half past eleven o'clock, and I have been in bed well over an hour."

That she had been in bed was evident. Staring at her, Steven was momentarily robbed of speech. Her gleaming black hair was tousled, and her eyes were glazed with fatigue. Her robe accentuated the fullness of her hips, and her self-conscious tugging at the neck of her gown drew his gaze to her breasts. Rose's dishabille lent to their conversation an intimacy that aroused Steven.

He should have felt guilty for disturbing her rest, but instead, a bolt of erotic pleasure shot through Steven. Rose's bed-rumpled look inflamed his curiosity. A mental image of her, naked against a backdrop of tangled sheets, flashed in his mind's eye.

"Are you all right?" She stood at the sideboard, too close, apparently, for her own comfort, for her hands continued to flutter at the neck of her robe.

"Would you care for a drink?" he asked.

To his surprise, Rose nodded. Sipping the ruby liquid, she peered suspiciously at him. The silence that enveloped them was filled with awareness. Rose was sweet and virtuous, but like most little lambs, she recognized a wolf when she saw one licking his chops. When at last she spoke, her cheeks were touched with color and her lips were stained with purple.

"Why did you come here in the middle of the night?"

He told the truth, for once. "I wanted to see you. And Stevie."

"He is fast asleep, sir."

"I would hope so." Steven spied a droplet of wine on Rose's lower lip, and suddenly wanted to kiss her. But he did not dare risk insulting her further. The near brawl he'd commenced on her parlor floor that afternoon with Devon Avondale was sufficiently outrageous to garner Rose's permanent scorn.

Her tongue darted along her lower lip, and the droplet of wine disappeared.

With a gulp, Steven pulled at his suddenly constricting collar.

"I believe, sir, that if you are going to persist in coming round, we should establish some ground rules."

"Let me guess. You have a list of rules that you wish for me to follow."

Her lips tightened. "Ridicule me if you like, sir. But in the future, I would prefer that you not pay house calls after eight o'clock in the evening. It is disruptive to my staff, not to mention my sleep." She touched her hair. "Goodness, tomorrow I shall have purple shadows under my eyes."

Her vanity struck Steven as charming. With a chuckle, he said, "And what is next on the list of things I am prohibited from doing, Rose?"

"You may not wrestle on the floor with Mr. Avondale."

"I do apologize for that." He took a step nearer to her.

Instead of retreating, Rose placed her empty glass on the sideboard and folded her arms across her chest. "You may not interfere with my attempts to discipline the children."

"Dear woman, I have witnessed no such attempts. As far as I can detect, you are allowing them to run around like wild animals. Stevie is filthy, Katie is a hellion and Mollie, bless her heart—"

"You don't have to tell me, sir. I can see for myself what Mollie's problem is. She thinks it is her duty to care for her brother and sister. I fear that she has lost a great deal of her childhood beneath the strain she has lived under."

It occurred to Steven that had he not failed so dismally in his efforts to rehabilitate Katherine, little Mollie and her siblings would not have suffered so. Rose's compassion for the children emphasized Katherine's unfitness as well as his callous neglect of them. What would have happened to the poor little wretches if Rose had not happened into their lives? he wondered. Had he any right at all to deny her the right to raise them now?

While he mulled over his inadequacies, Rose continued. " 'Tis Katie whom I worry most about, though. She is so angry all the time."

"She has every right to be, I suppose," Steven said. "Up till now, she hasn't had much of a life."

Rose released an unexpected giggle. "You have to admit, it was funny when he quite deliberately put his dirty little hand on Katie's clean white apron."

As he laughed, an emotion that Steven had not expected welled up inside him. Discussing the children as if they were a shared responsibility, *as if they were his and Rose's responsibility,* deepened the intimacy he felt toward her. "I would like to see Stevie," he said impulsively.

"Right now?"

"Now."

"But sir, he is asleep."

"We'll just take a peek, then. There's no need to wake the child."

"But Steven—"

"Come on, then, I won't take no for an answer." Steven guided Rose to the parlor door and up the steps. At the landing, he said, "Now, which door is it?"

With a little huff of exasperation, she led him to the door at the end of the hall. She placed her fingers on her lip, then carefully pushed the door open. A wedge of light from the gas lamp on the hallway table spilled into Stevie's bedchamber. He was asleep, all right, one arm thrown over his eyes, nightshirt rucked up about his legs, counterpane kicked to the foot of the bed. Had Rose not tiptoed in to cover the child, Steven would have done so.

He stood behind her as she rearranged the bedclothes. When she straightened, he slid his arm about her waist. For a long time, the two stood in Stevie's room, staring at the child as if he were the most fascinating creature on earth.

"Hear how he breathes," she whispered.

"Yes, he is very sweet when he is asleep," Steven agreed, unable to resist the urge to nuzzle Rose's neck.

Slowly, she turned into his embrace. With her arms still clasped over her chest protectively, she gave him a puzzled stare. "Did you love his mother very much?" she whispered.

"We'll wake Stevie," he replied, leaning forward to kiss her.

"He's a sound sleeper," she whispered back, pressing her palms against his chest.

Thwarted, and uncertain how to answer, Steven sighed. "Very much indeed."

"Was she very beautiful?"

"Yes." *But not so beautiful as you.* "She was also a very troubled woman. She, ah, drank too much whiskey and smoked opium, not an uncommon vice among women who fall into prostitution."

"Does it make you uncomfortable to talk about Katherine?"

"Yes." Steven thought that kissing Rose might distract her, but it did not seem likely she would allow such a thing to occur until she received satisfactory answers to her questions. If she were a lawyer, he would have deemed her a worthy adversary. "Yes, it makes me uncomfortable."

Rose nodded toward the door, and the two quietly padded out of Stevie's bedroom and into the hall.

"You see, Katherine was not a prostitute when I met her." Now that he was talking, Steven felt the need to explain that Katherine was not an evil person. "In the beginning, she hid her problems from me, and by the time I realized how addicted to opium and whiskey she was, it was too late."

"Too late for what, Steven?"

"Too late to help her, I suppose. Though I tried, God knows. I checked her into hospital, but she ran away. I took her to the country, where she couldn't escape, and she got better, but the minute we returned to the city, she began drinking and smoking again. I consulted every doctor in Dublin, and a couple in London and Edinburgh, too, but they all told me the same thing."

"Which was what?"

"That I could not help Katherine until she decided that she wanted to be helped."

"And when Stevie was born? You really didn't think the child was yours?"

Steven pinched the bridge of his nose. Embarrassed, he averted his gaze. "Katherine was so small and fragile, and sickly most of the time . . . well, it wasn't difficult for her to hide the symptoms of her pregnancy. I never really knew when she conceived. Often, I would go for weeks without visiting her."

"Didn't you miss her?"

"I did not allow myself to miss her. I thought missing Katherine was a sign of weakness on my part. The demands of my work made it easy for her to deceive me, too, now that I think on it. At any rate, I had some fuzzy knowledge that a baby was on the way, and then, poof! It had arrived and already been dispatched to the arms of one of Mrs. Bunratty's servants!"

"Katherine never allowed you to see the babe?"

"I caught glimpses of the child, and of Mollie and Katie, too." Steven looked Rose dead in the eye. "Look, perhaps I did not want to be a father. Perhaps it was easier for me to just believe what Katherine said, that the child wasn't mine, and that I shouldn't give the notion a second thought."

"What made you change your mind, then, Steven? What made you think you might actually want to be Stevie's father?"

You, he wanted to shout. *You! You forced me to confront the child and to think about my responsibilities toward him. If truth be known, you shamed me into realizing that I could not live with myself if I turned my back on my son.*

"It seems the forces of good and evil are conspiring to make me a better man."

"I don't understand."

"No, I don't suppose you do."

He could have told her more. But Steven did not want Rose to know how deeply she had affected him. That knowledge would have given her an infinite amount of power and control. He did not want Rose to know how empty his life had been until she had come along, or how happy it made him to be in a house with children. And he most certainly did not want Rose to know that he could not erase her from his thoughts, or that he could not forget how exciting it had been to kiss her and hold her. "Kiss me, Rose." He reached for her.

She held him at arm's length. "I don't know if I should, Steven. You see, it is difficult for me to understand how a man could feel nothing for his own child."

Panic twisted in his chest. He could not respect a man who cared nothing for his child, either. "I suppose I can't expect you to hold me in high regard, Rose."

Turning her head, she pressed her lips tightly together. The indictment in her silence was crushing to Steven.

Stepping back, he murmured, "Good night, then. I shall not trouble you any further. I appreciate your allowing me to see Stevie."

"Good—" Rose was cut off by a wail that sounded in the room just opposite where they stood. "That sounds like Katie!"

Steven followed her into the bedroom where the twins were. In the huge tester bed they shared, Mollie was sitting up and staring at her sister who lay on the pillow beside her, crying and holding her stomach. Quickly, Steven lit the lamp beside the table while Rose attempted to determine the cause of Katie's outburst.

"My tummy hurts!" Katie moaned.

Rose lifted the counterpane, pulled up Katie's cotton rail and examined the child's stomach.

"What is the matter with her?" Mollie asked, clearly frightened out of her mind.

"I confess, I do not know." Rose's voice was soothing, but Steven could feel the worried tension rolling off her body. Turning to him, she said, "Her skin is hot and clammy, but I see no wounds or injuries."

"Here, allow me." Leaning over Katie, Steven gave her a sympathetic smile as he moved his palms along her bare belly. "Does this hurt?" he asked, gently pressing his fingers into her left side.

"Ohhh! Please, sir, stop, I did not mean to be a bad girl, I promise I will never be bad again!"

When the child nearly bent double from pain, Steven knew precisely what the problem was. "You are not in pain because you have misbehaved, dear," he said quietly, laying his hand on her sweaty little forehead. To Rose, he said, "I fear her appendix will have to be removed by a surgeon."

"A surgeon?" Rose gasped. "Are you certain, Steven?"

He nodded, omitting the fact that he had seen several of Mrs. Bunratty's girls suffering from identical symptoms. If an infection was raging in the child's body, the need for surgery was urgent. "She needs to go to hospital, Rose. *Now.*"

Hearing the word *hospital,* Katie grew agitated. "I do not want to go there," she pleaded.

Wide-eyed, Mollie added, "I don't want her to go there, either. 'Tis a bad place! Women who go to hospital rarely return."

Steven's heart nearly burst at the sight of Mollie's terror. The child's understanding of the world was based strictly on what she had learned at Mrs. Bunratty's. No doubt she had witnessed some of the women there fall prey to terrible illnesses. Steven knew that some of them contracted communicable diseases or suffered with complications resulting from pregnancy. Others, like Katherine Rowen, struggled with addiction and mental illness. Mrs. Bunratty sent them to hospital only when their conditions became dire. It was not surprising that few of them returned.

Reaching over Katie, he gave Mollie's shoulder a firm squeeze. "Don't worry, darling, I will take good care of your sister. I won't let her out of my sight. And she will return in a few days, as good as new. I promise."

"What do you mean, you won't let her out of your sight? I hope you don't think I am going to allow you to take Katie—"

"Madam, you have no choice." Even as he spoke,

Steven began to wrap Katie in a blanket. Scooping her limp body off the bed, he held her against his chest. Her head fell onto his shoulder and her arms laced around his neck. Meeting Rose's gaze, he wished he could hold her, too, but the most he could do was assure her he would take good care of Katie. "You need to stay here with the other children."

"I want my ma," Katie whimpered.

"I will go with her," Mollie said, hopping out of bed. "I have to, you know. She can't take care of herself!"

"I will take care of her, Mollie," Steven said firmly, but gently.

Mollie wrapped her arms around Rose's waist, and she hugged the child snugly to her side. Together the four of them walked out into the hallway.

"Where will you take her?"

"To Meath Hospital." With precious cargo in his arms, Steven descended the steps carefully. "Luckily, my carriage is just outside. Katie will most likely be operated on this night. As soon as I have word from the surgeon that she is all right, I shall send a message by porter."

"Oh, Steven, I am frightened out of my mind."

"I know, dear." In the foyer, he leaned toward her and planted a kiss on her forehead. Then he leaned down and planted one on the top of Mollie's head, too. Tears slid down the child's cheeks, causing Steven to wish he could pull her into his arms for a long embrace. But Katie's need to get medical attention was paramount.

"You two ladies will simply have to trust me," he said.

Rose draped his coat over his shoulders and patted his hat on his head. "I trust you," she whispered, reaching up to kiss him lightly on the cheek.

Steven stepped into the blistering cold night air. He hurried to the waiting carriage and instructed his driver to proceed to Meath Hospital as quickly as possible. As the carriage rumbled through the icy streets, Katie whined and cried, squirming uncomfortably in his arms. With each passing minute, her situation grew graver and Steven's fear intensified.

He had not been able to save the child's mother. He had not been able to save his own mother, his father or his sister. If he could not save Katie, self-loathing would destroy him.

Ten

"Good heavens, Mrs. Sinclair, how long have you been here?" Mrs. Bleek's voice sounded in the threshold.

Startled, Rose looked up and bade the other woman enter the parlor. "Most of the night, I'm afraid." Half sitting, half reclining on the sofa, Rose had been sipping from a tepid cup of tea since dawn and occasionally looking at a passage in the Bible on her lap. Putting the book aside, she now swung her feet to the floor.

Mrs. Bleek took the cup and saucer from Rose's hands. "Forgive me for saying so, but you look a fright, mum. Anything I should know about?"

"Obviously, you haven't looked in on Mollie and Katie yet."

"It's a mite early for those two. I reckon they'll be squawking soon enough, though."

"Katie won't. She's been taken to hospital by Sir Steven Nollbrook."

Mrs. Bleek's pale face blanched even whiter. "What in Erin's name is wrong with the child?"

"Sir Steven thinks it is her appendix. She woke up last night feverish and in great pain."

"How did Sir Steven happen into the picture?"

"He was . . . er, visiting when Katie fell ill."

"I didn't hear anything and my quarters are just down the hall from the girls' room!" The nanny's brow furrowed with suspicion.

Sighing, Rose pressed her fingers to the sides of her head and massaged her temples. "Steven and I were just outside Stevie's door when Katie woke up. Everything happened very quickly, Mrs. Bleek. It was hours before Mollie settled down enough to go to sleep. I've been here ever since, waiting for a message to be delivered from Steven."

"You poor thing! You need to get some rest yourself."

"I can't," Rose objected. "Not until . . ."

Rose was silenced by a knock on the front door. Showing unusual speed for a woman her age, Mrs. Bleek raced out of the parlor and down the steps. In less than a moment, she returned with a small vellum envelope. Rose leapt to her feet, practically snatching it from the nanny's fingers.

Her own hands trembled as she ripped open the envelope and unfolded the single sheet of writing paper. In the instant that it took for Rose's vision to focus on the distinctive male handwriting, she considered the almost unreal possibility that Katie had succumbed to her illness. The pain that stabbed her heart caused her vision to blur and her mind to momentarily cease functioning. A week ago, she had not known of Katie's existence, and now the child's life meant everything to her.

The words faded and danced beneath Rose's gaze.

"Well, what does he say?" Mrs. Bleek questioned.

She willed herself to read Sir Steven's message aloud.

Dear Rose,

A surgery was performed on Katie in the wee hours. Her appendix was removed and she is now recovering. The doctor says she will make a full recovery and can return home in three days' time. I will wait here until she awakens, then I will come and fetch you for a visit.

Love,
Steven

" 'Tis good news, mum." Mrs. Bleek's eyes sparkled with unshed tears. "Will you permit me to help you to bed now?"

In the wake of the good news, relief poured through Rose. She gasped with pure joy. The mantel of worry and fear she had been wearing instantly lifted.

But the weight of her exhaustion came crushing down on her, too. Suddenly, Rose's knees buckled and she would have collapsed in a puddle if Mrs. Bleek had not been there.

"Oh, dear!" The older woman wrapped her arm around Rose's waist. Together, the two made it up the stairs and into Rose's bedchamber. Sitting on the side of her bed, Rose kicked off her boots and allowed Mrs. Bleek to help her out of her dress. Then, wearing nothing but a thin cotton chemise, she crawled beneath the covers. Her eyes were already shut as Mrs. Bleek tucked the counterpane around her. Smiling, Rose murmured, "Thank you," and drifted into sleep.

When she awoke, her room was bathed in shadows. She slowly swam back to consciousness, aware of a strong male presence in her room. The haze of her sleep lifted, and she inhaled deeply, stretching her legs beneath the blankets. A sense of well-being and safety eased Rose's awakening. Opening her eyes, she found herself staring into Sir Steven's dark, penetrating gaze.

He sat on the edge of the bed, half smiling at her. "Good afternoon," he drawled. "I hope you had a good rest. You needed it."

She glanced at the windows, noting that the blinds had been pulled low. "Afternoon? What time is it?"

" 'Tis after noon, dear. Don't worry." He found her hand and held her fingers to his lips. "I told your servants to stay below stairs and walk on tiptoe so that you could sleep."

"Katie?"

"Doing quite well, I am happy to report. She even ate a spoonful of flavored ice before she went back to sleep herself. I think she will be falling in and out of a deep sleep for another day or so. At least, her tummy doesn't hurt anymore."

"What about Mollie and Stevie?" A frisson of panic raced up Rose's spine. Mollie had been so frightened the night before, and little Stevie was bound to be equally confused by the news of his sister's hospitalization.

"Mrs. Bleek and Mr. Avondale have taken Stevie and Mollie to Clery's." Steven chuckled. "They have been well informed that their sister is doing much better and that the doctors are taking excellent care of her. They were just as concerned about your welfare, truth be known. But by now I suspect Stevie is inspecting an array of toy soldiers and Mollie is choosing a new baby doll. Really, you needn't worry about them at all."

Gratitude flooded Rose's emotions. Dashing a tear from her cheek, she whispered, "Thank you."

Silence covered the room, linking Steven and Rose in a web of physical awareness. Their fingers intertwined as he shifted his weight and leaned over her. His gaze bore into hers, and the smell of his skin surrounded her. Mesmerized, Rose studied the crinkles bracketing his eyes, the lines in his forehead, the dark shading of his beard. The strength and intelligence of his features comforted her.

Tentatively, he kissed her lips. Then, drawing back, he gave her a long, half-lidded stare. "Do you want me to leave, Rose?"

Her heart fluttered. She could think of a hundred reasons why he *should* leave, chief among them the impropriety of having an unmarried and obviously very virile man in her bedchamber. But she could only think of one reason why he should stay, and that was her desire to be kissed by him.

"Don't go," she murmured, as he covered her mouth with his.

Perhaps Rose's dreamlike state was caused by exhaustion. Or perhaps the emotional trauma of Katie's illness suppressed her inhibitions. Whatever the reason, she gave in to her wantonness as if to do so was the most natural thing in the world.

Indeed, it did seem natural. Amazingly, it seemed *good* and *right.* Rose wrapped her arms around Steven's shoulders, pulling him closer to her and deepening their kiss. His startled groan excited her, prompting her to gasp and guide his mouth toward the bare, sensitive skin of her neck.

Steven's coarse beard drew gooseflesh on Rose's shoulders. He rained kisses along her décolletage, burying his nose in her cleavage, inhaling her perfume. Arching her back, Rose pressed her breasts to his lips. Through the thin muslin of her undergarment, Steven gently suckled her nipples, catapulting her to the next plateau of pleasure.

A wild realization streaked through Rose. The children and Mrs. Bleek had gone to town, and her servants had been given strict instructions to stay away. She was quite alone with Sir Steven, and she could do with him exactly as she pleased. She was, after all, an adult woman, a widow, with physical needs she had long ignored. Who was to say that making love with Sir Steven was wrong or right? Who would know what she did in the privacy of her bedroom? Who would care?

As if he could read her mind, Steven stood up and slowly removed his clothes. Rose's gaze was riveted by the sight of a man yanking out his shirttail, unfastening the buttons of his trousers, sliding his unmentionables down his taut, muscular legs.

Her throat constricted and her mouth went dry. For a long moment, Steven stood at the side of the bed, stark naked, inviting her to look at his body.

"Have you no shame?" Rose asked quietly, unable to disguise the amusement in her voice.

"Do you see anything I should be ashamed of, Rose?"

"On the contrary, I should think you are quite proud of that." With a giggle, she held up the counterpane.

As he slid into bed with her, Steven smiled devilishly. Supporting his weight on his forearms, he wedged his hips between her legs. Then, while staring into her eyes, he moved against her, slowly at first, then in a more urgent rhythm. Instinctively, Rose widened the space between her thighs and drew up her knees. Through the snippet of fabric that separated her from Steven's nakedness, she felt a tantalizing length of hard male muscle. Hunger gripped her. Longing to feel him inside her, Rose grasped Steven's waist and moved against him, adjusting her position until his shaft hit a certain spot between her legs, the spot where all her nerves seemed to center.

Her ability to speak coherently abandoned her. Gasping, Rose struggled to maintain even a semblance of composure. But pleasure overwhelmed her, and she feared she would displease or disgust Steven by making too much noise. Clamping her lips shut, she muffled her voice by turning her face into the crook of his neck. A kittenish whimper escaped her lips, and she shivered with tightly repressed longing.

Steven's whisper raised the delicate hairs on her neck. "Rose, darling, don't hold back. I want to make you happy."

Her hands explored his muscular backside; she stroked his buttocks and pulled his hips more snugly into the cradle of her parted legs. Words she'd never spoken rolled to the tip of Rose's tongue, but she dared not give expression to the wicked desire that threatened to consume her. Biting her tongue, Rose writhed beneath Steven and moaned.

He wanted more from her. "Come on, Rose, tell me what you want," he urged her. *"Say it.* Whisper it to me, that's a good girl. You can tell me anything."

"Anything?" It was hard for Rose to believe that she could trust a man with her innermost thoughts. It was hard to believe that a man—any man, much less Sir Steven Nollbrook—cared what she wanted in bed.

"Your secrets are safe with me, Rose," he assured her.

She believed him.

And suddenly, she was free to tell him what she wanted, to tell him everything that her body needed and her soul hungered for. She told him she wanted to feel his naked chest against her breasts, and he stripped off her chemise, then lay flush against her. She told him precisely where she liked to be touched, and he touched her there, expertly manipulating the little bud of flesh between the folds of her womanhood.

At last, she told him her deepest, darkest secret. And Steven unhesitatingly obliged her, entering her body gently and slowly.

A flash of pain and pleasure tore through her. Shocked by the avalanche of sensations rolling over her, Rose let out a scream that was, to her ears, frighteningly immodest.

To her immeasurable relief, Steven seemed not the least nonplussed by her unladylike conduct. He was, however, concerned that he had injured her. Stilling his movements, he rasped, "Are you all right? Shall I stop, darling?"

She did not comprehend how he *could* stop, although he did seem to possess more control over his urges than had her late husband, Winston, who, in the time Steven had already taken to make love to her, could have taken his pleasure, shaved and read *The Irish Times* from cover to cover.

Unable to hide her happiness, Rose shook her head and smiled. Her fingers coiled in his hair, damp from his exertions. "No, Steven, please don't stop." Her muscles gradually relaxed, and her tension dissipated. Liquid heat gushed between her legs, heightening Rose's arousal. Even if Steven could have stopped, she couldn't have. She needed to feel his body inside hers. She needed to feel his weight pressing into her. She needed to feel him needing her.

A sort of purr, completely unbidden, escaped her lips, surprising Rose. Laughing out loud, she hugged Steven's shoulders, tasted his skin, breathed in the smell of him and wrapped her legs around his waist. She moved freely now, jutting her hips toward his, whispering against Steven's neck, telling him what she wanted and what she liked.

At last, his movements quickened and, thrusting even deeper inside her, Steven groaned. His release seemed to lock them even closer together, momentarily vanquishing the need for words. Rose kissed the lids of Steven's closed eyes, sighed her contentment, and held him while his breathing returned to normal.

Even his shallow snores pleased her.

Steven awoke, surprised to find that he was lying on his back, alone, in Rose Sinclair's otherwise empty bed. The room was lit by a single lamp on the bedside table, and a clock on the mantel indicated it was near supper time. His lower body was strategically draped with wilted sheets, and his clothes were neatly folded and laid across the arm of a chair. Rose, evidently, had quit her bed and dressed, for her rumpled chemise hung over the footboard and her sturdy boots were absent from the spot near her dressing table where they'd been earlier in the day.

He quickly dressed and stole out of the room, apprehensive that he might encounter a curious servant, embarrassed that he'd fallen asleep after making love to Rose. She thought him a cad, no doubt. He was certain that his performance had convinced her of the correctness of her initial impression of him. He was a selfish failure of a man.

Childish voices trickled up the stairs. The children were in the parlor, talking with Rose. Mrs. Bleek's voice mingled with the others. At the landing, Steven froze and listened, his ears pricking, his head buzzing with a strange resentment at being left out.

Little Stevie's reedlike voice was easily discernible. "Is Sir Steven my father, or isn't he? Miss Tweedy said he was. She said I was to ask for him and show his card until somebody got him to admit he was my da."

Cups and saucers rattled nervously. Mrs. Bleek could be heard clearing her throat.

Rose answered at length. "Would you like for Sir Steven to be your father, darling?"

"I don't rightly know. It's not like we ever saw him very much. I don't s'pose I really care. I don't s'pose he does, either."

Mollie spoke up. "He's not your father, Stevie. If Katie were here, she'd tell you that you're a little fool for believing anything Miss Tweedy says. Mother never said Sir Steven was your dad, now did she?"

"Mummy didn't say much at all," Stevie admitted softly.

The hair on Steven's neck bristled. He felt queasy and light-headed. The realization that he had failed Stevie slammed into him like a runaway train. The boy needed a father, that was true enough. But he needed a real father, not a miserable cad who had spent the better part of four years ignoring the child. The fact that Sir Steven had planted his seed inside Katherine Rowen did not make him Stevie's father.

And with that realization came the certain knowledge that he had no place in Rose's life, and no business attempting to insinuate his way into it.

Rose needed a certain sort of man, and he was not it. Rose was good and virtuous; Steven was driven by ambition. Rose reached out to people and helped them. Steven made his living off other people's misfortunes, and went to great pains to avoid intimacy.

Gripping the mahogany handrail, he paused. The

last two days had been a whirl of emotions, inciting him to decisions that now seemed imprudent and impulsive. Recalling Letterfrack's taunting threats, Steven thought how easily he'd been played for a dupe. Letterfrack had offered to foil Rose's adoption attempts for a sum of money. The burly lawyer had offended Steven's legal sensibilities, offering him a challenge that could not be refused. He had played Steven like a drum, but for what purpose? Steven wasn't certain. He would deal with Letterfrack later.

In the meantime, as he slowly started down the steps, he flashed on little Katie's face. She had been so fragile and so dangerously near death when he had rushed her to hospital. The news of her recovery had imbued him with such joy that he had rushed back to Rose Sinclair's home like a puppy with a bone clasped between its jaws.

Understandably, Rose was overwhelmed by relief. Her gratitude toward Steven made her vulnerable to him. She, too, had done something that was utterly uncharacteristic of her. She had been intimate with a man whom she considered a degenerate, a man incapable of loving even his own son.

Stevie's voice filtered up to him. The child chattered away, as yet unfettered by the humiliation of having a father who was, by all accounts, a failure. Well, Sir Steven was not a failure as a lawyer, but he was in every other aspect of his life. Perhaps that was why he worked so hard at being the best barrister in Dublin. He knew he could never be a good father, husband, friend, son, brother or lover. He did not have it in him. If his failure to save his mother and sister from poverty and disease hadn't proven that, then his failure to save Katherine Rowen from addiction and prostitution had.

Inserting himself into Stevie's life would only doom the child to a miserable future.

With his gut twisting and his heart aching, Steven continued down the steps. At the parlor door, he hesitated. Standing in the threshold, his gaze swept the room, lingering on little Stevie for a beat, then skipping to Rose.

Her violet eyes were round and inquisitive. Her glossy black hair had been combed and arranged in a neat little bun. The sexy hellion that Steven had made love to just hours before had once again transformed herself into a prim and proper lady. Had Steven been inclined to analyze his feelings, he would have been forced to admit that the contradictions in Rose's personality confused and excited him.

But having overheard his son's condemning statements, Sir Steven doused any hopes he had of ever again being intimate with Rose Sinclair. It wasn't fair to her; it wasn't fair to Stevie.

"Are you leaving now, Sir Steven?" Rose's cheeks blushed bright red. Her gaze darted to Mrs. Bleek who, perched on the edge of a chair, turned her head and appeared to be deaf to the conversation.

The children, their mouths forming twin ovals, stared at him. "Where did he come from?" Mollie asked.

"Don't you remember that it was Sir Steven who took your sister to hospital? Well, he stayed up with

Katie all night, and he was so tired when he returned that he fell asleep in one of the servants' rooms."

"Is she all well now?" Stevie asked.

"When will she be home?"

"You promised to take me to visit her," Rose reminded him.

"Would you walk me to the door, Mrs. Sinclair?"

"If you'll excuse me, Mrs. Bleek." Rose preceded Steven down the steps, then stood in the foyer, a look of mild bewilderment on her pretty features. "You look as if you are ill, Steven. Perhaps you need to eat something."

He pinched the bridge of his nose. "Christ on a raft," he muttered under his breath, hardly able to steal a glance at Rose. After a moment, however, during which she stood and stared expectantly at him, his training as a courtroom actor took over. Forcing himself to meet Rose's gaze, he said, "Perhaps you should ask Mr. Avondale to accompany you to Meath."

She stiffened perceptibly. "Why not you? What has happened?"

He could not tell her what he had overheard. Steven could not justify sharing his misery with her. It would only make Rose feel terrible, too; she was that compassionate.

"I've changed my mind, Rose. You were right. I am not cut out to be a father. I have come to the conclusion that it would be in everyone's best interests if I made a clean exit from Stevie's life and never troubled him again. I will, of course, send you an ample amount of money each month to support my child. Legally, he is my responsibility."

"I don't understand," she whispered, sooty lashes fanning her cheeks. She blinked back her tears and squared her shoulders. "What in heaven's name has caused you to change your mind?"

"Aren't you happy, Rose? Isn't this what you wanted? Didn't you hire Letterfrack to make certain Stevie would be yours and I would never lay claim to the child? Well, you can tell him now that I am willing to sign a termination of my parental rights. He's done his job. You should compensate him handsomely."

"I wanted to adopt the children, yes. Mollie and Katie have no father." She stammered, clearly puzzled and overset. "They should stay together, the children. You can't be expected to take three little children into your life. I thought that if I took them all—"

"You wanted to adopt them all and exclude me from their lives completely."

Her chin quivered. Their lovemaking had likely confused her, but it *was* what she wanted. When the glow of their intimacy faded, she would realize that her instincts had been correct in the first place, and that Steven was not a fit father for Stevie. "At first, I thought it best that you distance yourself completely from Stevie."

"And you still do. I may be the child's natural father, but I have never taken responsibility for him. You said it yourself last night. You can't respect a man who could treat his child as shabbily as I have treated Stevie."

"That was last night—"

"Nothing has changed since then."

"You saved Katie's life."

"I took her to hospital." Steven shrugged. "Any man in my position would have done the same. 'Twould have been murder not to."

Anger snapped in Rose's eyes. Through tightly compressed lips, she practically hissed, "Don't tell me you weren't concerned about that child's health, Steven. I saw it in your eyes. I heard it in your voice. You were frightened out of your mind, just as I was. You rushed her to the hospital as quickly as you could. You saved her life!"

"Perhaps," he replied curtly. "But that does not mean I want to be a father to any of those three children."

"Oh? And when did that realization hit you, sir?"

"When I was in bed with you," he answered smoothly. If he was going to injure Rose, he might as well cauterize the wound. A clean exit was infinitely kinder than a messy one. "When I was in bed with you, Mrs. Sinclair, I realized how highly I value my freedom. And my bachelorhood."

"Are you suggesting that our lovemaking was nothing more than a—a physical release, a sexual fling, an illicit tryst?"

"You're the one who had sex with a man you have said you couldn't respect. You tell me, Rose."

As her indignation flared, the lines of her features, particularly her cheekbones, sharpened impossibly. "What sort of man are you?" she breathed.

"Exactly the sort you should run from."

"I don't believe you. What we shared last night—"

"*Was nice.* And that is all it was."

A prickly silence descended. Steven schooled his

expression into one of icy dispassion and met Rose's gaze without flinching.

"Liar." With military precision, she reached out and slapped his face.

Stung, and grudgingly impressed by the force of her blow, Steven turned on his heel and left. Of course he was lying. But he would rather Rose regarded him as a liar than as the wretched, ineffective man he was.

Eleven

Rose sat in a wooden chair beside Katie's bed. Despite the bustle in the children's ward, Katie slept peacefully and there was no need to wake her. Mr. Avondale stood, flipping through the sheaf of medical reports attached by a string to the metal railing of the bed.

"You don't have to stay all night," Rose said absently. She felt guilty at having usurped Mr. Avondale's leisure time. It seemed the handsome man who lived at the far end of Fontjoy Square was always sacrificing his time and labor to help one of the four women who had moved there nearly six months earlier. Evidently, he regarded himself as their collective caretaker or chaperon. Rose thought she understood why. It was human nature to want to be needed by someone.

"Don't be silly, Rose. I consider you family, you know that. Which means that Katie and Mollie and Stevie are my family now, too."

"That is very kind of you." Her throat constricted.

"Is something else the matter, dear?" Mr. Avondale replaced Katie's charts and, folding his arms across his chest, stared inscrutably at Rose. "I noticed Sir

Steven's carriage in front of your house. I don't mean to pry, but I couldn't help noticing he stayed most of the night."

Her face burned with embarrassment. Did everyone in the neighborhood know that she'd been in bed with Sir Steven Nollbrook? Was she insane when she thought she could do whatever she pleased in the privacy of her own bedchamber without fear of inciting scandal and recrimination? "After he returned from taking Katie to the hospital, he was exhausted. I allowed him to sleep in the guest quarters."

Clearly skeptical, Devon rubbed his lower lip. "I see."

"You don't think very highly of the man, do you, Devon?"

"He fathered a child with a prostitute, then abandoned them both. That does not speak very highly of his moral standards, Rose."

Keeping her voice low so as not to disturb Katie, Rose said, " 'Tis a bit more complicated than that, Devon. He told me a little about Katherine Rowen. She was not a prostitute when she met him."

"That's even worse, Rose. Then why didn't he stop the woman from ruining herself?"

"Perhaps for the same reason I was unable to change Winston Sinclair's behavior. People are what they are, Devon. And if you think you change someone just because you love them, then you are destined to a miserable existence. That much I learned in my marriage, and rather early on, I might add!"

Devon pulled up a chair and sat beside her. Taking her hand in his, he leaned toward her and spoke earnestly. "That does not excuse Nollbrook's total disregard for little Stevie's life."

"He did not know the child was his."

"How is that possible?"

Why she felt the need to defend Steven's actions, Rose could never have explained. She was, after all, so angry with him and his mistreatment of her, she would have slapped him herself if he had entered the hospital ward that very minute. But as Millicent had already pointed out, Rose historically defended anyone under attack. And it was plain to see that Devon Avondale was judging the man based on a distorted view of the facts. "You don't know him," she finally said, with a little huff of exasperation.

"Tell me, then, Rose, what do *you* know of him? Do you think he is an honest fellow?"

"I think he is a very . . . *troubled* man. And a very lonely one, too."

"Did he attempt to make any untoward overtures toward you last night?"

Lips pressed firmly together, Rose shook her head. Steven had done nothing to her that she hadn't wanted, nor, indeed, that she hadn't asked for. If Devon Avondale knew that Sir Steven had laid a finger on her, he would do far worse than slap the man.

"You're a terrible liar, Rose," Devon said softly.

Looking at Katie, she brushed a tear from her cheek. "Perhaps so, but he had agreed to a termination of his parental rights."

"Not in exchange for—"

"God, no!" The suggestion was laughable. Patting Devon's hand, Rose assured him that was not the case.

"On the contrary, I believe that the small dose of domesticity that he received at my house has quite convinced him that he does not want to be bothered with fatherhood."

"That only confirms my original suspicion that he is not much of a man."

Rose was too exhausted to argue the point. Besides, she was not at all certain how she felt about Sir Steven. His behavior after their lovemaking was so rude and callous that it bordered on bizarre. That the man would have abandoned his notion of getting to know Stevie, and given up the idea of playing an active role in the child's life, just because he suddenly realized that he valued his bachelor freedom above all else was ludicrous. That he would experience this epiphany while he was making love to Rose was simply too far-fetched an explanation to be taken seriously.

No, there was some other reason Sir Steven had bolted that afternoon. Something else, other than his need to preserve his precious bachelorhood, had frightened him off. Rose did not believe for one second that Steven had considered their lovemaking *"nice."* Though she hadn't had sex in years, even Rose knew that the sex she had with Steven was unusually powerful and intense. Pondering the mystery of Steven's behavior, Rose fell silent.

"You should be happy," Devon said at length. "The man will soon be out of your life. Letterfrack will draw up the necessary paperwork, and Sir Steven will never be heard from again. No doubt he will be elated to have escaped his parental responsibility."

"Yes," she murmured. But would she be happy when Sir Steven was officially and legally out of her life? "Yes, I will be thrilled when the adoption is completed."

"I am sorry if the man, ah, hurt your feelings, Rose. Please don't think anymore on it. You have plenty of friends who will help you raise these children. I, for one, intend to do everything I can—"

"I appreciate that, Devon. Really, I do." She did not mean to cut him off so abruptly. But really, he did not understand. As much as Rose loved Devon Avondale, he did not understand.

Like it or not, she had a bond with Sir Steven Nollbrook. He was Stevie's father; his son was Katie's and Mollie's half brother. Her own deceased husband was Katie's and Mollie's father . . . It was only right that she and Steven raise these children together . . . *together.*

Looking at Devon, she read the hurt in his eyes. "I am sorry, but I believe I must talk to Sir Steven once more before he terminates his parental rights."

"I don't understand, Rose. Do you want to adopt Stevie, or don't you?"

"I want the child to be mine. Of course I do!"

"Then leave Steven Nollbrook alone. He is a conniving lawyer who does not possess an ounce of integrity. He will never be a fit father for Stevie, Rose."

"But is it fair to Stevie to cut him out completely?"

"Is it fair to you to have this rogue coming in and out of your life, toying with your affections, undermining your attempts to provide a stable, moral environment for your children? I am not a fool, Rose. I know what happened last night! That man has taken advantage of you! You are not thinking clearly about what is in Stevie's best interests."

Stunned by the ferocity of Devon's dislike for Steven, Rose stiffened. "Thank you for your help, Devon. I don't want you to think me ungrateful."

Standing, he sighed. "I did not mean to insult you, Rose." His voice was raw with emotion as he scooped his hat off the table, stood at the end of the bed, and nervously fingered the brim. "You are very special to me, dear. I know you do not understand—"

She stared at him in bewilderment. Was the man about to confess some heretofore suppressed romantic interest in her? Truth be known, she thought he was infatuated with Lady Claire Kilgarren, the aristocratic blond beauty who lived at Number Three Fontjoy Square.

They locked gazes, and his cheeks instantly darkened. Despite the gray at his temples and the lines that furrowed his forehead, the man looked suddenly very young and uncertain. His blue eyes blinked rapidly and his Adam's apple bobbed as he stammered out an explanation. "Don't misunderstand. I have only the most honorable of intentions toward you. I think of you, Rose, as my . . ."

"If you say *mother,* I shall slap you silly."

Her levity lightened the moment, and Devon chuckled. "No, but *sister* doesn't seem appropriate either. Suffice to say, Rose, I would do anything to make you happy. I am indebted to you. More than you will ever know."

His statement did not make a bit of sense. Not only

had the man patched her roof, mended her fences, repaired her plumbing and provided cab service to and from the city proper for the past six months, he had done so willingly and free of charge. The ladies of Fontjoy Square frequently started sentences with, *If it were not for Mr. Avondale . . .* They had all learned to depend upon him, and they all cherished his friendship.

But none of the ladies who had moved to Fontjoy Square about six months earlier was in a position to return Mr. Avondale's kindnesses. They had all, with the exception of Lady Dolly Baltmore-Creevy, been near destitution when they arrived. There was no way on God's green earth that Devon Avondale owed anything to Rose Sinclair.

A tiny trickle of suspicion wriggled up Rose's spine. Was it possible that Devon Avondale was the anonymous benefactor who had saved her from poverty and donated to her the Georgian mansion she now lived in?

"Was it you?" she blurted. "Was it you who gave me my house?"

He frowned. "What are you talking about Rose? I was under the impression that your late husband willed you that house."

That was what Rose had told everyone in the neighborhood. It was too humiliating to admit otherwise when Millicent Hyde and Lady Claire Kilgarren related how their fathers had provided homes for them, and Lady Dolly said her late husband had left her Number Two Fontjoy Square.

"Are you telling me that someone other than your late husband gave you your home at Number Four?"

"Indeed not." Flustered, Rose made a dismissive gesture and dropped the subject. Devon's guileless look convinced her he was not her mysterious benefactor. Besides, she had other more pressing matters to worry about, such as Katie's health and Stevie's adoption. "I'm sorry, Devon. I am tired and not making any sense."

He smiled. "Katie is going to sleep all night. Why don't you let me take you home?"

"No. I would rather stay. Mrs. Bleek will be with Mollie and Stevie. I want to be here when Katie awakens."

"As you wish." He leaned over, kissed Rose's cheek and discreetly pressed a couple of paper bills into her hand. "When you want to go home, summon a hackney cab."

She started to protest and hand the money back, but she knew Devon would insist and she lacked the energy for any further arguments. Returning his smile, Rose said, "Thank you."

"Thank you, Rose," he replied. Then he patted Katie's head and walked briskly from the children's ward as if he had serious business to attend to.

Outside Meath Hospital, Steven sat in the compartment of his carriage, watching the pedestrians navigate the treacherous, icy streets while he mulled over his conversation with Rose Sinclair. When Devon Avondale exited the hospital's front entrance and leaped into his waiting carriage, Steven's entire body tensed. He hated that man.

Every time he thought of Avondale's superior sneer, Steven's insides burned. When he thought of Avondale's influence over Mrs. Sinclair, Steven's blood boiled. Avondale was precisely the sort of man Steven disliked—handsome, arrogant, outspoken and self-righteous. A man like Avondale would judge Steven Nollbrook harshly and without compunction. Avondale thought Nollbrook was a cad. But Avondale knew nothing of Steven's life and even less about his feelings.

Avondale, Steven concluded, knew nothing of the hardships Steven Nollbrook had grown up with in Waterford. Judging from his aristocratic bearing and looks, Avondale enjoyed inherited wealth and a fine pedigree. He had probably never worked a full day in his life. He had never been hungry. He had never been ashamed of a father who, on a good night, stumbled home drunk, and on a bad night, slept in whatever foul pub he fell down in. Avondale had never experienced self-loathing and doubt.

As Avondale's carriage rumbled off, Steven sighed and leaned his head against the leather squabs.

What am I doing here? Isn't it enough that I have made a fool of myself over little Stevie and Rose Sinclair? Isn't it enough that I have proven myself to be an irresponsible failure, a man who has not only failed to save his mother and his sister, but the mother of his son . . . and his son, too?

It was wrong to even *consider* playing a role in Stevie's life. Rose Sinclair had been right from the start: Sir Steven Nollbrook was an unfit father and a morally bankrupt individual who valued his personal freedom, his wealth and his reputation as a lawyer far too highly to care for a child.

Closing his eyes, he recalled the moment he laid eyes on Rose. He thought she had come to blackmail him, and so his first instinct had been to deny he was Stevie's father. His well-honed sense of self-preservation had compelled him to turn the woman away with mean words. He was a ruthless lawyer, for God's sake, a man who would not be rooked, cheated, tricked or taken advantage of. He knew a scam artist when he saw one.

Oh, but he had been so wrong about Rose Sinclair. He had realized his mistake the moment he slammed the door in her face. When he saw her next, he was even more impressed with her feminine virtues, her integrity, her selflessness and her nurturing demeanor. She could not have been more unlike Katherine Rowen. And he could not have been less deserving of Rose Sinclair.

She had convinced him that perhaps he could be a father to little Stevie. Perhaps Sir Steven had even harbored a remote fantasy that he and Rose might raise Stevie and the twins *together.* When he kissed Rose, she responded so passionately that for a fleeting moment, he believed she might love him. He had even felt *lovable.* He had imagined himself to be the sort of man who might have a family, who might go home each night to a loving wife and a house full of happy, chattering children. He had, not for the first time, mistaken lust for love.

Sadly—but luckily, since there was yet time to correct his mistake—Steven's epiphany came after he made love to Rose. Their encounter had left him shaken and confused. He had made love to hundreds of women in the past, but he had never experienced the depth of emotion that Rose inspired. She had a sort of power over him. With her, he felt vulnerable and fulfilled at the same time. She had a unique sensuality that was both innocent and wanton. Summoning the memories of their sexual encounter, Steven's lower body stiffened. He ached to have Rose again. He loved her—and that was why he needed to get as far away from her as he could.

Because everyone Steven had ever loved had abandoned him.

Steven had no business sitting in his carriage outside Meath Hospital. The knowledge that Rose Sinclair was inside, undoubtedly keeping a vigil at Katie's bedside, had lured him there. He had gained some perverse pleasure from being so close to her, yet his inability to see and talk to Rose was an even greater source of pain.

Just as he lifted his arm to knock on the ceiling door and tell his driver to return him to his offices, the door to the carriage compartment swung open, admitting a blast of cold air and a bark from Devon Avondale. Steven's surprise was quickly quelled by anger and resentment.

"What the hell are you doing here?" Devon growled, hovering in the doorway.

"Get out of my rig," returned Steven.

"I'll leave when you do, sir."

"This is a public thoroughfare, Avondale, and I have every right to park here. You, however, are trespassing inside my personal carriage. Why don't you just leave?"

"I did leave, but I spied your *personal carriage,* and decided to turn around and park behind you. I thought my eyes had deceived me. I wondered if any man could have as much gall as you!" Avondale leaned menacingly into the compartment. "But now I see for myself. You are truly an evil man!"

"Get out before I put you out."

"You can go the devil where you belong! You'll leave this place now, or—"

"Or what?" The hair on Steven's nape bristled. He itched to plow his fist into Avondale's patrician nose. "I warn you, Avondale, I will defend myself."

The men stared challengingly at each other for a moment, neither of them flinching or backing down. Steven was poised on the edge of his seat, ready to spring. Devon was a hair's breadth away from lunging into the carriage. Then, when the two were on the verge of clashing, a deep voice startled them both.

"And what would be the trouble here, laddies? Eh?" A uniformed constable peered over Devon's shoulder.

Pushing back against the squabs, Steven released a sigh of pent-up anger. He did not truly want to fight Devon, but his warped sense of honor demanded that he not retreat from the man. "There is nothing the matter, officer."

The constable looked skeptical. "I heard some fightin' words, though, and I'm right sure of it."

Releasing his hold on the frame of the compartment, Devon stepped backward to ground. "No problem, sir. Sorry for your trouble."

" 'Tis a wee bit too cold for a friendly chat, gentlemen. Aye, and me eyes are not blind! I can recognize a fight when I see one brewing. I strongly suggest you two part company now . . . while you're both a'wearin' your own heads!"

Steven smiled grimly. "Good day, Avondale."

"Don't forget, Sir Steven," the man replied. "I have warned you now."

"Get out of here!" cried the constable.

A bitter satisfaction roiled through Steven as his nemesis was forced to trudge off in the direction of his own carriage. Through his rear window, Steven watched until Devon had climbed into his carriage and driven off. When the constable was nowhere in sight, Steven disembarked his own rig and walked into Meath Hospital.

Letterfrack was at his desk when Devon brushed past Mr. Hare and stepped into the silver-haired lawyer's inner office.

"What's the matter with you, Avondale? I won't have you barking at Mr. Hare in that manner! He was only doing his job. I am not receiving visitors at the moment, you see. Got a trial I am preparing for."

"What I have to discuss with you is far more important than any trial, Letterfrack."

"Make an appointment," the lawyer growled.

"My appointment is right now." Devon sat in the chair opposite Letterfrack's desk while Mr. Hare stood in the threshold, sniffing the air like a frightened animal who senses a storm brewing.

"Get out of here!"

"Is that any way to talk to a paying client?"

"You're not my client, Mrs. Sinclair is!"

"But I am paying her bill, and I want some answers, Letterfrack. For starters, what the hell did you tell Sir Steven Nollbrook that made him think he wanted to be a father?"

The older man snorted derisively. "I don't know what you are talking about. I did my job, that's all. Mrs. Sinclair told me that she wanted to adopt Sir Steven's son. Well, it is my obligation to obtain the man's consent. Or, if he does not consent, then I must try to find another way to effect my client's wishes."

"Speak English, man," Devon demanded, furious and frustrated by Letterfrack's legal obfuscations.

But as was customary with lawyers, the more Letterfrack explained, the more murky the situation became. "You cannot terminate a man's parental rights without his consent, Avondale."

"Why notify the man of the adoption proceedings at all? He made it plain he wanted nothing to do with the child. Initially, he even denied little Stevie was his! You should have simply left the man alone. You could have told the courts that Stevie's father was unknown. His mother was a prostitute, for God's sake!"

"And a very well-known one, unfortunately. Her relationship with Sir Steven was not a secret, either."

Letterfrack's bushy eyebrows arched. "If Mrs. Sinclair lies to the court concerning her knowledge of the child's father, she risks having the entire adoption overturned at a later date."

Exasperated, Devon sighed. "Rose would never lie to the courts anyway." In reality, he would not have wanted her to. "But suppose Sir Steven changes his mind—"

"Which is not outside the realm of possibility, is it? People change their minds every day, Avondale. An unmarried bachelor enjoying his freedom may think he wants nothing to do with a bawling snot-nosed infant. But suppose he later gets married and finds to his horror that his wife cannot produce a boy child to inherit his wealth? What if Sir Steven decides he wants Stevie after all? As the child's natural father, he would have the right to assume custody. 'Twould be a tragic result, would it not?"

Devon shuddered. "Yes. I suppose that makes sense. Tell me, then, what you know of Sir Steven's intentions. For the life of me, I cannot figure the man out! First he doesn't want to be a father, then he thinks he might, then—"

Letterfrack's chortles were nauseating. "That's human nature, isn't it? The man was presented with a baby he didn't know existed, or if he knew it existed, he went to great pains to pretend he didn't. His heart is at war with his head, I'm afraid."

"I don't think he has a heart," Devon said sourly. After a moment, he said, "What can we do now? To get the man out of Mrs. Sinclair's life, that is, and finalize this adoption. The stress and uncertainty of it all is wearing on everyone's nerves, mine included. And now your client is talking about meeting face-to-face with Sir Steven again. Surely, you do not approve of such a thing!"

"Of course not." Letterfrack's amusement vanished. Leaning forward, he peered at Devon through narrowed eyes. "She's a fool if she attempts to match wits with that man. He's a clever one, Sir Steven."

Devon sighed. "I am willing to pay anything to end this mess!"

"Anything?" The chair supporting Letterfrack's bulk squeaked as he leaned back and patted the tips of his fingers together. "Mr. Hare, would you close my door, please?" When the little man had disappeared, Letterfrack stared hard at Devon as if appraising his strength of character. Or perhaps the depths of his pocketbook. "You are quite devoted to Mrs. Sinclair, I take it?"

"Money is no concern, if that is what you are getting at."

"If Sir Steven is having difficulty making up his mind, I do believe I can help him."

"How so?"

"Witnesses can be produced whose testimony would be embarrassing to Sir Steven."

A moment of silence passed while Devon digested what he had heard. His gut churned. What Letterfrack was suggesting, the bribery of witnesses, possibly even the subornation of testimony, was illegal and immoral. With his blood thrumming in his veins, Devon stood. His fists coiled at his sides, but he suppressed his violent impulse. As rude and offensive as Letterfrack was, attacking him would only hinder Rose's cause.

Letterfrack shrugged lightly. " 'Twas merely a suggestion, Avondale. If you haven't the stomach for it—"

" 'Twas an idiotic suggestion," returned Devon, backing away, staring at the man he had hired to represent Rose Sinclair, wondering if there existed a single lawyer in Dublin who could be called honest and trustworthy.

He thought about firing Letterfrack on the spot. But he dared not. At present, Sir Steven seemed to be leaning toward terminating his parental rights. Another lawyer, new to the case, might muddy the waters even more.

Too angry to continue a civil conversation with the man, Devon hastily left Letterfrack's office. On the street, he breathed in the frigid air, relieved to be out of the vile lawyer's presence. In the carriage heading toward home, he ticked off his options in his head. Letterfrack, it seemed, had failed to understand the importance of Rose Sinclair's adoption application.

His only alternative was to attempt to reason with Sir Steven Nollbrook. Touching the side of his face, Devon winced at the memory of Steven's arm flung back, that powerful fist suspended in the air, prepared to strike. If Rose had not intervened, Devon most likely would be nursing a broken jaw.

He did not like or respect Sir Steven, and he did not relish initiating a dialogue with the man.

But for Rose's sake, he had to. Silently, he considered what needed to be said to Steven. Eventually, a grim smile flickered at his lips. For while Devon could not in good conscience participate in the bribery Letterfrack had suggested, he was not at all above threatening to kill Sir Steven if he did not do the honorable thing and leave Rose Sinclair and little Stevie alone.

Twelve

Stalking through the tiled corridors of the hospital, Steven berated himself and Devon Avondale. Had it not been for the other man's crude challenge, he would have followed the dictates of his conscience and driven away from the hospital without speaking a word to Rose Sinclair. But Sir Steven Nollbrook could not tolerate defeat, and he would not back down in the face of Avondale's threats. Cowardice was not among Nollbrook's defects—or so he told himself as he pushed open the door to the children's ward.

Immediately, his gaze fell on her. At the far end of the room, Rose, head lowered as if in prayer, sat beside Katie's bed. His heart skipped a beat and his mouth went dry.

She did not see him at first.

'Tis not too late to turn around and leave!

Steven's being there was a flagrant contradiction of his resolution to stay out of Stevie's and Rose's lives.

Leave, man! Leave before she lifts her head and sees you!

But Devon Avondale had thrown down the gauntlet, and Steven, true to his character, had snatched it up.

As Rose's head popped up and her violet gaze met

his, Steven experienced a dizzying moment of indecision and doubt.

Was he so much a coward that he was afraid to appear weak? Or was surrendering to his love for little Stevie, not to mention his obsession for Rose Sinclair, in truth, a sign of strength?

Rose gasped. Blinking, she wondered if her eyes were playing tricks on her. Perhaps her feeble mind had conjured an image of the man she longed for. Her fantasy had taken shape; it was an apparition she was staring at. But as Sir Steven slowly walked the length of the children's ward, Rose's mind grasped the reality of his presence. *He had come.* Contrary to the heartless, hurtful words he had uttered earlier that day, he had come.

He stood at the foot of the bed, gazing at Katie. When he looked at Rose, his eyes were moist. But the softness in his expression quickly vanished. Rose's senses went on full alert as she watched him tamp down his emotions. The control that Sir Steven Nollbrook exerted over himself was formidable.

"I am surprised to see you here, Steven. I understood that you did not want to involve yourself in my family."

"I will leave if you would prefer."

She took a moment to consider whether she wished Steven to leave. The rational part of her brain told her she should banish Steven from her sight. He had insulted her virtue and her integrity, and he had proved himself to be a rogue.

But her heart was not in accord with her intellect. Rose had been severely wounded by Steven's cruel words, but she had not believed them. Her feminine instincts told her that he loved little Stevie and that his interest in her was more than a passing fancy, or a sexual fling. He had, after all, rushed Katie to hospital as if the child were his own. He had saved Katie's life. No matter what else happened, Rose would forever be grateful to Steven for that.

"No, I do not wish you to leave. Not now, anyway."

"After what I said this afternoon, you would be well within your rights never to speak to me again."

"Sir, there comes a time when pride must take a back seat to one's nobler inclinations."

"Are you inclined to forgive me, then?"

She permitted herself a wistful smile. "How can I remain angry with the man who saved Katie's life?"

He scoffed. "I did nothing of the sort, Rose. 'Twas the doctors who saved little Katie."

"You got her here, and that was no small feat given the icy condition of the streets. Thank you, Steven. No matter if we take opposite sides in the future, I thank you for what you did for Katie."

He swallowed hard. "You are welcome."

The silence that followed was not uncomfortable. In fact, Rose enjoyed the peacefulness that connected them while they watched Katie sleep.

At length, a man dressed in a long white coat entered the ward and, after making several visits to other children in neighboring beds, stopped at Katie's bedside. "I am Doctor Conolley," he said, extending his hand to Sir Steven. "And you are the child's father, I presume."

"No." Steven stood beside Rose. "This is the child's mother, Mrs. Rose Sinclair."

Doctor Conolley gave her a warm smile. "Your daughter is healing nicely, ma'am. But due to the anesthesia that was administered during surgery, I am afraid she will sleep throughout the night. You might as well go home and get some rest yourself."

"But what if she wakes up? What if she needs something?" Rose could not bear the thought of Katie awakening in a strange place and being frightened. The child had been through so much already.

"The nurses will attend to her, Mrs. Sinclair. Trust me, she is in good hands."

"I do not want to leave." Rose returned the doctor's smile. "Thank you very much, but I will stay right here."

"Ma'am, please." The kindly gentleman's voice took on a firmer tone. "We do not encourage parents to spend the night with their children in the ward. Can you imagine if all the parents of all these children held a vigil here each night? The nurses would not have sufficient room to move around."

Frankly, Rose did not care whether the nurses had room to move around. And as sympathetic as she was to the plight of the other children on the ward, her paramount concern at the moment was Katie's welfare. "I am not going to leave Katie's bedside, and that is that, Doctor Conolley." Smiling determinedly, Rose met the doctor's rheumy gaze.

"I must insist."

"I won't go."

Huffing, the doctor turned to Sir Steven. "You must talk some sense into this woman! She cannot stay here all night, I tell you."

Inhaling deeply, Rose looked at Steven. Her pulse reeled and her flesh warmed as he stared back at her.

Without hesitation, Steven said, "If the lady wishes to stay, then she shall stay."

"But sir!"

Steven smoothly produced his calling card and handed it to the doctor. "Any mother whose daughter had undergone surgery would be anxious, would she not, Doctor? My client is no exception. If you force her to leave, you will only increase her agony. And if you do that, well, then, I shall be forced to sue you for compensation."

"Sue me?" The doctor's eyebrows shot up. "Are you serious?"

"I have never been more serious in my life." Steven's cold expression emphasized his threat.

As the doctor retreated, he sputtered his outrage. "You are a disgrace to your profession, sir. Threatening to sue me . . . for what? Have you no scruples?" But it seemed he could not get out of Sir Steven's sight quickly enough.

When the door to the children's ward swung shut behind the doctor, Steven smiled sinisterly. "Coward."

Rose could not suppress her amusement. Chuckling softly, she stood and laid her hand on Steven's arm. "You should be ashamed of yourself, Steven. You practically frightened the poor man out of his wits."

"I could go and apologize," Steven mockingly suggested.

"Don't do that." Rose gave an unladylike yawn. Then she placed her hands at the small of her back and twisted her waist, grimacing at the soreness in her muscles. Belatedly, she realized why her body ached so. Making love to Sir Steven in the wee hours of the morning had involved body parts long forgotten. "Oh, dear, I think a little walk would do me good. Would you care to stroll down the hallway, sir? Just to stretch our legs?"

"Love to." He held out his arm.

Rose smoothed the sheets around Katie's shoulders and patted her hair. Then she allowed Steven to guide her out of the ward and down the long stretch of hallway that seemed to wind around the entire building. Given the parade of sick and ailing people they passed, theirs was not, by any objective standard, a very romantic promenade. But it was good to feel Steven's body against hers. Rose's tension eased as they walked arm in arm through the crowded passage.

"Has Stevie adjusted well to living in your home?" he asked her casually.

Halting, she faced him. "As well as can be expected, I believe. The only predictable thing in those children's lives at Mrs. Bunratty's was unpredictability, you know. They are quite adaptable, all three of them."

Steven's broad, intelligent forehead wrinkled. "I hope my questions do not upset you, Rose."

"I would expect you to be interested in your son's development."

"Does he miss her? Do the girls?"

At first, Rose did not understand his question. Steven's pained expression made it clear, however, that he was referring to Katherine Rowen. "Oh! I am certain they miss her. But she was gone three months before Miss Tweedy brought them to me. They are little realists, if nothing else. They have witnessed far more human tragedy than children their ages should have to see."

"She was not a very good mother." His gaze skittered off, as if he were embarrassed for Katherine Rowen's failings.

Rose, acutely aware that her proximity to Steven invited disapproving glances, took another step closer to him. She did not care what people thought. "You mustn't blame yourself, Steven. You were powerless to change Katherine or to cure her of her addictions."

"Perhaps." His eyes watered, but his jaw hardened. "But I was not powerless to change my own behavior. When I learned Katherine was pregnant, I should have insisted that she tell me the truth."

"She lied to you. You could not have known for certain."

He shook his head dejectedly. "I wanted to believe her lies because I was too selfish and irresponsible to be a father."

Rose struggled with her dilemma. Her maternal instincts told her to protect Stevie, Mollie and Katie. In his vulnerable state, Steven could easily be persuaded to sign a termination of parental rights. If Rose affirmed Sir Steven's perception that he had failed his child, she could proceed with the adoption without delay or protest.

But in the short time she had known him, Rose had developed a strong and bewildering affection for Sir Steven. Despite his thorny exterior, she sensed a heart as soft as oatmeal. The man was like a child, needy and scared. Practiced in the art of appearing tough and unafraid, he hid his weaknesses well. Notwithstanding his insecurities, which Rose reckoned were invisible to the general populace, he was the most enigmatic and attractive man she had ever met. He was intelligent and intense. And he was an amazingly skillful lover.

"You said you wanted to spend some time with Stevie," Rose said slowly. Even as she spoke, she wondered whether she was doing the right thing. "If you still want to, you are more than welcome in my home. I only ask you, Steven, please do not take little Stevie away from his sisters and me. 'Twould be a horrible tragedy were the children to be separated."

Without saying a word, he planted a chaste kiss on her cheek.

At that moment, the doors at the end of the corridor burst open. A team of doctors and nurses, all of them shouting, pushed a wheeled structure into the hallway. As the commotion neared, Rose saw that the structure was laden with a body draped in a white sheet. She turned her head as the entourage passed, disturbed by the glimpse of bloodied linens.

A wave of queasiness washed over her. Her knees wobbled and her vision blurred.

"Rose, are you all right?"

A suffocating weariness bored down on her. In the dim recesses of her mind, Rose heard Steven's voice, but she could not force herself to frame an answer. As she slid into blackness, she felt the safety of his arms closing around her, and she succumbed.

Pandemonium erupted around them. The man who lay on the gurney absorbed the full attention of every member of the hospital staff. No one turned a head when Steven caught Rose in his arms and pushed through the swinging doors into the main atrium of the hospital.

Outside, he was grateful for the bracing, icy air. He strode toward his carriage, yelled for his driver to open the compartment door, and deposited an unconscious Rose on the leather bench seat.

"Want me to drive ye somewheres?" The driver looked quizzically from Rose to Sir Steven.

"Like where, man? *A hospital?*" Steven grabbed a lap blanket and tucked it around Rose's body. "No, thanks, just make certain no nosey constable bangs on the door again, will you?"

"Right-o," the burley man said, intuitively drawing the shade before he closed the door.

For what seemed an interminable length of time, Steven sat on his haunches in the shadowy compartment, studying the paleness of Rose's skin, the reassuring pulse in her throat and the perfect lushness of her slightly parted lips. Just when he feared she would never awaken, just when a bubble of panic had begun to form in his belly, her eyes flickered open.

"Where am I?" she asked groggily.

"You are in my carriage, parked just outside Meath Hospital." He rubbed the back of her hand to warm her. "You fainted in the hallway. There was nowhere for you to lie down, other than a hospital bed. So I brought you here. Are you warm enough?"

Her gaze focused and she nodded. "Katie?"

"Fast asleep. When you feel better, I will take you back inside."

"The doctor said—"

"The doctor will not object to your remaining at Katie's bedside as long as you please. Don't worry about that."

"Thank you," she whispered.

An awkwardness Steven had not known since he was a boy silenced him. There were a thousand things he wished to tell Rose Sinclair, but he could not articulate one of them. He thought she understood much of what he felt, and he was thankful that she did not press him for explanations or apologies. She was a patient, indulgent woman, the kind of woman a man would like to come home to.

Yet she was incredibly exciting to be with. Staring into her liquid gaze, Steven could not resist drawing her fingers to his lips.

"I want to tell you something," he said, chuckling at his own sudden backwardness.

"You can tell me anything, Steven."

"Do you know what it feels like when your horse leaps over a hurdle for the first time, or your carriage goes too quickly over a bump in the road?"

"You feel as if your heart is floating."

"That is how I feel now, Rose." He leaned forward and tentatively tasted her mouth. Then he drew back, eager to see her reaction.

She swallowed hard, and her eyes blinked rapidly, as if she were startled. But after a beat, she smiled and rewarded him with a throaty, feminine giggle.

"Don't stop, Steven," she said, reaching for him. "Lie beside me."

But the leather bench was too narrow for them to lie on, so Steven arranged a pallet of blankets on the floor and gently pulled Rose to the floor of the carriage compartment.

Perhaps the brief senselessness that she had suffered had robbed her of her inhibitions. Even as Rose pressed her mouth to his, Steven could hardly believe that she really wanted him. She had, after all, properly pegged him as a rogue. She was not the sort of woman who would indulge her sexual urges by dallying with a morally inferior man. He could only conclude, therefore, that her attraction to him was the symptom of a temporary lapse of judgment.

A gentleman would not take advantage of a woman's diminished capacity.

But I am no gentleman!

"Oh, Steven," she breathed against his neck. "I want you."

He rose on his elbows, putting distance between them so that he could catch his breath and speak rationally. "Rose, it was wrong of me to force myself upon you."

"I do not recall your forcing me to do anything, dear." She pulled at his lapels.

"I fear that you will regret—"

She made a *shushing* sound. "Do not talk back. You have been a bad boy long enough."

And with that, Steven's doubts were swept away. Rose Sinclair wanted him to make love to her, and he would be a disobedient cad to disoblige her.

Lowering himself, he fit his body atop hers. Her mouth was sweet and warm; kissing Rose was a sort of lovemaking in itself. Closing his eyes, Steven allowed himself to leisurely explore her lips and tongue and teeth. He felt her smile against his lips, and he smiled, too. The contentment of being with her thrilled him. He would have been happy if their lovemaking had progressed no further.

But when she gasped and her back arched, he reacted to Rose's heightened arousal by pressing himself more snugly to her. "I want you, too, Rose," he whispered against her neck. To his own ears, he sounded like a supplicant. "Will you . . . will you give me what I need, please?"

She kissed his forehead, his eyelids and his lips. "I'll take care of you, darling. Don't worry. You can tell me everything. You can come to me anytime that you need me."

"I need you, Rose."

"I won't leave you then."

A floodgate burst deep inside Steven. In his mind's eye, he saw his mother's face, etched with wrinkles. She'd looked fifty when she was thirty. He'd spent his entire life feeling as if he were a failure because he was unable to save her and his sister.

But where was Steven's mother when he was ten

years old and his father stumbled into the house drunk and beat him to within an inch of his life for no reason at all?

And he'd spent the better half of the last decade drowning in guilt because he could not save Katherine Rowen from her addictions.

But where was Katherine when he'd needed her? And why hadn't Katherine loved him enough to try to live in *his* world, to try to give back to *him* an ounce of the love he gave to her?

Suddenly, Steven realized that he was terrified of loving—loving anyone, a child or a woman—because he feared he would be abandoned.

So when Rose told him that she would never leave him, and that she would take care of him and fulfill his needs, Steven was filled with a sense of longing. For years, he had not known what he needed or wanted. And now it—or rather, *she*—was in his arms. And little Stevie, who was his child—*and hers*—was within his reach. He wanted to hold on to them, and possess them, and never let them go.

He wanted to be as close to Rose as he possibly could.

He wedged himself between her legs, moving his hips against hers. Her arms wound around his neck and her knees slid up his thighs. Reaching down, Steven grasped the hem of her long skirts. Thank God she was not wearing a bustle, he thought, as he ran his hand up her woolen stockings.

He found the bare skin at the top of her thighs. Rose squirmed and gave a little moan. Her legs actually quivered and goose bumps materialized beneath

Steven's fingertips. The intimacy of touching her naked flesh thrilled him. Emboldened by her uneven breathing, he slipped his fingers beneath her pantaloons.

She clasped her hand on his wrist.

"Do you want me to stop?" As much as he did not want to, Steven would have if Rose showed the slightest resistance.

Relief flowed through him when she whispered, "No. I want to show you what I like."

Pushing off the floor of the carriage, he kneeled between her legs. Mesmerized, he watched her pull her cotton drawers aside.

Her smile was uncertain and coquettish at the same time. "Do you like that, Steven?"

Gazing at her body, now totally exposed, his mouth went dry. "Yes," he managed to say.

The heaviness in his lower body grew more urgent by the second. But rather then taking her too quickly, Steven was happy to delay his pleasure. He had never seen such a beautiful sight as Rose touching herself.

Their body heat had warmed the tiny compartment. Steven yanked off his necktie and shrugged out of his coat. Without taking his eyes off Rose, he unbuttoned his shirt and the front of his trousers. Then he grasped her knees and parted her legs a bit wider so that he could see everything, every inch of Rose's incredibly beautiful body. When he could not see enough, he turned and lit the small gas lamp beside the door. Illumined, Rose's thick black curls glistened, and tantalizing trails of gossamer spilled down her thighs.

Arousal thundered through Steven's body as he watched.

Lazily, Rose parted the folds of her flesh with one hand. Then, with her other hand, she ran her fingertips along the slick, wet folds. Her touch must have aroused her because she drew in a quick, sharp breath and whispered Steven's name. He thought he would go insane if he did not sheath his body in hers, but somehow he managed not to. Gripping the soft flesh of her thighs, he groaned with a mixture of pain and pleasure.

Her gaze raked hungrily over his bare chest, then dipped lower and fixed on the dark curls showing in the opening of his unfastened trousers. Her tongue moved along her lower lip, and her hips lifted provocatively. Steven ached to touch himself, but if he did, he would not be able to bridle his excitement. Hardly able to draw a breath, he nearly lost control of himself when Rose's slender finger disappeared inside herself.

Her tiny moans drove him to the brink of his composure. The heady aroma of musk filled his nostrils, dizzying him. Unable to contain his passion any longer, Steven lowered his mouth to the juncture between Rose's legs.

"Steven! Good God, what are you doing?"

He lifted his head and met her startled gaze. "Dear woman, you hardly strike me as innocent. Surely you know."

"I never said I was innocent, Steven," she said huskily. "But I have never made love to anyone but my former husband."

"Really? You appear to be quite well versed in pleasuring yourself."

"If you knew what sort of lover Winston was, you would understand how I acquired that skill."

"Are you telling me that you have never been kissed like this?"

"I am telling you that I learned how to pleasure myself because no one else has ever taken an interest."

"Well, I am very interested," Steven replied, dipping his head and giving her a wicked little flick of his tongue.

Her head lolled. "Oh, God," she murmured. "I have never, ever—"

"Never?" His words were muffled, but the vibration of his voice clearly aroused her. "Well, then, darling, it is high time you experienced this."

Rose's fingers grappled in his hair as he expertly lathed her flesh. Slipping his hands beneath her hips, he lifted her buttocks and held her open body snugly to his mouth. He kissed her everywhere, gently and not so gently. He nipped her thighs and ran his coarse beard along her skin. He buried his face between her legs and breathed in her perfume.

No woman had ever been as delicious to him as Rose was. Tasting her, Steven grew intoxicated. When, at length, she tugged at his shoulders and drew his face to hers, his cheeks were drenched. She framed his face with her hands, staring incredulously at him. Then she kissed him full on the lips and drew his tongue into her mouth.

Thirteen

A warning bell sounded in Rose's head, reminding her that she was making love to the enemy. Sir Steven had not yet decided whether he wanted to be a part of his son's life. There was still the chance that he would object to Rose's adoption application. And, like a spineless fool, Rose had invited the man to spend more time with Stevie, and Mollie and Katie—*her family.* What had she been thinking? She should have insisted that Sir Steven stay away from her. She should have encouraged him to think of how greatly he valued his bachelor existence.

Of course the last time he made love to her, which wasn't so very long ago Rose recalled with a twinge of guilty pleasure, he had arrived at the startling conclusion that he was better off a bachelor. So, perhaps he would have the same reaction to *this* encounter. Perhaps, Rose thought, the more she made love to him, the more Sir Steven would want to remain a bachelor.

Preposterous! Once again, Rose was simply rationalizing her need to feel his body against hers, to hold on to him a moment longer before he vanished from her life, to feel needed by him.

He did need her. Perhaps he did not realize it, but Rose knew that he did.

Steven groaned, signaling the urgency of his desire. Rose helped him out of his shirt, then slid her hands over the muscles of his bare back. A tremor of pleasure rocked her body as she pressed her lips to his shoulder. Gently, she sucked at his warm, fragrant skin, tasting him, nipping at him, hungrily running her tongue over his chest and nipples.

She had never wanted so much of a man before. Even in the very beginning of her marriage, before Rose discovered that her husband was cheating on her at every opportunity, when the romance was new and she was naïve enough to believe that their lovemaking represented their love for each other, she had never wanted Winston Sinclair as wholly or completely or as urgently as she wanted Steven. And, given that Steven was the one man who could deprive her of everything she wanted, namely, a family, her obsession with him did not make sense.

Despite her fears, however, she could not release Steven, not now. The sound of their labored breathing and the heady aroma of their exertions filled the tiny compartment. Their hips moved together rhythmically, and as more clothes were tossed aside, pulled off or even ripped off, they discovered more places on each other's bodies that brought wilder pleasure and greater arousal.

Arousal fueled Rose's brazenness. Shifting to her side, she gave Steven a little push so that he was flat on his back. Straddling him, she leaned forward, at first kissing his lips, then working her way down his chest, the tip of her tongue moving along the trail of fine hair that ran from his belly to beneath the waistband of his trousers.

"Oh, God, Mother of Erin, Jesus Christ . . ." His mumbling took on a more sanguine tone as Rose tugged his pants down his legs.

When he was stark naked, she sat astride his thighs, staring unabashedly at his rigid erection.

"Rose, I cannot stand much more—"

"Oh, be a good boy," she purred, delighted that her boldness seemed to arouse him even more. Then, slowly, and acting purely on primal instinct, because she had never done such a thing in her life, Rose lowered her mouth to Steven's body.

Tentatively, she placed her lips on the tip of his penis. She licked and kissed him, fascinated with his taste, the softness of his skin, the hardness of his muscle. He reacted instantly, moaning his pleasure-pain and thrusting his fingers in her hair.

She would not have thought it possible, but his erection swelled to even greater proportions. Holding him with both hands, Rose parted her lips wider and slid her mouth down the length of his shaft. She felt him at the back of her throat, and, without being told what to do, she knew to move her mouth up and down Steven's penis until he was writhing with pent-up desire.

She tasted him everywhere, breathing in his unique masculine scent. It felt good to have Steven inside her; it felt right to kiss him everywhere, even in the most intimate parts of his body. Above all else, it felt incredibly wanton and wicked.

"Rose, if you don't stop, I will not be able to control myself," Steven rasped.

Aware that he was on the verge of release, Rose carefully and tenderly squeezed the base of his penis. For a moment, she remained hunkered over him, quietly, her lips pressed to the thatch of crisp dark hair beneath his belly. Then, when his breathing returned to normal, she sat up and set about leisurely exploring Steven's body.

She was grateful for the flickering lamplight behind her because she wanted to see everything. Gently, she cupped Steven's most sensitive anatomy. Aware that he was watching her, and aroused by his heated gaze, she caressed and kissed his inner thighs. Then she put her hand between his legs and stroked the smooth area between his manhood and his *derrière.*

The sound that escaped his lips was one of utter agony. Suddenly, Rose could not wait a second longer to feel Steven inside her. Resting her palms on his chest, she positioned her hips over his. As she locked gazes with him, the tip of his penis teased her soaked curls.

She lowered herself onto him, gasping as he filled her, crying out when he thrust his body upward to touch that hidden spot deep within her, moving her hips back and forth, gripping him with her inner muscles.

"I want you to make love to me, Steven," she whispered.

Through clenched teeth, he returned her sentiment, though in far more graphic words than Rose had used.

But his salty language only served to push Rose over the brink of her desire.

They rocked against each other, at first gently and slowly, then desperately as their passion rose to a crescendo.

Mere seconds passed before Rose felt the first spasms of her release. Abandoning any vestige of propriety or decorum, she told Steven precisely what she wanted and needed from him.

And he gave it to her, hard and fast.

Together—fingers intertwined, gazes riveted on each other—they reached their climax.

Afterwards, the lay beside each other, too overwhelmed with emotion to speak, too content to interrupt the silence. When Rose finally struggled to her elbows and looked at Steven, she wondered what she would say to the man whom she loved, the man who stood between her and the solid unity of her precious newfound little family.

As it turned out, there was no need to say anything. Steven's eyes were closed and his lips were slightly parted. He snored peacefully as she quietly got into her clothes. When Rose was fully dressed, she kissed him lightly on the forehead.

"Good-bye, darling."

He roused, gazing at her with a slightly confused expression. Grasping her shoulders, he said hoarsely, "Where are you going?"

"Back to hospital, to spend the night with Katie. Remember? You made everything all right with Doctor Conolley. Thank you, Steven." She patted his hand and reached for the doorknob.

"Don't go." He struggled to his elbows, belatedly noticing his nakedness. Grabbing his trousers, he thrust one leg into them. "Rose—"

"Good-bye," she said over her shoulder and swiftly leapt to the ground. Embarrassed, she threw the driver a quick smile and raced for the hospital door. Outside the carriage, the air was frigid, and she was not wearing her cloak and bonnet. Her heart galloped as she entered the children's ward. Now that her body was satisfied, her conscience nagged at her to face reality.

She should not have made love to Sir Steven Nollbrook. She was foolish, trifling with a man who could ruin her life. The sight of little Katie lying flat on her back, as helpless as a rag doll, brutally chastised her.

But she loved him, and she could no longer ignore that fact.

Leaning over Katie, loving stroking the child's hair, Rose wondered how on earth she was going to rid herself of a man she loved.

But rid herself of him, she must. Because as much as she adored making love to him, keeping little Stevie and the twins together was a far more important objective.

Rose spent the next three days at Katie's bedside, returning to Fontjoy Square only once each day, and that was when Devon Avondale retrieved her from the hospital and drove her home for a quick bath and a change of clothes.

On the day Katie was to be released from the hospital, Rose stood in the girls' room, a small portmanteau open on the bed. "I haven't much time, Mrs. Bleek. Dr. Conolley says Katie can come home this afternoon."

"And a blessed event that will be," the older woman replied as she handed Rose a set of fresh underclothes and a clean frock for the child to wear home.

Rose neatly folded a miniature pair of woolen stockings and laid them inside the valise. "I feel as if it has been eons since I have laid eyes on Mollie and Stevie. Are they holding up all right, Mrs. B.?"

"I would say so, Missus. They seem to roll with the punches, those two. And they trust what Sir Steven's been a'telling them. They know Katie is coming home soon, and they know she is being well taken care of."

"Sir Steven has been here?" Rose felt a sharp pull in her chest.

"Why, yes, ma'am, I thought you knew. He's been here every day this week, tending to the children, playing ring-around-the-rosie with them yesterday, if I recall correctly. He even sat in the classroom with little Stevie for an hour this morning, working with the boy on his alphabet." The governess clucked her tongue. "I don't know what they taught the child at Mrs. Bunratty's, but it wasn't reading and spelling, I warrant you that."

Paralyzed with fear, Rose asked the dreaded question. "How does he get along with the children, Mrs. Bleek?"

"Why, didn't you hear what I just said? Oh, dear me, I don't mean to be harsh. We're all tired and worried about Katie, aren't we? But the answer to your question is, Sir Steven gets along with the children famously. Little Stevie especially. But Mollie, bless her wee heart, she just adores him, she does!"

With a heavy sigh, Rose tucked the extra pair of unmentionables between Katie's stockings and apron. She should not be surprised by Sir Steven's interest in his own son, she silently scolded herself. But a part of her was. A part of her truly wanted to believe the man was as callous and uncaring as she had thought he was when she first met him. If he were, it would be so much easier to divorce herself from the notion that she loved him.

"Do you think he would make a good father?"

" 'Tis not for me to say," Mrs. Bleek replied in an uncharacteristically timid voice. "But I expect so. He loves the child; Miss Rose. That much is as plain as the nose on my face."

Snapping shut the leather case, Rose turned to Mrs. Bleek. "Is Mr. Avondale below stairs?"

"Waiting for you, ma'am. Now there's a fine gentleman! Too bad he and Sir Steven hate each other so much!"

Too distraught to respond, Rose swept out of the room. Her worst nightmare was materializing; she had finally acquired a family and it was about to be ripped asunder.

Devon Avondale stood in the foyer with his coat on, waiting to accompany Rose back to the hospital. When he heard footsteps descending the stairs, he looked up. Dismay and anger engulfed him as Sir

Steven reached the landing with Mollie and Stevie in tow.

Rather than rushing to Devon, the children clung to Steven's hands.

"Hello, Avondale." Steven's smile was wide and, to any casual observer, would have appeared completely sincere.

But Devon's antennae instantly thrummed with suspicion. He knew that Steven was a man of low morals, a man who could not possibly love those children *or* Rose Sinclair. Devon also knew that Rose, despite her desperate wish to hold on to her fledgling family, possessed a curious interest in Steven, perhaps even harbored a secret attraction toward him. Well, virtuous women were often fooled by ruffians and seduced by rogues. Devon hardly blamed Rose for her innocence.

But Sir Steven represented an enormous threat to Rose's happiness and he could not be trusted. His presence at Fontjoy Square was unacceptable.

"Hello, Mollie and Stevie. What have you two been about this morning?"

"We've been reading Shakespeare," Mollie answered. "Or rather, Sir Steven has been reading it, and we've been listening."

"Don't like it very much," put in Stevie. "I prefer Miss Tweedy's limericks. They're a good bit easier to remember, if you ask me."

"Have you seen Katie?" Mollie inquired. "Is she coming home soon?"

"This afternoon, as a matter of fact," Rose answered as she descended the steps into the foyer. She cast a sidelong glance at Sir Steven, but Devon could not read the message that passed between them. Then she gave the children hugs and kisses, asked them how their lessons were going and assured them that Katie was fine. "Run along to the classroom," she said, patting Stevie's behind as he scampered up the stairs.

When the children were gone, she looked warily from one man to the other. Devon stared at Steven, itching for him to make a rude remark or an aggressive gesture, anything that would justify Devon's planting a fist in the man's face.

Steven, however, smiled knowingly. He even had the gall to kiss Rose on the cheek.

"You needn't stay here any longer, Steven," she said, blushing. "Though I do appreciate your efforts with the children while I was sitting with Katie."

"I look forward to seeing her," Steven replied, apparently unwilling to accept Rose's hint.

Devon's suggestion was less subtle. "I want you out of this house before we return from hospital. Do you understand me?"

Steven's glare was chilling. "This is Mrs. Sinclair's home. You have no right to put me out. Only she can make that decision." He turned to her. "And you have no right to keep my son here if you toss me out, Rose. You know that."

Seething, Devon bit out his final warning. "You will be gone when we return." He would have liked to tell Steven that he had every right to determine who could or could not occupy Rose's house. After all, he had given it to her. But even Rose did not know that, so he could hardly make it a basis for evicting Steven.

"And if I am not?"

"Then we will finish what we started a few days ago. Only this time, you will be the one lying in a hospital bed!"

"Stop it!" Rose cried, clamping her hands over her ears. "I will not tolerate this sort of behavior in my home. 'Tis hardly a good example for the children, and believe me, they are well aware of the hatred you two feel for each other."

Subdued by the thought that he was endangering the children, Devon took a step backward. To his surprise, Rose's outburst and the mention of the children's welfare seemed to quell Steven's anger as well. Both men nodded curtly; then Steven turned on his heel and went upstairs.

"Why do you allow him in your home, Rose?" Devon asked her when they were in the carriage.

Biting her bottom lips, she shook her head. Tears glistened in her eyes as she shrugged and murmured, "I do not know."

With a heavy sigh, Devon folded his arms across his chest. Clearly, something had happened between Rose and Steven, something that had greatly affected Rose and confused her. Vaguely, he wondered if they had—

But no, that was impossible. Rose was as prim and proper a lady as one would find in Dublin. She would never have allowed that ruthless charlatan to get beneath her petticoats.

Would she?

"If he has hurt you, Rose—"

"No, of course not!"

"If he has touched you—"

"Please, Devon!" Sniffing, she held a linen square to her nose. After a moment, her tears dried and her emotions calmed. "I do not wish to discuss this with you."

"I am here to help you," he said softly, wounded that he was being excluded from her confidence.

"Yes, I know." She offered him a watery smile. "And I appreciate that. But there are certain things you cannot possibly understand. Such as how badly I want a family, Devon. A whole family, not a splintered one."

His throat constricted and his mouth went dry. Did she really think that Devon Avondale could not understand *that?* Closing his eyes, he forced down the emotion Rose's remark had provoked. All he had ever wanted was a good woman to love and a family to take care of.

But Mary's death had robbed him of his love. In the aftermath of her death, he thought he would go insane. Then he read his wife's diary and realized what her parting words had meant. He found the four women who had befriended Mary during her life. He repaid them for loving Mary by giving them houses to live in. The ladies who moved to Fontjoy Square had become Devon's family. And now Rose's children were his family, too.

If Sir Steven Nollbrook did anything to harm, injure or endanger his family, Devon would kill the hateful barrister without batting an eyelash.

It was Rose who did not understand how deeply afraid Devon was of losing everything that he loved.

No one could ever understand . . . no one except Mary, that is.

And, then, dear diary, the very worst thing happened. In another day and age, or at a different time in my life, it might have been the very best thing. But you could not have convinced me of that then. I thought my world had ended. Worse, I thought I had destroyed my family's life, as well, by bringing so much shame and scandal down on their heads. If anyone knew what I had done, and the consequences of my recklessness, the sun would cease to shine and the earth would spin off its axis.

So I told no one of The Pregnancy, no one except, of course, Padraig, and my very dearest friend Rose Humphrey, who promised never to tell a soul, and to this day, I do not believe she has.

You asked me once if I had ever suffered from a debilitating illness when I was young, or sustained an injury that might have prevented me from getting pregnant. I said no, and I answered truthfully, but I wasn't wholly honest with you. Oh, Devon, I am so sorry! All these years, you thought it was you who could not father children. No, dear, it was I who could not conceive, and I am going to tell you what happened that summer that led up to my being unable ever to bear another infant.

Padraig, of course, was frightened out of his mind. His father would kill him, he said, or worse, send him to boarding school in Scotland where he would never be seen or heard from again. He was quite maudlin in his reaction to my dilemma, now that I look back, and I call it "my" dilemma, not "ours," because I do not think Padraig ever considered the baby his responsibility. It was only his problem because of the threat that my father might demand some sort of contribution or retribution from Padraig for having despoiled me.

I was crushed, naturally, by Padraig's reaction, and so as the summer progressed and I saw less and less of my sweet, red-haired accomplice, I began to wonder what I should do about the growing fetus in my belly.

Rose said I should tell my parents, that perhaps there was some medical way to stop the babe from growing or from coming out. That shows you how innocent we were! We had no idea whether the pregnancy could be reversed! We only knew that if nothing was done, the child would, in nine months time, emerge from my stomach in the most painful, not to mention shameful, manner.

And I, in my naïve, schoolgirlish dream state, even harbored the silly notion that perhaps I really wasn't pregnant, that I had contracted some deadly disease that thwarted the flow of my menses. At night, I prayed that this disease would manifest itself in some other, less embarrassing way, so that I could be treated and cured. But of course that never happened, and the summer passed in a blur of sand and sea water and sleepless nights.

As I said before, I told no one, meaning I did not tell my parents. Only Rose and Padraig knew, and after two months, Padraig was so terrified that he would be snatched up by the scruff of the neck at any moment and deported, he was totally useless to me. Oh, I nurtured no hard feelings toward the lad. He was nearly as young as I, and he was only half responsible for my condition. It was not as if he had forced me to do anything I did not want to do.

Dear Devon, forgive me for making you my confidante all these many years later. 'Tis such a boorish thing for a wife to do to a husband, but you see, Rose is not around, and I do so badly need to tell someone before I die about this in the event that the child ever appears and begins asking questions about his mother . . . But that will never happen, will it? At any rate, I suppose you deserve an explanation from me after all these years.

You could guess the rest of my story, couldn't you, Devon? When the summer ended, Rose and I returned to Dublin and our respective households, although—and I believe this was somewhat of a surprise to our parents, who occupied two entirely different social spheres—we remained fast friends.

And as our sun-kissed skin faded to paleness, we might have forgotten all about Padraig and his father's sparkling hotel but for the subtle swelling of my lower belly and the thickening of my waist. Like many very young mothers, I never looked very pregnant, even in my final month. Mother merely thought I was putting on a little much needed weight, and Father kept remarking that I was turning into a beautiful young woman, and that my complexion was actually "glowing."

But only Rose knew the truth, and Rose, by this time, had sworn to tell no one.

You might wonder what our plan was. Were we going to make a last minute attempt to abort the fetus, or wrap it in a swaddling blanket and leave it in a basket at the edge of the Liffey? I swear, I do not know what I planned to do! Though I was an extraordinarily able pupil, literate in French and Latin, as well as Spanish, sophisticated in so many other ways, I could not bring myself to plan for the eventuality of the birth of my own child.

Rose, God help her, visited nearly every weekend, and while we closeted ourselves away in my room, pretending to embroider or to practice the pianoforte, she tried her best to convince me that I should tell someone of the imminent arrival of another child in the world.

"What if something goes wrong, Mary?" she would ask me in that sensible, motherly tone of hers. "A doctor or midwife should be in attendance when the child is delivered just in case something goes wrong! You must tell your parents, Mary, you simply must."

But I could not. I knew what sort of hue and cry would be raised by my father if I did. He was not the sort who tolerated mediocrity—my friend Dolly, who told a lie in Switzerland to save me from my father's ire, could testify to that.

Instead, I prayed for what I called a "reverse miracle," a divine intervention of sorts that would make the fetus inside my stomach disappear. When that did not happen, I prayed for a quick, painless and discreet delivery.

Poor Rose. It all sounds so nonsensical now. She must have been beside herself with worry and regret. I'm certain she thought she bore some responsibility in my getting pregnant; that's the way she is, carries the weight of the world on her shoulders, that one. After all, she knew when we were in Killiney that I was sneaking off to be alone with Padraig, and she never tattled on me.

The night the baby came, we were in my quarters in my parents' house in Dublin. Luckily, my little son decided to make his arrival during a weekend, when Rose and I were sequestered in my bedchamber, and Mother and Father were attending the opera.

My cries were muffled by the bed sheets I stuffed into my mouth. The pain was unlike anything I have ever known, even worse than the pain I am suffering now, Devon. And there was blood everywhere . . . Oh, God, I was horrified that I and the baby would die! Rose turned as pale as a birch tree, but when the baby finally slipped into her arms, looking for all the world as if he had been through an ordeal worse than mine, she gently bathed him in the basin and wrapped him in a towel. She cut the umbilical cord with a pair of shears; we had learned that much from reading the books our mothers did not want us to read!

Then she placed the child on my breast and sat on the bed beside me while I stared in amazement at this wondrous little creature that I had given birth to.

"What are we going to do now?" Rose asked, smiling as the baby wrapped its tiny fingers around her thumb.

A black cloud of confusion and resentment descended on me. I cannot explain what came over me, Devon, except to say it was as if my emotions ran away from me, and despite my fascination with the little child I held in my arms, I wished I had never lain with Padraig, or gotten pregnant, or allowed this baby to live in my stomach without doing something before which would have stopped it from growing! Oh, horrid thoughts tumbled through my head, and my chest ached, and all I wanted to do was go back in time and undo what I had done!

Closing my eyes, I turned my head on the pillow and sobbed. "Take this thing away from me," I said, and thrust the baby toward Rose.

I was too humiliated by my own behavior to look at her, but I could hear her moving about the room, packing a small valise, then putting on her coat and shoes.

"Are you certain, Mary?" she asked, standing at my bedside.

"I don't care what you do with it, or where you take it! Throw it in the river, if you must. Just get it out of here before Mother and Father return!"

Do you think me a terrible person yet, Devon? Well, before you judge me too harshly, rest assured that I spent years reliving that moment, wishing I had kept that child, hating myself for tossing it out.

But it was Rose who saved me from total self-loathing. She left quietly, and as she did, I opened my eyes in time to see her slipping out of my room, a small suitcase in one hand and what appeared to be a bundle of rags, but which was really my baby, cradled in the crook of her other arm. I did nothing to stop her. She could have destroyed my baby and I would have done nothing to prevent her from doing so.

She did not destroy the child, though, Devon. On the contrary, she took it to a society known as the Dorcas Society for the Aid of Illegitimate Children. I have no idea how she knew of this place, but she did. Someone there took the child in, and placed it in a home with parents who could not conceive an infant but who desperately wanted to have a family. Ironic, isn't it, Devon? Because of my transgressions, I made a family for another couple, strangers to us, but failed to give you what you wanted most from me, children.

Well, there you have it. The postscript to this story, if you haven't figured it out already, is that when Rose returned, I was lying unconscious in a pool of blood. The mattress was soaked through and my lower body was completely awash in it. As fate would have it, Father and Mother happened home from the opera at just about the same time, and I was wrapped up in blankets and—I am told this, for I do not recall a thing—Father instructed the coachman to drive as fast as he could to Meath Hospital.

There, the doctors managed not only to save my life but also to do so without informing Father that I had just been delivered of a newborn infant. They knew, of course, but they also knew my father would strangle me if he learned the truth. And so they became conspirators, too, along with Rose and the Dorcas Ladies. I believe it was as a result of my mishap that I was never able to become pregnant with your child, Devon, and for that I am eternally sorry.

Ah . . . speaking of eternity, darling, do mention to Rose that I love her dearly for saving my son and finding him a loving home. I have missed him constantly, and I have regretted not being a part of his life, but I have never—at least not since that awful night when he was born—regretted giving birth to him.

She was a strong, brave young woman, Devon. By now, I suspect, she has a brood of her own—

grandchildren, perhaps, who knows? Lucky children!

Oh, Devon, please, please forgive me. . . . I love you so!

Fourteen

Rose strode the corridors of Meath Hospital with a spring in her step. Not since she had laid eyes on Mollie, Katie and Stevie had she been as happy. The trauma of Katie's sudden illness had dissipated with the child's recovery. Having Katie at home, safe and sound in Fontjoy Square, seemed a miracle for which Rose would be eternally grateful.

As she walked up the steps that led to the fourth floor and the children's ward, Rose reflected on the tragedy that had befallen Mary O'Roarke that odd summer in Killiney, so many years ago. The girls had been so innocent in the ways of men that they could hardly believe Mary had gotten herself pregnant. They had been so young and foolish that they actually believed no one would notice Mary's swelling belly.

The amazing thing was, no one did!

But since she'd gone to work at the Dorcas Society, Rose had met many young girls in their ninth month of pregnancy whose stomachs were flatter than hers was now. If a girl was young and thin, she could easily hide her growing babe. Mary's parents, bless their fool hearts, had actually been thrilled to see their lanky daughter add some pounds to her frame.

Rose had never forgotten how frightened Mary was that night; nor had she forgotten the deep depression Mary had fallen into after the child's birth. In addition to nearly bleeding to death, Mary had suffered enormously from guilt and resentment. Though she feigned a complete and total recovery—even gallivanting off to Europe within weeks of her release from the hospital—Rose knew better than anyone how greatly affected Mary was by her pregnancy, the birth of her child and the subsequent deception she concocted to avoid her father's censure.

After Mary returned from her European holiday, she never spoke to Rose Humphrey again. Despite Rose's numerous missives, Mary refused to visit the Humphrey household. When Rose paid an unexpected call on Mary, she was told by a flustered servant that Mary was "unavailable to visitors."

It did not take long for Rose to realize that she was part and parcel of a memory that Mary wished to erase. Rose could hardly blame her. Giving up her child to an anonymous couple must have weighed heavily on Mary's conscience. She must have lain awake at nights wondering if her son was cradled in another woman's arms, and if he was happy and well taken care of. She must have wondered how different her and her son's life would have been if she had faced her father's anger and kept the child.

Not that Rose thought Mary erred in giving up her child for adoption. Indeed, it was more humane than tossing the infant in the Liffey, as Mary had suggested that night. But Mary was not rational that night. She was young and frightened and confused. She made a series of mistakes and one compounded the other. In her right mind, she would never have hurt a child, any child, much less her own. Mary O'Roarke was the sweetest, gentlest girl Rose had ever known.

She was a bit wild, perhaps, Rose thought with a sliver of a smile. But what was so terribly wrong with that? Since she'd fallen in love with Sir Steven Nollbrook, Rose had decided that *naughty* was not altogether such a bad thing.

The memory of her lovemaking with Sir Steven brought a sudden wave of heat to Rose's face. The thought of facing the man when she returned home made her head swim. She had no idea how she was going to force him out of Stevie's life when she couldn't get through a day without thinking of him, without yearning to feel his naked body beside hers, and without aching to have him inside her.

Devon Avondale was an added problem; the two men detested each other. Rose would consider herself fortunate if they did not brawl in her foyer.

She would worry about that later, she thought, entering the children's ward. Right now, all Rose wanted to do was gather up her dear little Katie and take her home.

She walked the length of the ward, her gaze searching for Katie. She stood at the foot of Katie's hospital bed, curious to see that the sheets had been changed and a fresh blanket had been tucked around the mattress. But where was Katie?

Laying the portmanteau on the mattress, Rose reached for the sheaf of medical papers that hung on the metal railing on the bed. Scanning the most recent entry, she saw that Katie had been "discharged" an hour earlier.

She wasn't really worried. She told herself that the child had probably gone to the water closet, or was waiting to be met in the foyer on the ground floor. At worst, Rose thought that Katie had gotten lost and was wandering the halls of the labyrinthine hospital. Turning, she caught the attention of a passing nurse.

"Excuse me, but do you remember a little dark-haired girl named Katie who has been occupying this bed for the past five days?"

"Oh, to be certain, mum, and she was a sweetie, that one, wasn't she?"

Rose forced herself to smile. "Her chart says she has been discharged."

"Yes, mum. The surgeon removed her appendix, but she recovered quite nicely."

"Yes, I know that. I am her mother."

The nurse looked puzzled. "Her mother, you say?" Her eyes darted about the ward as she scratched her chin. "Well, if you are her mother—"

Rose's heart sank. "Yes?"

"Then who was the lady who took her home?"

Outside, beneath the *porte cochère* in front of the hospital, Devon flung open the door to his carriage and leaped to the ground. Scanning the stream of people flowing out the great double front doors, he felt a tingle of disquiet. Rose had asked him to remain with his rig while she fetched Katie, but that was nearly an hour ago. He was eager to get her and Katie out of the biting cold and into the relative warmth of his rig. He was eager to get them home.

The moment he saw Rose running toward him, without Katie, he knew something was wrong.

"She's gone, Devon!" The wind whipped at her hair and bonnet. "Katie's missing! Someone came and took her from the hospital over an hour ago!"

"Who?" Even as he asked, Devon feared the worst.

"I've asked every nurse on the floor, but the most I can find out is that she left in the company of a young woman with red hair, wearing an elegant dove-gray walking suit with a fashionable bustle." Tears pooled in Rose's eyes.

Devon gripped Rose's shoulders. "Do you know anyone who fits that description?"

"Clodagh Tweedy," snarled Sir Steven, throttling an imaginary throat. "It has to be her. Red hair, expensive clothes. And when I get my hands on her—"

"There'll be no killing," interjected Dick Creevy, entering Rose's parlor. Joining his neighbors, he stood next to his wife, Lady Dolly.

Flanked on the sofa by Millicent and Dolly, Rose dabbed a linen square at the corner of her eye. She was grateful to her friends for rallying around her, and to Mrs. Bleek for calmly occupying Stevie and Mollie in the classroom while this crisis was going on. In the chair opposite the sofa sat Lady Claire Kilgarren. Devon stationed himself at the mantelpiece. And Steven, who had been pacing the length of the carpet ever since receiving the news of Katie's abduction, now stalked to the sideboard and poured himself a hefty shot of whiskey.

"What was Clodagh Tweedy doing in Meath Hospital?" Millicent asked.

"Doubtless her presence there was no coincidence," Devon replied. "She went there for the specific purpose of spiriting Katie away with her."

Having doused his anger with liquor, Steven returned to the center of the room. "Well, I for one am not going to stand by and allow that lousy little bit of baggage to ruin Katie's life. Nor Rose's. Nor Mollie's and Stevie's for that matter!"

Dick Creevy gave the barrister an appraising look. "Sir Steven Nollbrook, are you? We have not been formally introduced, but I know you by reputation."

"As I do you," Steven said shortly.

"I'm sorry," Rose murmured. "My manners . . ."

"What do you intend to do, Nollbrook?" Creevy asked.

"I intend to pay a visit to Mrs. Bunratty's, that's what. And when I find that stringy-headed little whore—"

"Watch your language, man!" Devon's voice boomed. "There are ladies in the room!"

"I vote for summoning a constable," said Creevy calmly. "There's no sense tearing into Mrs. Bunratty's establishment in the state you're in, old man, no offense. I fear you will do something impulsive. You might even endanger the child's life, sir."

"There isn't time to summon a constable!" Steven roared.

Rose pushed off the sofa. Keenly aware of Devon's

disapproving look, she went to stand by Steven. Gently, she laid a hand on his arm. "Mr. Creevy has a point."

His jaw hardened to stone. If Rose had never seen the tender, loving side of Steven, she would have been terrified by the crazed look that flashed in his eyes. "Rose," he whispered, drawing her into his arms. "I will not let anyone take Katie away from you."

"I'll go with you," she said quietly.

"No."

By his tone, Rose knew there was no use arguing with Steven. Besides, she believed him. Behind her, Dick and Devon continued to discuss what little was known about Katie's disappearance, and Devon even went to the writing desk to pen a message to the constable, but none of that mattered to Rose at present. Steven quietly promised her that he would bring Katie home, and she believed him.

When he left the room, Devon looked up, startled. "Where in the hell is *he* going?"

"To Mrs. Bunratty's, I suppose," Rose answered.

"Is he mad?" Dick exclaimed.

"Stop him!" Devon yelled, crossing the parlor floor, as quick as lightning.

But it was too late. Below stairs, the front door slammed shut. Carriage wheels rumbled down the street. Sir Steven was on his way to Mrs. Bunratty's, and Rose had no doubt in her mind that he would find Katie and bring her home—or that he would die trying.

* * *

Steven had not been inside Mrs. Bunratty's for over a year, not since his last, painful encounter with Katherine Rowen. Up till then, he had nurtured the ridiculous hope that she might get well, or that he might find a cure for her. But after the birth of little Stevie, her downward spiral continued unabated, except for the occasional forced trip to the country or a sanitarium. At last, Steven had realized the extent of his failure. Katherine did not love him enough to even want to get well.

Monto had not changed since he had last visited. Nor had the grimy streets and the guilty expressions on the faces of men scurrying in and out of whorehouses. Steven's stomach churned as he approached the nondescript entrance to the place where Katherine had lived, where he had loved her, and where his son had been conceived. To think he had abandoned his son to the denizens of this place horrified him. He was glad Rose was not here. She was too innocent and good a woman to even witness the sort of degradation and degeneration that flourished in a place like this.

He could never live in Rose's world. He knew that now. It was his fault that Katie had been kidnapped by Clodagh Tweedy. He did not know why the woman had committed this despicable act, or what she intended to gain from it, but Tweedy was from *his* world, and he had contaminated Rose's world just by being near her. His gut told him Tweedy wanted something from *him.* His conscience told him that if he had stayed away from Rose, Katie would never have been abducted.

If he had to stay away from Rose and Stevie in order to protect those three children, he would gladly do so.

He did not bother knocking, but pushed open the door and paused. As his eyes adjusted to the shadows, the familiar furnishings of Mrs. Bunratty's place came slowly into focus. Heavy velvet drapes blocked the daylight while thick Axminster carpets absorbed the sound. Lamps with fringed shades, porcelain bric-a-brac and claw-footed furniture filled every nook and cranny of the whorehouse. Dark mahogany paneling and rich portraits of nude ladies on the walls created a masculine, clubby ambience.

After a moment, he realized he was not alone.

"What brings you here, Sir Steven?" A curtain of beads parted and Mrs. Bunratty's bejeweled bulk appeared. She stood at the foot of the grand spiral staircase holding a small glass filled with ruby liquid.

"I'm here to see Clodagh Tweedy." He took a step forward, then halted, afraid of his violent impulse toward the woman. "Don't bother showing me the way. I know where she is."

Smiling slyly, she stood aside. "She lives in Katherine's former quarters, dear. She took over most of Katherine's customers, you know."

Mrs. Bunratty's jibe threatened to undo him, but Steven battled his rage and pushed past her. Above stairs, he went directly to Katherine's old room and rattled the brass doorknob. From within sounded Clodagh Tweedy's voice. "You're early darling. I told you not to come until—"

The door swung open to reveal Tweedy's startled

face. She tried to close it, but Steven was faster and stronger than she. As he pushed open the door and stepped inside, Tweedy stumbled backward.

"What the devil are *you* doing here?"

"You appear genuinely surprised, Clodagh. Did you really think you could get away with it?"

"Get away with what?" she asked, innocently.

"Congratulations, dear. Your acting skills are nearly as finely honed as mine."

"Our occupations are not that different, then, are they?"

"You had best tell me where Katie is. I wouldn't want to have to strangle that pretty little throat of yours."

Swallowing hard, she retreated toward her bed. Her eyes blinked wide and her face blanched. "You wouldn't hurt me, Steven. You were never the type to be cruel or violent. Katherine said so—"

"Leave Katherine out of this!"

"I don't see how we can, really. Not if you're looking for Katie. She's the one who went and died, leaving those children to me and Mrs. Bunratty to look after."

"You did as fine a job as she, didn't you?"

"I did a better job than *you,* Steven! You turned your back on that little boy! You refused to even acknowledge he was your own. You can't very well criticize me for taking those young'uns to the Dorcas Ladies, now can you?"

Her words wounded him because they were true. The condemnation of a moral bankrupt like Clodagh Tweedy soundly affirmed Steven's estimation of himself as worthless and unlovable. Yet during the last few weeks, he had witnessed the power of a woman's love for three helpless children. Deep in Rose's thrall, Sir Steven had admitted—to himself, at least—that he was Stevie's father. Quite naturally—for that was what all decent parents did, wasn't it?—he had fallen in love with Stevie. But surprisingly, he had fallen in love with Katie and Mollie, too.

"Perhaps taking those children to Rose Sinclair was the only decent thing you've ever done, Clodagh, though I question your motives even now. Why did you? Why did you give up on blackmailing me and suddenly decide to take the children to the Dorcas Society?"

Her gaze fell to the floor. "I had me reasons," she mumbled. "I heard about that Mrs. Sinclair. Everybody in Monto knows of her. They say she's got a soft heart. It wasn't no good, them kids livin' here. When I saw I couldn't get you to take 'em off me hands, I thought it was best to find 'em a good home, if I could."

Something about Tweedy's explanation rang false. Slowly advancing on the fidgeting redhead, Steven said, "Tell me where the child is, Tweedy, and I'll see to it that the judge is lenient with you when you are sentenced for kidnapping."

"Sentenced?" Her green eyes popped wide open. "For kidnapping?"

"You couldn't blackmail me, so you took the children to the Dorcas Society and left them with Rose Sinclair." Steven's memory reeled back to his conversation in the pub with Aloysius Letterfrack. "You were watching Rose's every move, weren't you? You knew she wanted to adopt all three of the children. You approached Letterfrack and told him what you know."

Her chin wobbled. "No!"

He continued to theorize as he closed the distance between himself and Tweedy. "Letterfrack advised me to pay you a bribe, to buy your silence so that you wouldn't testify you saw me visiting Katherine at Mrs. Bunratty's. Without someone like you to tie me to Katherine, I could easily have denied that I was Stevie's father!"

"I don't know what you're talking about, sir!" Her hand flew to her throat and she reared back against her night table.

Steven hovered over her, disgusted by her display of ignorance and her show of fear. "Letterfrack should have known that I would never pay a bribe to a witness! Never!"

"I never told Aloysius any such thing! I swear I didn't! After you refused to pay me anything, I just wanted to get rid of the children!"

"When Letterfrack was unsuccessful in persuading me to pay a bribe, you waited. You knew Rose would fall in love with those children, didn't you? Any *decent* woman would."

She slapped his face and cried, "Stop it!"

Her defiance, however, served only to anger Steven even more. Stung, but unharmed, he leaned closer to Clodagh Tweedy. "When you were convinced of Rose's devotion to Mollie and Katie and Stevie, you decided to kidnap one of them. If you were watching

Rose's house, you knew when I took Katie to hospital. You fetched her from the children's ward today!"

"I did not!" Recoiling, Clodagh grasped the edge of the bedside table.

Steven was nose to nose with her. "You should have known someone would see you, though. Your red hair and your expensive clothes are hardly forgettable."

"More than half the women in Dublin have red hair!"

"But it was you who took Katie. Now where is she, Clodagh. Tell me now before I—"

The crack of a gunshot deafened him. For an instant, staring into Clodagh's gaping expression, Steven was stunned and confused. His right shoulder burned, his chest ached and he could not fill his lungs. Instinctively, he clutched his shirtfront. Something wet and warm oozed onto his fingers; looking down, he saw that his hands were covered with blood.

"You idiot, you've killed him!" Clodagh Tweedy cried.

Unbalanced, dizzied and bitterly angry, Steven made a slow, painful turn. The figure he saw standing in the doorway gave him a malicious smile. The last thing Steven saw before the floor rushed up to greet him was a flash of red hair and the swirl of a dove-gray cape.

In her foyer, Rose held up Devon's black sheared-lamb overcoat while he thrust his arms into the sleeves. She understood Devon's and Dick's determination to pursue Steven. The barrister had flown out of the house in a murderous rage, and it would do no one, including Katie, any good if he strangled Clodagh Tweedy as he had promised.

Secretly, however, Rose was gratified by Steven's quick reaction. For a man who prided himself on maintaining perfect self-control, he had shown a tremendous amount of *uncontrolled* emotion when he learned that Katie was in danger. The man could no longer pretend he had no paternal instincts. His reaction had been as primal as that of a mother lion protecting her cub.

"The man's a fool!" Devon muttered, wrapping his muffler around his throat.

Dick Creevy gave Rose a knowing look. "Oh, I wouldn't call him that."

"Well what *would* you call him?" Devon asked bitterly.

"He is obviously very determined." Dick pulled on a pair of woolen gloves. "But I suppose that is the secret of his success as a barrister. He is the sort of man who does things his way. My guess is, more often than not, he gets what he wants."

"Arrogant, hot-tempered, fool that's what he is! And I hope to God I never see him in Fontjoy Square again!"

The knock that sounded at the door was barely audible above Devon's rantings. Rose opened the door, and a gust of cold wind swept through the foyer.

A small boy, his head covered only by a battered felt cap, stood in the doorway. "Two pence, mum," the porter said, holding out a fluttering piece of paper.

Her mouth went dry as she took the paper from the

boy's ragged mitten. Devon flipped the child some coins, and off he ran. Closing the front door, Rose studied the crudely scrawled message she held in her hand. The handwriting was childish in its appearance, but the message was cruel.

"Oh, my God!" She grabbed a marble-topped table for support. Fearful that her legs would collapse, she handed the paper to Devon.

He quickly scanned the note. "Well, Dick, we will not be chasing Steven to Mrs. Bunratty's after all. It appears our kidnapper has invited us to visit her at the Dorcas Society's headquarters. We are to be there before eight o'clock tonight."

" 'Tis nearly seven now." Dick snatched the piece of paper. "And that's not all. The kidnapper wants us to bring along five hundred pounds in exchange for Katie."

"Where will I get that sort of money?" In the blink of an eye, Rose's hopes for seeing Katie returned safely home were dashed. She realized now that Steven had not helped at all by rushing off to Mrs. Bunratty's. Thank God Devon Avondale and Dick Creevy were more level-headed, cautious men. "I have only a few pounds to my name!"

Dick frowned. "I don't keep that much hard currency in my house, but I can raise half."

"I can raise the other half," said Devon.

"I will pay you both back," Rose promised. She shouted for her cloak and hat, and while her servant assisted her in putting them on, she told the two gentleman, "I will sell my house if I have to!"

The men assured her that she would not be forced

to sell her house. Then Dick, Devon and Rose left in Devon's carriage, stopping to pick up the necessary ransom money before they headed to Monto as quickly as the driver could take them.

The first flurries of snow fell in Mabbot Street as Devon's carriage rumbled to a stop opposite the glossy red façade of The Shebeen pub. "Wait here," Devon instructed Rose as he pushed open the carriage door.

"You are insane if you think I am going to stay here." Rose leaped to the ground before either man could stop her.

Dick wrapped his arm around her shoulder. "I am afraid I agree with Avondale, Rose. We don't know what sort of trap Miss Tweedy might have set. I must insist you remain in the carriage."

She put up a valiant protest, but in the end, Rose knew she would only be a hindrance to the men if any complications arose concerning Katie's release.

"All right, then. Here is the key to the front door." She laid the flat skeleton key in Devon's open palm. Then, reluctantly, she climbed back into the carriage compartment and watched as Dick Creevy and Devon Avondale crossed the empty street and entered the Dorcas Society's front office.

In the hushed stillness of the carriage interior, Rose reflected on what had happened in the previous two weeks. What she had always wanted, a family, had fallen into her lap and she had grabbed it. She saw the succeeding events as acts in a play. Enter Sir Steven Nollbrook, whose very existence threatened to rob her of the children she'd fallen in love with. To deepen the plot, she fell in love with him. Ironically, in doing so, she helped Steven discover that he was capable of loving, too.

Then one of her children was snatched from her, and Steven, driven by his newly found paternal instinct, rushed off to become the hero of this melodrama. But tragically, his efforts were misdirected and he was in the wrong place to save little Katie. Now, it would be Devon and Dick, her neighbors, who would rescue the child. And she knew that if Devon crossed Mabbot Street with little Katie in his arms, she would be eternally indebted to the man. When he banished Sir Steven Nollbrook from Fontjoy Square, she would have nothing to say about it.

Perched on the edge of the leather squabs, Rose watched and waited. Her heart skipped erratically as the minutes ticked by. This was her black moment, the moment when she realized that she could have her children, or her lover, but that she could not have both.

Pressing her forehead to the cold glass, Rose sighed. She would never love another man the way she had loved Sir Steven. But Katie, Mollie and, yes, little Stevie, too, were now her responsibility and her paramount concern. If Sir Steven objected to her adopting the little boy, she would fight him tooth and nail. If she spent the rest of her life a spinster in order to provide them a good, loving home, she would.

No questions asked. No doubt about it.

Fifteen

Steven struggled to the brink of consciousness. The pain in his shoulder was now a blinding throb, robbing him of breath. The brush of a coarse rope carpet burned his cheek. His eyes opened to the sight of a wicker screen and an overturned chair. The smell of gunpowder and blood filled his nostrils. He was on his belly, arms stretched out and legs splayed wildly. He started to call for help; he needed medical attention and he ached too much to move. But the harsh whispers overhead silenced him. He closed his eyes and listened.

"You've shot him dead, you idiot!" Clodagh Tweedy's voice was unmistakable.

"I didn't mean to kill him!"

"Well, you did! Whatever for? What's going on?"

"Grab your coat. You're coming with me."

"Where? I don't want to go! I've had enough of you and that nasty Letterfrack. He can do his own dirty work from now on, and you can tell him I said so."

"Tell him yourself, Clodagh. You'll be seeing him in just a little while." A scuffling sound accompanied the footsteps that crossed the floor. "Now that's a good girl. Don't make me use this again. You can see I will if I have to."

She spat, whether at her abductor or on the floor, Steven did not know. A hand slapped her face—hard—and she grunted. There was a moment of silence, then Clodagh said thickly, "You've split my lip. I'll tell Letterfrack! He'll take care of you."

Her threat was met with a sinister laugh.

She moved about the room—clumsily, judging by the rattle of her toiletries and the scrape of her boots on the carpet. She must have taken a pretty hard knock from her visitor. "Where are you taking me?" she asked at length.

"We're going to the offices of the Dorcas Society, if you must know."

"Whatever for?"

A heavy sigh. "I don't suppose it hurts none to tell you now. It will very soon be over, after all."

"What will be over?"

"Letterfrack's greatest scheme, dear, his final bid for fortune if not fame, and his most clever one to date, if I may say so myself."

"I don't understand. Sir Steven was unwilling to pay either me *or* Letterfrack for my silence. And Mrs. Sinclair was unwilling to pay for my testimony. What else do we have to sell? Why not call it a day? It didn't work out. There'll be other sheep to fleece another day."

"The wolf is already at the door, Miss Tweedy."

"You've knocked out one of me teeth, you bastard." She spat again.

"Shut up, or I'll knock out the rest!"

"What's at the Dorcas Society? It's late, and they're closed!"

"Haven't you a brain in your head? Did you think that Letterfrack would just forget about this little caper? When he could not extort the money from Sir Steven or from Mrs. Sinclair—"

"—or from that nice man, Mr. Avondale. I seen him comin' out of Letterfrack's office. Handsome one, he is."

"Aloysius came up with the bright idea to kidnap the little one."

"Stevie?" Clodagh yelped.

It took every ounce of self-restraint Sir Steven possessed to remain quiet. But lacking the physical strength to overpower anyone, much less someone with a pistol, he deemed it more prudent to lie quietly . . . and listen.

"No, not Stevie, but the little girl who went to hospital to have her appendix removed. She was to be released to her mother this afternoon, but you got there first."

"What do you mean? I haven't been out of this room all day!"

"Just get your coat on, and let's go! Mrs. Sinclair was to show up with the ransom money before eight o'clock, and it's half seven now. We'll be entering from the rear door so that we won't be seen from the street, but Aloysius will be annoyed if we're late!"

"She's going to get her baby back, isn't she?"

"What do you care? You haven't a motherly bone in your body!"

"P'raps not, but it don't seem fair to take the lady's money and still not give her the child back."

"I'll put it to you this way, Miss Tweedy, darling. Not everyone who is invited to this party is going to be leaving alive. And the child has seen me."

"Do you mean to say that Katie can identify you?"

"She knows a redheaded woman took her from the hospital. If I know Letterfrack, he's had her pretty well drugged since I delivered her to him. She won't remember details."

"You *are* sick! Why do I have to be there?"

Another malevolent chuckle. "It'll be great *craic,* sweetling, you'll see." Footsteps moved toward the door. "Are you quite certain Nollbrook's dead?"

"Don't he look dead? Bled like a stuck pig, that one did. Aye, he's dead for sure."

"Think I should shoot him again?"

"And put another bullet hole in Mrs. Bunratty's carpet? I wouldn't if I were you, unless you want to lose a few of your own precious teeth!"

Steven did not exhale until the door had closed and the pair of footsteps had faded down the hall.

Pushing off the floor and scrambling to his knees set off an explosion of pain in his head. After what seemed an eternity, but really was only a matter of minutes, he managed to get to his feet. Collapsing on the bed, he gasped for breath.

The bullet had missed his heart, that much was clear, but he had lost a great deal of blood and his wound required the attention of a surgeon. If he had been concerned about his own welfare, he would have pulled the bell cord, summoned a hackney cab and driven straight to hospital.

His own welfare, however, was the least of his worries. Rose, and presumably Avondale and Creevy, for Steven could not imagine their allowing her to drop off the ransom money alone, were walking into a trap.

Somehow, though streaks of white-hot pain were now shooting down his right arm, Steven managed to get out of Mrs. Bunratty's house and into his own carriage, still parked in the street. His driver, appalled at his condition, bandaged and wrapped the wound as best he could.

"Let me take you to a doctor, sir, please!"

But Steven would not hear of it. "Mabbot Street, and as fast as you can go. *Now!*"

Devon carried a small pistol while Dick held the leather bag containing the ransom money. The men stole quietly through the front office. Once they were past the storefront window, the street lamps outside provided little or no illumination. Luckily, Devon found a branch of candles. Having lit them, he led the way up the rickety stairs, calling, "Katie! Katie, where are you?"

At the landing, the men paused and stared down a long, shadowy corridor. A scrabbling sound raised the hairs on the back of Devon's neck. "Do you hear that?" he whispered.

"It's coming from the second room on the left," Dick replied.

Indeed, a sliver of light could be seen beneath the

door Dick had indicated. From within, footsteps moved across the floor. A deep masculine voice and a high-pitched feminine one mingled, then faded to whispers. A muffled cry was heard. Then Katie's voice rang clear. "Mr. Avondale! I'm here! I'm here! Help me!"

Both men bolted into action. Tossing caution aside, they ran down the hallway to the second room on the left and barreled through the door.

The sight that greeted them drew them up short. Hearts pounding, eyes blinking in astonishment, they froze in their tracks.

In the center of the room, back-to-back in matching wooden chairs, sat Katie and a woman Devon had never seen before. Though Katie had screamed Devon's name just a moment before, her mouth was now stuffed with a linen handkerchief, as was the mysterious red-haired woman's. Both the woman and the child were bound to the chairs, their wrists secured behind them and their ankles tied snugly together. And both of them appeared unconscious. Katie's head lolled to the side, and her eyes were half shut and glazed. The red-haired woman's chin had fallen to her chest and unnatural gurgling sounds emanated from her throat.

From the ceiling hung a crude lamp that cast a pool of light around the captives. Outside that circle was nothing but blackness.

Dick lurched forward, but Devon grabbed his arm and held him back.

"Who is there?" Devon demanded, addressing the

shadows. "Show yourself, and my friend here will give you the ransom money. Not until then."

The sight of Katie, apparently drugged and helpless, filled Devon with rage. Mindful, however, of Sir Steven's knee-jerk reaction, which everyone now considered a blunder, Devon reined in his passions and proceeded carefully. "Come out, I tell you, or I shall start shooting at shadows!"

As he expected, a figure materialized from the darkness at the edge of the room. What Devon did not expect to see was Aloysius Letterfrack walking toward him.

"Letterfrack!"

"The lawyer?" Dick asked incredulously.

"Thank God you have arrived," the silver-haired man said, approaching Devon with his hand extended. "Oh, put away the pistol now, there is nothing to fear. As you can see, the kidnapper is already subdued."

Devon lowered his gun while Dick rushed forward to untie Katie. The red-haired woman whom Letterfrack had identified as Katie's captor remained bound and gagged, her body disturbingly lifeless.

"Take Katie to the carriage," Devon instructed Dick. "And take the money with you."

"By all means, get the money and the child out of here!" Letterfrack said. His gaze tracked Creevy like an eagle's as the famed pugilist easily hoisted the child into his arms and left the room, leather valise tucked under his arm.

"I don't understand," Devon said. "What has happened here?"

"I am afraid we have been the mutual victims of a

very cruel scam, Mr. Avondale. I arrived shortly before you did, sir, and I was confronted by that despicable little hellion you see tied to the chair there. Silly trollop! Thought to take my money and shoot me, I suppose. But I disarmed her instead."

With a flourish, Letterfrack produced a pearl-handled pistol from beneath the waistband of his trousers.

"You took her gun away?"

"Aye, and tied her up, too."

"Why subdue the child?" Devon's fingers tightened around the stock of his own pistol. Ominously, he took note that Letterfrack did not tuck his weapon away, either. "Why tie up Katie?"

"She was already bound and tied when I arrived, sir."

"But she was not gagged. I heard the child scream. 'Twas her voice that led me to this room, as a matter of fact."

"Ah, yes, well, you see, I started to untie the child when I discovered her in that abominable condition. When I pulled the kerchief from her mouth, she screamed. Understandably, she was frightened and uncertain whom to trust."

"But you stuffed the gag back in her mouth."

"I heard footsteps, sir. How was I to know it was you coming up the steps? How was I to know whether Miss Tweedy had an accomplice, come to back her up? So I muffled the child's voice and stepped back into the shadows. When I saw that it was you, I emerged. Simple as that."

"You move quickly for a man your size."

"I'm lighter on my feet than I look, sir."

Letterfrack was *considerably* lighter on his feet than he looked. In fact, Devon was downright skeptical that events had played out just as Letterfrack described them.

After an awkward moment, Letterfrack said, "I am sorry to have played an unwitting role in it, but it seems Miss Tweedy's criminal enterprise has made fools of us all."

"The woman who delivered Katherine Rowen's children from Mrs. Bunratty's establishment is a more accomplished criminal than I had thought," Devon remarked.

Pensively, Letterfrack stroked his puckered lips. "I see you have an intimate knowledge of the facts surrounding this sordid tale of woe."

"Tell me, how was a sophisticated lawyer like *you* victimized, Mr. Letterfrack?"

Looking sheepish, the man shrugged a hefty shoulder. "I allowed myself to become, ah, *friendly* with Miss Tweedy. Against my better judgment, I, ah, *patronized* her for quite some time."

"Though I do not approve, many men visit prostitutes."

"I have a family, Mr. Avondale, and a reputation to uphold. Perhaps you understand what I am saying."

"She was blackmailing you."

"Precisely."

Devon considered what he had heard. "A bold scheme indeed, if she planned to lure us both here at the same time to collect her double payoff."

"I believe she planned to board a ship for Scotland

tonight. She would have left Ireland a very wealthy woman, sir, if her plan had gone as intended."

"And the precise details of her plan? I'm curious, Letterfrack. When did you receive a note to meet her here?"

"What difference does it make?"

"Just curious."

Letterfrack waved the tip of his gun in the air. His lips parted, but before he could speak, the unmistakable pop of gunfire sounded from the street.

Rose's heart leapt at the sight of Dick Creevy emerging from the Dorcas Society offices with Katie's disturbingly limp body in his arms. On his shoulder rested the child's head, and beneath his arm was tucked the leather valise that had contained the ransom money.

Unable to wait a second longer to take the child in her own embrace, Rose pushed open the carriage door, jumped to the ground and crossed the street at a run.

"What is the matter with her?" Rose brushed the hair out of Katie's eyes. "She looks as if she is—"

Before Dick could answer, however, a series of terrifying events occurred so quickly that Rose would later have difficulty describing what happened.

Out the door of The Shebeen ran a figure clad all in a black cloak with a black beaver hat pulled low over his eyes. Inexplicably, he ran at full speed toward Dick and Katie and Rose. There was no time to sidestep the man or run. Paralyzed by shock, Rose gaped as the man barreled toward her. When he collided head on with Dick and Katie, she was knocked to the ground, where she lay stunned and badly bruised.

"Run to the carriage!" Dick yelled at Rose.

But she had no intention of leaving the scene without Katie safely in her arms. Though her legs were so badly bruised and scraped that they could barely sustain her weight, she scrambled to her feet and reached for the child. To her horror, the black-clad man produced a gleaming pistol and waved her away from Dick and Katie.

"Best to do what the gentleman says, ma'am. Go back to your carriage, and you'll not be harmed." The assailant's voice was vaguely familiar, but Rose's thoughts were in such disarray that she could not immediately identify him.

"Let me take Katie with me," she pleaded. "Please."

"Be quick about it, then." The black-clad man danced nervously from one foot to the other.

"Get in the carriage and stay there," Dick whispered as he handed Katie to her.

Rose nearly collapsed beneath the weight of the child. Moving clumsily, she scuttled back across the street, cursing her luck that a constable was nowhere to be found when she needed one. And where were the patrons of The Shebeen? Couldn't anyone inside the pub see what was taking place just outside the storefront window? Or had the weather driven all the pub patrons home to their hearths and families?

As she opened the door to the carriage, Rose took a sharp inhale. Avondale's driver was slumped on the squabs, hands bound behind his back and a bloody gash on his forehead.

Meanwhile, now that Rose was safely in the carriage with Katie, Dick had no intention of letting his assailant get away. The silver-nosed pistol staring him in the face was a deterrent, to say the least, but Creevy had never walked away from a fight, even when the odds were stacked heavily against him.

"Toss me the money, then," the black-clad man said.

"Not until you take off that hat and show your face."

A set of oversized and protruding front teeth gleamed in the dark. "You're fit for the loony bin if you think I am going to unmask myself. Now, toss over the money or I will shoot you and simply take it off your dead body."

"Shoot me if you like. You'll only end up hanging from the end of a rope, and for what? The valise is empty, old man."

"Empty?" The man snorted his derision. "There's five hundred pounds in that satchel, and I know it!"

"Really? You don't think Mr. Letterfrack has already collected the payoff and disappeared down the back stairs? Why, when I saw him last, he was tucking the money in a leather file case, the sort he takes to court, no doubt, and laughing uproariously. It's never wise to do business with a man who's a bigger cheat than you, you know."

The black-clad man's shoulders sagged and the tip of his pistol lowered just a fraction. Seeing his opportunity, Dick seized it. Quick as lightning, he threw one leg up in the air and kicked the pistol out of the assailant's hand. A gunshot cracked the icy air. When the weapon clattered to the ground, both men dove to the icy street and grappled for it.

Seconds later, much to Dick's relief, Devon Avondale plunged into the street and fired a shot from his own gun. The black-clad assailant went still, the sound of his wheezing the only evidence that he was still alive.

"Where's Letterfrack?" On his feet, Dick dusted off his clothes.

"I left him upstairs with Tweedy, the kidnapper," Devon replied.

Just then, another shot sounded, this one from inside the Dorcas Society's offices. Devon and Dick exchanged puzzled glances.

"What the devil is going on in there?"

Dick's gaze was riveted to the front door of the building. When another gunshot popped the silence, he tightened his hold on the leather valise and glanced in the direction of Avondale's carriage. "We had best get Rose and Katie out of here."

An eerie silence had descended in the street. For a moment, the two men stood staring at each other and the façade of the Dorcas Society. Only Letterfrack and the kidnapper had been left inside, and the red-haired woman was bound to her chair and appeared completely helpless. Had someone else been in the building, someone whom Dick and Devon failed to see?

"Stay with Rose and Katie, then. I'll go back inside," Devon suggested.

But before he could re-enter the building, Sir Steven

Nollbrook emerged. And, to the utter surprise of both Dick and Devon, he carried in his arms the limp, doll-like body of the red-haired kidnapper.

"Who was shot?" demanded Devon, a trifle peevishly to Dick Creevy's ears.

"If you must know, *I was.*"

Dick indicated the woman whose body lolled in Steven's embrace. "Is she dead?"

"Drugged," Sir Steven replied. "Chloroform, most likely. And Katie, too. They'll sleep it off, but they will have some damnable headaches when they come to."

"I don't understand," Devon said. "Where's Letterfrack?"

"Warming his feet, I suppose." Steven's lips twisted. "In Hell."

"You shot him?" Devon took a step toward Steven. "But why?"

"Because he and his assistant, Mr. Hare, conspired to kidnap Katie, that's why. I suspect that Letterfrack and Clodagh Tweedy have a longstanding, ah, business relationship. I would not be surprised to learn that Tweedy told Letterfrack what she knew concerning the paternity of Katherine's children many months ago. That accounts for Letterfrack's sudden coldness toward me."

"But did you have to kill him?" Dick asked.

"Would you have preferred I let him slip down the back stairs and make his getaway? He heard the gunshot that was fired. He knew that that bumbling fool Mr. Hare had upset his entire scheme."

When neither Dick nor Devon responded, Steven

sighed his exasperation. "Has either of you noticed that I have been shot myself? Not just by Letterfrack, who took offense to my detaining him, but also by Letterfrack's assistant. I went to Mrs. Bunratty's before I arrived here, if you recall. While I was questioning Miss Tweedy, she received an unexpected gentleman caller. It was Mr. Hare. Bastard shot me in the right shoulder."

Upon closer inspection, Dick saw that both of Steven's shoulders were soaked with blood. "Why did he do that?"

Steven gave a grim chuckle. "Stick to boxing, Dick. A world-class detective you are not. Foolishly, he shot me because he feared I had caught on to his and Letterfrack's nefarious plot The irony is, though, I had not. I thought it was Clodagh Tweedy who kidnapped Katie. Had I killed the redheaded woman, we would all have presumed she was the guilty party."

"You're saying she did *not* abduct Katie from Meath Hospital?" Devon asked.

"Look inside his jacket pocket," Steven suggested, nodding toward the unconscious Hare.

Devon leaned over the body sprawled on the street. Flinging open the black cape, he reached inside Mr. Hare's jacket, and as he groped around, his expression changed from one of skepticism to disbelief. "What the hell is this?"

Straightening, Devon held up his arm. Clutched in his glove was a copper-colored wig, glinting in the street light.

Dick muttered a colorful oath and unthinkingly clapped Steven on the shoulder.

"That hurt," Steven said brusquely.

"Good God, I am sorry!" Dick hastened to take Clodagh Tweedy's body out of Steven's arms. The woman was heavier than she looked.

Steven stumbled as he stepped into the street.

Devon, offering his arm to Steven, continued to gape at the wig in his hands. "Hare wore a wig—"

"You're a clever one, you," bit out Steven, leaning forward and walking with obvious difficulty. "Tweedy was guilty of blackmail, nothing more. Letterfrack orchestrated the kidnapping plot."

"But he dressed Hare up in a wig so that he could shift the blame on Tweedy! I suppose he would have killed her if you hadn't happened along." Devon wrapped a supportive arm around Steven's middle. "Good job, Steven. I take back all that I said about you."

"Christ on a raft," Steven muttered in response. As the men approached the carriage, Steven's head lowered and his shoulders slumped. Each step he took appeared more painful.

When the carriage door swung open, and Rose Sinclair leaned out of the compartment, Steven's lips curved in a smile. Relief flashed in his gaze and it seemed for an instant that his strength had returned.

But when he reached for the doorframe and tried to lift his boot to step into the rig, his eyes rolled back in his head and he stumbled. Devon caught him before he hit the ground.

"Is he all right?" Rose cried.

"He's been shot," Dick said, clambering into the carriage with his own unwieldy and as yet unconscious cargo. The sight of Avondale's driver, slouched in the corner of the cab, holding a wet towel to his head, drew him up short. "What happened to you?"

"What does it look like, Mr. Creevy? Someone sneaked up behind me and rung me bell, they did!"

"No doubt to render him unable to assist us," Dick said, pulling Steven's motionless body into the crowded compartment. "Can you drive, man?"

"Aye, and I can for sure." Tucking the bloodied towel into his pocket, the driver leapt out of the carriage. From the ground, he said, over his shoulder, "Anywhere you want to go, Mr. Avondale, I can take you there. And I'll be mighty pleased to get away from this spot as fast as these horses can go."

"To Meath Hospital, then." Devon pulled the door closed and looked around the cabin. Meeting Dick's gaze, he said, "I have a premonition, Creevy, that this is going to be a very long night."

Sixteen

By the time Sir Steven arrived at the hospital, he had lost an enormous amount of blood and his lips had turned an alarming shade of blue. Doctors on call swiftly wheeled him into surgery where he was worked on for over two hours.

Katie, meanwhile, having been administered only a minute amount of chloroform, was examined at Meath Hospital and released to Rose's care. Because Rose wished to remain at the hospital until Sir Steven's surgery was finished, the child was driven home to Fontjoy Square by Dick Creevy and Devon Avondale.

Seated on a hard wooden bench in a waiting area that was cold enough to hang meat in, Rose struggled not to burst into tears when Doctor Conolley emerged from the operating amphitheater.

"Is there a relative?" the doctor asked, wiping his bloodstained hands on the front of his long white coat.

A wave of nausea swept over Rose at the sight of so much of Steven's blood. She was grateful when Mr. Avondale stood and addressed the doctor.

"We are not relatives, doctor. We are the man's . . . friends."

"Then I suggest, sir, that you contact the man's closest relatives."

"Good God," exclaimed Devon. "He is not going to die, is he?"

"He has never mentioned any relatives to me," Rose said quietly, saddened by the thought that she knew so little of Steven's life.

"What about his son?" the doctor queried.

Rose and Devon exchanged puzzled glances, then stared at the doctor.

"In his state of delirium, just before we administered the anesthesia to him, he asked for his son. He gave the impression they are very close."

"Little Stevie is too young to visit his father in hospital," Rose replied softly.

"At any rate, Sir Steven is not safely out of the woods yet," Doctor Conolley said. "One bullet wound alone would not have been so bad. But with two . . . well, he lost so much blood, you see. All we can do is wait and watch and pray that he recovers. He is very weak presently, but if he makes it through the night . . . well, then, I think he will survive."

"May I see him?" Rose asked, standing.

The doctor was disinclined to allow Rose access to the recovery room where Sir Steven had been stationed. "He will be unconscious for quite some time, Mrs. Sinclair."

But Devon Avondale was every bit as abrasive as Steven had been in persuading the doctor he should let Rose do as she wished. Within minutes, she was seated in a chair beside Steven's cot, holding his hand and staring at his unnaturally bloodless complexion.

Devon promised to return in the morning to fetch her home.

The night passed with excruciating slowness. Nurses filed in and out of the recovery area, routinely monitoring Steven's pulse and checking for fever. Despite the incessant probing and poking, however, he lay deathly still.

In the unrelentingly stark hospital atmosphere, Rose reviewed her life. Strangely, she could not remember much about her life prior to the children entering it. Try as she did, she could hardly picture Winston Sinclair's face!

Indeed, it seemed she had blossomed in the past two weeks. After years of locking her emotions in the closet, Rose at last had taken them out, unpacked them and fully explored them. What a relief to realize she could still feel alive! Her sterile marriage had not destroyed the secret, feminine essence of Rose's true personality.

The moment Miss Tweedy asked her to take Katie and Mollie and Stevie into her custody came to Rose's mind. She wondered how different her life would have been if she had simply refused. She would not have suffered the heartbreak of seeing Katie nearly die, and she would not have known the fear of losing little Stevie in an adoption contest. She would be at home now in her comfortable home in Fontjoy Square, knitting or reading or baking bread. Her stomach would not be churning with apprehension. Her body would not be aching for the touch of a man.

In the silence of the recovery room, she allowed herself a private chuckle. She had no regrets. If she had been able to foresee the future when Clodagh Tweedy marched into the Dorcas Society's offices, she would have not have turned those children away. The moment she made the decision to take them into her heart and home, she fell in love with them. That would never change.

Despite her efforts to keep a watchful vigil, Rose's shoulders eventually slumped and her chin fell to her chest. In her fitful sleep, she imagined that Sir Steven was making love to her, kissing her everywhere, whispering secrets against her neck. Inevitably, she felt the liquid warmth that flowed through her body every time that Steven touched her. Her subconscious conjured wicked images of Steven's naked body hovering over hers. Even in her dreams, she could not escape the overwhelming desire she had for the man.

At the sound of his voice, thick and raspy, her head snapped up. Blinking the sleep from her eyes, Rose met Steven's glassy gaze. She reached for his hand and held it against her breast. Leaning over the side of the cot, her heart near bursting with emotion, Rose smiled.

"Hello, there," she whispered. "How are you feeling?"

"Like someone has been embroidering on my shoulders."

She held a glass of water to Steven's lips, and he sipped thirstily. "You are going to be all right, darling."

"Katie?" He had a coughing spell that left him exhausted.

"Doctor Conolley said she had been administered

a very small dose of chloroform. Mr. Creevy drove her home last night."

"And Miss Tweedy?"

"She is in the women's ward, sleeping off the effects of being drugged. If you had not happened along when you did, Steven, Letterfrack would have killed her."

"I shudder to think what would have happened had Avondale not been so quick-witted." After a length, Steven said, "You are to be commended, Rose. Your friends love you."

"I believe you have won their respect as well, Steven."

"Undeservedly." Steven closed his eyes and swallowed hard. "Last night, Rose . . . when I thought I was going to die . . . I had to face the hard truth."

Rose's throat constricted. He was going to tell her that he wanted Stevie to live with him. He was going to tell her that he realized how deeply he loved his son, and that under no circumstances would he allow the child to be adopted. With a thundering heart, she managed to whisper, "And what do you believe to be the truth, Steven?"

"That yours is the better home for little Stevie."

She thought she had not heard him correctly. Conflicting feelings of relief, suspicion and sadness roiled through her. "I don't understand," she said slowly.

He looked her straight in the eye, but for once there was none of the bold arrogance in his expression that Rose had come to expect. "He needs stability—"

"You are stable."

"I work all the time, Rose."

"Yes, and you have made enough money in your lifetime to support three families," she argued. "You can simply work less."

His lips quirked. "He needs a mother."

Words escaped her. Little Stevie *did* need a mother. Rose was in total agreement on that point. But he did not have one. What he had was a *father.* And it seemed criminal to deny the child knowing that father.

She opened her mouth to protest Steven's abdication from his son's life. Then she snapped her jaw shut. What was she thinking? Since she had begun the process to adopt Stevie and Katie and Mollie, she had prayed that Sir Steven would terminate his parental rights. She had hoped against hope he would say exactly what he had just said, that he was not cut out to be a father, and that Rose Sinclair was the more fit custodian for little Stevie Rowen.

Steven's termination of parental rights, would, after all, enable Rose to keep all three of the children together.

"It would be tragic if the children were separated," she murmured.

"Just so." Steven sighed. He seemed resigned to his decision.

"I suppose it is the right thing to do. . . ."

"He is not attached to me now. He does not even know whether I am his father. Perhaps you will meet a man in the future, Rose, a suitable husband who will be a good father to Stevie."

Her hand fluttered at her throat. The thought of her remarrying was ridiculous, not because she was too old, or because she could not attract a man, but because she could not fathom the notion of loving anyone other than Sir Steven. But she could not tell him that!

"Perhaps," she replied.

"If not, Mr. Avondale and Mr. Creevy will always be around to take Stevie to horse races and ballgames and such. Creevy can teach him to protect himself with his fists. That's a thought, now, isn't it? And Avondale seems a good enough fellow, even if he does despise me. Has reason to, I s'pose."

Silence spilled into the room. For a long time, Rose sat quietly, bewildered by her warring loyalties.

"I thought you would be happy," Steven said.

She thought he had fallen asleep. Patting his hand, Rose lied, "Yes, Steven, I am happy."

Why, then, did she have the crazy impulse to talk Steven out of terminating his parental rights?

Her head throbbed and her body ached from the bruises she had sustained when she was thrown to the ground in Mabbot Street the night before. Suddenly, Rose could not draw a deep breath. Her thinking was confused and her emotions were even more muddled.

Uncertain how to respond to Sir Steven's announcement that he was going to gracefully bow out of Stevie's life, Rose met his gaze and forced a smile to her lips. The prospect of all three children being kept together made her want to crow with delight. But the idea of Sir Steven giving up on his son made her want to cry.

"Are you certain, Steven?" she asked.

A tear glittered in his eye. But he quickly steeled his expression and nodded. "Yes."

Fortuitously, for Rose might otherwise have given in to her impulse to protest Steven's decision, a nurse, bustling with efficiency, entered the room. "Time to change Sir Steven's bandages," she chirped.

"Time for you to leave," Steven added. The warmth had left his gaze, and in its place was cold, unfeeling resolve.

Was it possible that he could believe he was an unfit father? Was it possible that he *was?*

Stunned and shaky, Rose stood beside the bed. "I'll be just outside—"

"You should go," he interrupted.

A lump formed in her throat. Rose took a deep breath, fighting to maintain control. Exhaling, she somehow found the inner strength to look at Steven. Leaning over, she lightly kissed his lips. "Good-bye, then."

" 'Tis best if I do not come around anymore, Rose. 'Twill be confusing for Stevie. You understand—"

Unable to speak, she gulped and nodded.

"I could come back," the nurse suggested.

"No!" Rose gathered her cloak and other belongings from the bedside table. "No, I am leaving."

Turning, she swept out of the room without a backward glance. She knew that if she looked at Steven, lying in that hospital bed, his body battered and bloody from his heroic attempt to save Katie's life, she would never have the courage to allow him to terminate his parental rights.

In truth, little Stevie could not have asked for a more loving father or a more noble man to model himself after.

Pushing out of the hospital's front doors and into the freezing cold, Rose tied her bonnet strings beneath her chin and fiercely yanked on her gloves. The sight of Devon Avondale's carriage parked beneath the *porte cochère,* waiting to return her to Fontjoy Square and to her family, should have gladdened her heart.

Instead, she felt like a condemned woman. And she could not decide which was the more heinous of the crimes that had just been committed—Steven's abandonment of his son, or her betrayal of Steven.

Two days after Rose left the hospital, a new lawyer by the name of Sean O'Witt appeared at Steven's bedside with a sheaf of legal papers. Procured by Avondale, O'Witt explained that he represented Mrs. Sinclair in her efforts to adopt Katherine Rowen's three children, Katie, Mollie and Stevie. According to O'Witt, Mrs. Sinclair was under the impression that Sir Steven Nollbrook, the youngest child's father, was agreeable to terminating his parental rights and entrusting the child to her custody.

"She is correct," Steven said.

Scanning the papers, his jaw clenched so tightly that his teeth hurt. Were he reviewing paperwork of such a delicate nature for his own client, he would have read the documents far more carefully. A cursory glance, however, assured him that his signature would result in the termination of his paternal responsibilities. Beyond that, he did not care what the papers said.

O'Witt thrust a pen in his hand. "Sign here."

Desperate to secure O'Witt's departure, Steven scrawled his name.

"Aye, and I don't blame you at all, laddie, for what you're doing." O'Witt winked. "By-blows can be an awful nuisance. You're lucky to be rid of this little leprechaun."

Steven's head fell back against the pillow. A black emptiness enveloped him. Had he the physical strength, he would have coldcocked that idiot O'Witt. Turning his gaze toward the wall, he stared at nothing.

"Best the young'uns stay together anyhow." Packing all his papers in his battered leather case, O'Witt chatted happily, as if nothing out of the ordinary had just taken place, as if Sir Steven had not just signed away his last chance at happiness.

A bitter taste rose in Steven's throat. "I'm certain you are right," he muttered.

"Oh, laddie! I know I am right. And who's the better mother for the children than Rose Sinclair? Mollie and Katie, after all, are her late husband's by-blows!" The man cackled gaily, obviously pleased with the hilarity of the situation.

Lifting his head, Steven gaped at the man. "Excuse me? What did you just say?"

"I said—" O'Witt momentarily froze. When he spoke again, he wore a rather sheepish expression. "You didn't know?"

"No."

"Well, I don't suppose it is something Mrs. Sinclair wishes to make public. She told me in confidence, you see."

And you are a fine confidante and counselor!

Not for the first time, Steven marveled at the buffoons who were routinely called to the bar in Dublin. It seemed any man who could scrounge the tuition to attend law school could practice law—regardless of his skills or moral integrity.

Eager to get more information out of the garrulous O'Witt, however, Steven said, "Now I think of it, she did mention something of the matter to me. I'm afraid my injury has rattled my brain a bit. Did Mr. Sinclair know that Mollie and Katie were his daughters?"

"Oh, yes, it was quite well known at Mrs. Bunratty's that he had sired two children with Katherine Rowen." O'Witt clucked his tongue. "Worse yet, it is said that Sinclair introduced the Rowen chit to whiskey and opium. She was young and innocent when he met her."

"How is it that you know so much, O'Witt?"

"I interviewed Mrs. Bunratty, you see, obtained her affidavit in support of Mrs. Sinclair's petition for adoption. You might be surprised, but Mrs. Bunratty is quite influential with some of the judges—"

"Doesn't surprise me."

"At any rate, according to Mrs. Bunratty, the children are three months older than was previously thought. Apparently, Katherine hid her pregnancy for quite some time."

"That's enough!" Steven's curiosity vanished. A cold shudder of disgust wracked his body. Katherine Rowen's deceit had been more grotesque than he'd thought. No doubt she was pregnant with Sinclair's children when she met him!

And Rose Sinclair had deceived him too. She had

known from the day she met him that Mollie and Katie were her late husband's children. Conveniently, she had omitted to tell him that fact.

Would Rose Sinclair ever have told him the truth about the twins' parentage? If Steven had chosen to play a vital role in Stevie's life, would he have been forever ignorant of the fact that Winston Sinclair was Katherine Rowen's lover?

Perversely, he felt as if he had been cuckolded again, this time by Rose Sinclair. Anger consumed Steven. He was glad he had opted out of Stevie's life. When his wounds healed and he was released from the hospital, he would never see her or think of her—or little Stevie—again!

O'Witt shrugged. "Oh, well. As I said, laddie, you are a lucky man to be out of this situation. I would not want to raise a child who had spent the first four years of his life in a brothel! Why, the boy will never be right!"

"Get out," Steven growled.

His sudden rudeness surprised the older man. With a huff, O'Witt snapped his briefcase shut and shuffled out the door. When he was gone, Steven closed his eyes and wondered how he could ever have been such a fool as to consider Rose Sinclair a paragon of feminine virtues. She was no better than Katherine Rowen. She was just as flawed as everyone else he had ever loved.

After she left Meath Hospital and returned to Fontjoy Square, Rose tried her best to forget she had ever met Sir Steven. The children, particularly Katie, needed her, and she had plenty to do without dwelling on the emptiness she felt inside her, or her sadness at Sir Steven's terminating his parental rights. Besides, she had legal matters to attend to, specifically her upcoming court appearance, at which her application to adopt Katherine Rowen's children would, if all went well, be granted.

Mr. Avondale quickly retained a new barrister named Mr. O'Witt who, while not as well known or successful as Sir Steven Nollbrook or the late Mr. Aloysius Letterfrack, held himself out as an expert in the area of difficult or contested adoptions. *Not that Sir Steven had lodged an objection to the adoption of Stevie Rowen.* On the contrary, Steven had willingly signed the termination papers presented to him, formalizing his intent never to see his son again.

Of course, that meant that Sir Steven would never see Rose Sinclair again, either. It had to be that way. Despite the pit that formed in Rose's stomach each time she thought of Sir Steven, she concluded that it was best for him to disappear completely from her life as well as Stevie's. It would simply be too confusing for the child if Sir Steven popped up at Fontjoy Square from time to time for friendly visits or romantic interludes.

Still, she longed for him. She spent long, restless nights staring at the ceiling, making lists in her head, trying to decide if she had done the right thing in encouraging Steven to give up his legal rights to his child. On one side of her mental ledger, she saw the tremendous advantages of having Steven excluded from her life. As soon as the adoptions were complete, all three of Katherine Rowen's children would be legally hers. The siblings would not have to be separated. They would grow up happily together in a warm and loving home.

On the opposite side of her invisible ledger, Rose marked the disadvantages to Steven's having forfeited his paternal rights. The child would be deprived of knowing a kind, conscientious father. Father and son would never experience each other's love. And Rose would never again feel the depth of emotion and passion she had felt when Sir Steven made love to her.

When she weighed the factors she had listed on either side of her mental worksheet, Rose feared she had made a horrible, tragic mistake. She had allowed fear and selfishness to color her better judgment. Because she had feared losing what *she* wanted, namely, to keep all three children in her possession, she had actively participated in depriving little Stevie of his father's society and love. Plagued by guilt, Rose wrote a half-dozen notes to Sir Steven, begging him to reconsider his decision.

But none of her letters to Steven were mailed. Rose simply lacked the courage to undermine the success of her own attempts to adopt Katherine Rowen's children. When Mr. O'Witt informed her that Sir Steven had signed the documents that terminated his parental rights, and that the presiding judge would undoubtedly grant her request to finalize the adoption decrees, she feigned relief and happiness. Secretly, however, Rose Sinclair was more unhappy than she had ever been.

On the day she was scheduled to appear in court,

she met Mr. Avondale in the foyer, her nerves jumpy from lack of sleep and worry. "I fear I have made a mistake," she told him, as he assisted her into his carriage.

She had expected that he would greet her announcement with disbelief, or that he would scold her for failing to protect her children's best interests notwithstanding the unpleasantness associated with Sir Steven's termination of parental rights.

But his reaction surprised her. "Giving up one's child is an awful decision," he mused quietly. "I expect Sir Steven has conflicting feelings about it himself."

As the carriage rumbled through town, Rose became reflective. "When I was very young, sir, my dearest friend had a summer romance with a dashing boy. When she found herself with child, she was tormented by confusion and guilt. For the longest time, she refused even to accept that she was pregnant. Then, when the babe came, she looked at it and wanted to be rid of it. I took it to the Dorcas Society because I did not know what else to do."

"It must have been a very difficult time for your friend . . . and for you, as well."

"Yes." Rose shut her eyes, remembering Mary's ordeal. "I have often wondered what happened to that child. And to Mary. She never spoke with me again, you see. Do you think I did the wrong thing, sir? Or did I ruin my friend's life? And participate in the ruination of an innocent child's life?"

Devon, seated on the squabs opposite her, leaned across and squeezed Rose's hand. "Both of you were very young and frightened. I think you have assumed the guilt of that episode for too many years, Rose. You must forgive yourself now. You ruined no one's life. You may even have saved one or two."

"I wonder what became of Mary . . ."

"I don't know, but I suspect she grew up to be a lovely, lively young woman. And I suspect she loved you dearly, Rose, for what you did for her. It may have been too painful a period in her life to relive. Perhaps that is why she failed to make contact with you afterwards. But she loved you, Rose, that I am sure of."

Rose stared quizzically at Mr. Avondale. The man was full of mysteries; often, he seemed to possess a supernatural awareness of the past lives of the ladies who lived in Fontjoy Square. But he could not possibly know Mary O'Roarke, or anything about that strange summer in Killiney. He could not possibly understand Mary's fear and Rose's guilt.

Yet somehow his kind words assuaged Rose's guilt. By the time the carriage pulled to a stop in front of the great stone courthouse, she realized that there was no tidy answer to questions swirling inside her. She could only do what she thought was best and what she thought was right for her children. She had to forgive herself for being imperfect. She had to look to the future and put her past mistakes and regrets behind her.

The weeks following Steven's injury passed in a blur of pain and anger. He tried to tell himself he had done the right thing by allowing Rose Sinclair to raise his child. Not only could she provide a better home for Stevie, she could also raise him along with his siblings, Mollie and Katie.

Yet he could not help but think he would be a good father, too. Hadn't he rushed Katie to the hospital when she was ill? Hadn't he done everything in his power to rescue the child from her kidnappers? Reviewing the events of the previous month, Steven realized that his paternal instincts were not as unevolved as he thought they were.

As he lay in his hospital bed, recovering from his wounds, Steven thought about his past, his parents and Katherine Rowen. He was not an unintelligent man; with nothing to do but stare at invisible spots on the hospital wall, he became acutely insightful.

With no court appearances to occupy his mind and no legal problems to solve for his clients, Steven was forced to examine the patterns that existed in his relationships. His conclusions were not flattering. At length, he admitted to himself that by the time he met Rose Sinclair, he was so afraid of being abandoned that he tried desperately not to fall in love with her.

As his shoulders healed, his introspective powers grew stronger. On the day he was released from the hospital, Steven walked into the blistering cold a new man, physically and emotionally. Though he still debated whether or not he should have signed the papers Mr. O'Witt presented to him, he concluded that he did so, in part, because he was afraid of loving his child too much, of being so vulnerable that he became a hostage to his emotions. He realized that he had never gotten over the fear of being rejected or abandoned by those he loved. He recognized that he had not failed his father, but that his father had failed him. He saw that Katherine Rowen's decline into alcoholism and drug abuse had not been his fault. And he understood that he could forgive himself for the mistakes he had made.

His one regret was that Rose Sinclair was not waiting for him when he walked into his cold and empty house. Despite his newfound insights into his own character and motivations, Sir Steven Nollbrook remained a lonely man.

The paneled courtroom was filled with litigants and spectators. When Rose Sinclair's name was called out by the bailiff, Mr. O'Witt stood and recited the pertinent aspects of her petition to adopt the three children born to Katherine Rowen. Somewhat theatrically, the barrister withdrew from his briefcase a succession of papers, and, after requesting and obtaining permission to approach the bench, he presented them all to the judge for his signature.

"Pray for judgment," O'Witt intoned.

Scratching his peruke, the judge studied the documents over the tops of his half-moon glasses. After a moment, he said, "Judgment is gran—"

"Just a moment." A deep baritone boomed authoritatively from the rear of the courtroom. "I have an objection to these proceedings, your honor."

Shocked, Rose turned and stared as Sir Steven Nollbrook strolled down the aisle and pushed through the little gate that segregated the spectators and the participants. He stood beside one of the long wooden counsel tables that faced the judge's bench, his battered shoulders square, his hands clasped behind his back. And despite his pale, slightly drawn complexion, he was the most handsome and compelling figure Rose had ever seen.

Her breath caught. The war that had raged in her heart now turned on this final engagement.

"What have you to say for yourself?" asked the judge.

Mr. O'Witt was clearly knocked off balance. "Your Honor, I object—"

"Hush, O'Witt! Sir Steven is an officer of this court and a well respected litigator. This court owes the man a hearing. Besides, the termination of a man's parental rights is a very serious thing. Speak, Sir Steven!"

"Your Honor, I was flat on my back in a hospital bed with bullet holes in both of my shoulders when I signed those papers."

Tearing her gaze off Steven, Rose searched the audience for Mr. Avondale's reaction. In response to her inquisitive look, he shrugged. But Rose's self-appointed guardian angel did not seem overly concerned by Sir Steven's appearance.

Poor Mr. O'Witt, however, was near apoplectic. "Your Honor! If Sir Steven is suggesting that I took advantage—"

"Silence, O'Witt!" the judge roared. "Sir Steven, if you lacked the capacity to voluntarily and intelligently waive your parental rights, I will ignore your written assent to this adoption. Is that what you wish me to do?"

"Before I answer that question, Your Honor, might I have leave of the court to ask Mrs. Sinclair a question?"

"This is highly irregular!" cried Mr. O'Witt.

"O'Witt," the judge snarled, "procuring the signature of an incapacitated man and attempting to deprive him of his child is highly irregular, too. I strongly suggest you step aside, counselor, and allow Sir Steven his day in court."

A hush fell over the courtroom while O'Witt, his face as red as a tomato, threw himself into a chair at the counsel table, crossed his arms over his chest and pouted. Steven faced Rose and, for a long, dizzying moment, simply stared at her. A shared intimacy crackled in the air like lightning's first warning. Meeting Steven's gaze, Rose was moved as much by the depth of emotion she saw in his eyes as by the heady feelings that engulfed her. Taking a step forward, she clung to the edge of the counsel table, uncertain whether her knees would support her.

Sir Steven closed the distance between them and stood toe to toe with her. "Mrs. Sinclair, I want what is best for my son. If you promise to love him—"

"Oh, Steven, he should be with his father!" she blurted. "That is what is best for little Stevie."

Propping his elbows on the table, Mr. O'Witt dropped his head in his hands.

Stevie leaned a bit closer so that his voice was not audible to the judge or the spectators. "I believe I could be a good father, Rose."

She could no longer contain her tears. Sniffling, Rose replied, "You will be a *fine* father."

"There is another alternative, of course, darling." Smiling, he tipped her chin. "While I was flat on my back in hospital, I had plenty of time to consider the options available to us—and to the family we share."

"The family we share?"

"It would be unfair to separate them. You said so yourself."

Her heart was near bursting. "They should stay together, Steven."

"And so should we." He kissed her, then, full on the lips, right in front of the judge and O'Witt and everyone in the courtroom. Applause erupted in the spectators' gallery, and the judge was forced to bang his gavel on the edge of his bench.

But when order in his courtroom had been restored, the judge leaned over his bench and smiled down at Rose and Steven. "Aye, you are good folk, and do you know it is your lucky day? For I have authority to marry you as well, my dear lass and laddie! Now are you prepared to say you love each other and that you are going to raise these three beautiful children as your own?"

Steven nodded.

Rose whispered, "Yes."

Mr. Avondale broke all the rules of decorum by leaping over the swinging gate and throwing his arms around the newly engaged couple. "Mary's green eyes are smiling on you," he said to Rose as he kissed her cheek.

And even Mr. O'Witt, who made a dramatic demonstration of ripping all his paperwork into pieces, was forced to agree that a more unusual case had never been heard in Dublin's chancery.

AUTHOR'S NOTE

In the late nineteenth century, the law in Ireland required that an actual or putative father be formally notified of an impending adoption proceeding. Of course, it was not uncommon for unmarried women to thwart this requirement by stating that the father was "unknown."

If, however, an unmarried man acknowledged paternity of a child, his legal rights would often take precedence over the mother's. Fortunately, the law in Ireland has evolved to recognize that parents have equal rights to the custody and control of their children regardless of the legitimacy of those children.

In telling Rose Sinclair's story, I applied the basic spirit of the Irish law as it was written in 1865, but I did not always strictly adhere to the details of the legal system.

If you liked CHILD'S PLAY, be sure to look for Cindy Harris's emotional conclusion to the *Dublin Dreams* series, LOVER'S KNOT, available wherever books are sold in April 2002.

Dolly Baltmore wasn't looking for passion when she had a bright idea to avenge her husband's murder. Millicent Hyde was only hoping for a little adventure when she found a wolf at the door. Rose Sinclair knew from the start that desire wasn't child's play. Yet each of them had conquered their past heartaches to discover that love was more than possible—it was irresistible. Lady Claire Killgarren isn't so sure, but with a little help from her newly happy friends, and one very special man, she's about to find that she'll give anything to be caught in a lover's knot . . . for all time.

COMING IN DECEMBER 2001 FROM ZEBRA BALLAD ROMANCES

__A ROSE FOR JULIAN: Angels of Mercy
by Martha Schroeder 0-8217-6866-2 $5.99US/$7.99CAN
Taking a position with Miss Nightingale is a dream come true for Rose. One patient in particular—Julian Livingston, an earl's son—inspires dreams of another kind. They are impossible dreams, for Rose believes that Julian will despise her if he discovers the shameful truth of her past. Can Julian convince her that he loves the woman she has become?

__JED: The Rock Creek Six
by Linda Devlin 0-8217-6744-5 $5.99US/$7.99CAN
Jed Rourke, a Pinkerton detective, finds a compelling reason to stay in Rock Creek—prim and sensible Hannah Winters. Hannah's brother-in-law has been charged with murder and she insists on helping solve the crime. Working with a woman is the last thing Jed planned on, but with Hannah, teamwork may just lead to a walk down the aisle.

__REILLY'S HEART: Irish Blessing
by Elizabeth Keys 0-8217-7226-0 $5.99US/$7.99CAN
Meaghan Reilly has never let being female stop her from doing anything, and now studying medicine is her only dream. Until Nicholas Mansfield, Lord Ashton, walks back into her life. Meaghan is certain that the nobleman is her destiny. If only Nick would ignore the duty that has brought him to Ireland and instead, embrace the passion between them . . .

__THE THIRD DAUGHTER: The Mounties
by Kathryn Fox 0-8217-6846-8 $5.99US/$7.99CAN
Mountie Steven Gravel wonders if business is the only thing on Cletis Dawson's mind. At every chance, marriageable middle daughter Emily is thrust into his path. Yet it's not gentle Emily who draws Steven's eye, but the oldest girl, Willow. Stubborn Willow is hardly willing to be courted—unless Steven can unlock the secrets in her wild heart.

Call toll free **1-888-345-BOOK** to order by phone or use this coupon to order by mail. *ALL BOOKS AVAILABLE DECEMBER 01, 2001*

Name ______________________________
Address ______________________________
City ____________________ State ______ Zip ______

Please send me the books that I have checked above.

I am enclosing $__________
Plus postage and handling* $__________
Sales tax (in NY and TN) $__________
Total amount enclosed $__________

*Add $2.50 for the first book and $.50 for each additional book. Send check or money order (no cash or CODs) to: **Kensington Publishing Corp., Dept. C.O., 850 Third Avenue, New York, NY 10022.**
Prices and numbers subject to change without notice. Valid only in the U.S. All orders subject to availability. **NO ADVANCE ORDERS.**
Visit our website at **www.kensingtonbooks.com.**